W9-CYH-810

TO BE CONTINUED...

AFTERWORD

I want to start off by saying, if you bought/downloaded this book, thank you!!! I hope you all enjoyed it as much as I enjoyed writing about Diamond and Koda. Let me know how much you enjoyed the book by leaving a review. It means a lot!

Also, add me on Facebook: Raya Reign
Join my Facebook reading group for sneak peeks and more: Raya's Reading Palace

Thank you for the support!

Coming Up Next!

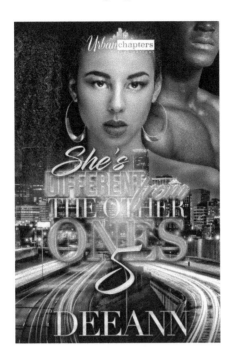

CPSIA information can be obtained
at www.ICGtesting.com
Printed in the USA
LVHW041950110119
603610LV00016B/323/P

IN THE ARMS OF A THUG

RAYA REIGN

**TEXT UCP TO 22828 TO SUBSCRIBE TO OUR
MAILING LIST**
**If you would like to join our team, submit the first 3-4
chapters of your completed manuscript to**
Submissions@UrbanChaptersPublications.com

"Keep in mind that I'm an artist, and I'm sensitive about my shit."

Erykah Badu

ONE

D IAMOND
    Sitting on my front porch, I watched as my neighbor came out of her door, and nippily made her way to her car. She was dressed in yellow from head to toe and even had the nerve to have on a hat. Nah, it wasn't a regular fitted cap. It was a church hat. A large ass, yellow church hat. I knew exactly who she was. I'd known her my entire life.

Ms. Robinson, or as the church would call her, Sister Robinson.

She basically watched me grow up. She watched all the kids of the church grow up, including her nasty ass son who didn't know how to keep his hands to his fucking self. His name was Christian Robinson. That nigga was sick in the head. That's all there was to it.

See, when I was a child, I didn't know what that meant. I had heard someone from the church say that about him, but I just couldn't understand why. But then, a couple of weeks after I wondered, something happened that changed my life forever.

I had an older brother, Michael, and an older sister, Apryl. When I was a little girl, I admired everything my brother did. I wanted to be just like him in every way, so I always followed him around. Of course, a sixteen-year-old didn't want a nine-year-old following him around while he was trying to hang with his friends, but that was something I didn't care about. My mom made him take me along with him anyway.

So, there I was, following aimlessly behind Michael while he talked and joked with his friends. Christian was there, along with another one of Michael's friends, whose name I didn't remember. Christian kept giving me this weird look. I didn't know what it meant, but I knew he was too damn old to be playing games with a nine-year-old.

"My mom thinks I did my homework before I came out here," Michael said with a light laugh. *"I ain't doing that shit, though. Fuck that."* Michael only cussed when he was around his friends. He knew not to talk like that when our mom was around.

"Shit, who you have homework for? Why teachers be giving out homework on the weekend anyway? What the fuck is that?" Christian asked, turning his head to glance at me again. This time, I rolled my eyes at him. What was he looking at? He was starting to irritate me.

"Miss Wilson," Michael continued. *"Math class. That shit won't be getting done. I don't give a fuck."*

That's when I heard the barking coming from behind me. I quickly turned around and saw the dog running straight toward us. I was terrified. I'd always been terrified of dogs. Even to this day, those mothafuckas still scared me.

"Oh shit!" Michael yelled, frantically looking around to see where he could run to. I stood frozen in place as the dog got closer and closer. They all took off running, not giving one little fuck about me. But since they were running, the dog followed them and left me alone.

I let out a small sigh of relief, but then I realized I had no idea where I was at. I was just following behind my brother, not looking at my surroundings, and now I was lost. I looked around, seeing trees, a couple of houses, and a corner store at the top of the street. I decided to just make my way to the corner store. Maybe that's where Michael went.

"Aye!" I heard once I started walking. "Aye, where you going?" I stopped walking and watched as Christian made his way toward me. I thought it was a little weird that he was walking by himself, but that didn't stop me from waiting for him to catch up to me.

"I'm going home," I let him know.

"Home? You don't even live that way. You live over there." He pointed in the direction behind us, and I quickly turned around. See, being a little ass girl, I thought since he was older and also my brother's friend, he would've helped me.

But, nah. I thought wrong.

"Well, since you know where I live, can you show me how to get there?" I asked, hoping he would say yes.

"Yeah," he said, giving me a small smile. "I'll show you."

"Thanks." I didn't know what it was, but I felt weird being with him alone.

We walked for maybe five minutes before he said, "Aye, lemme show you something right quick." He was making his way toward the woods, and I hesitantly followed behind him. I knew I didn't wanna go over there because my mom had always told me to stay away from trees. I wasn't even supposed to be going near them.

"What is it? Because my mom told me I'm not supposed to go near the—"

He forcefully pulled me by my arm, causing me to let out a loud shriek. That's when he covered my mouth with his oversized hand and told me to be quiet. I didn't know what was going on, so I just started crying. I was scared, I didn't know where my brother was, and I damn sure didn't know how to get home.

"Shut up, aight?" he said, looking me directly in my eyes. "Don't say anything." He was still pulling me further and further into the woods, and I was just letting him. As soon as he let me go, I had plans to run. I was going to run as fast as I could to get away from him. The only thing was, he never let me go.

He threw me to the ground where I landed on rocks and sticks. I was pretty sure my knees were bruised up because of the shorts I was wearing.

"Stop it!" I cried as he started unbuckling his belt.

"Didn't I tell you to shut up?" he asked, looking at me with cold eyes. "This will be over before you know it. Just don't say anything."

That didn't happen, though. I cried, screamed, and kicked the entire time he was on top of me. I couldn't bring myself to understand what was going on. Why was he doing this to me? A little girl? Why would he take my innocence like that when all I wanted to do was get home?

Once he was finished with me, he quickly got up, fixed himself, then took off running. I just laid there for a moment with tears coming from my eyes, not knowing what to do. I wanted to get up and run, but what if I ran into him again? I didn't want to see him, and he does something worse to me. Also, I was in a lot of pain, and I felt like I couldn't move.

It took me a little while, but I finally pulled myself up, pulled my shorts back over my behind, and started walking out of the woods. I still didn't know where I was at, so this time, I made my way to the corner store where I got a woman that I'd never met before to call my mom.

My mom was livid when she discovered what happened. She wasn't mad about me getting raped. She was mad that I wasn't with my brother. She was mad that I didn't run behind him when he took off running. In the entire situation, my mom wasn't mad at my brother at all. Nope, she was mad at me, blamed everything on me, and told me I had brought everything upon myself. Crazy, right?

But wait, it gets worse.

Being that my mom was who she was, she let everyone at the church know what happened, including Mrs. Robinson. She was so mad, she hit her son during service, and then she made him apologize to me. You know what my mom did?

She made me go up in front of the entire church and forgive him. She told me it was the 'Christian' thing to do. Yeah, I was young, but that shit didn't make sense to me. I knew what he did was bad, but everyone was looking at me like I was the one in the wrong? He didn't even get in trouble, and that was the day I stopped being a Christian.

"Hmph," I snorted as I watched her get into her car and pull off. She made sure to never be late to church. I couldn't understand it either.

I pulled a cigarette from the box, put it to my lips, then lit it. It was going to be a good day. I could feel it.

I was just about to walk back into my house when I saw the black Toyota pull into my driveway. I couldn't contain my smile even if I wanted to.

"Wassup, Dime?" he asked, stepping out of his car and making his way toward me.

"About time, nigga. It took yo' ass a whole two hours to get here." I stood up and folded my arms as Lawrence stood in front of me.

"To be honest, I didn't wanna get out my bed. You called me early as fuck on a Sunday, asking for some damn pills. Man, I just wanna relax with my girl today. I don't need none of that—"

"Okay, nigga," I snapped with my hand out. "Give me my shit so you can get the fuck outta here. All this talking ain't even necessary."

He shook his head with a small laugh, then reached in his pocket and handed me a bag full of pills.

"Here, man," he said, putting the bag in my hand. "I thought you said you were done with this pill shit. What the fuck happened?"

I pulled some money from my bra and put it in his hand.

"That shit ain't none of your business, Lawrence," I let him know.

"I mean, nah, but when I see someone I care about killing themselves with drugs, I feel like—"

"Boy, fuck you." I laughed. "You care about me? You didn't care when you let your girlfriend put me out, knowing I didn't have anywhere to go."

"She walked in on us fucking! What did you expect to happen, Diamond?"

I shrugged. "I don't know. Thanks for my shit, though. I'll hit you up when I need some more."

"Which will probably be tomorrow," he muttered as he turned to leave. I ignored him as I walked back into my house.

My home wasn't anything special. It was a small, one-story house, and it wasn't in the best neighborhood. I barely had grass in my front yard. I had one chair on my porch, and my shit needed to be pressure washed. I just didn't feel like paying anyone to do that shit. It didn't bother me that much.

I could barely keep myself together as I knocked everything off my coffee table, pulled a few pills from the bag, then crushed them up with the bottom of a glass I had laying around. I could've been normal and just swallowed the pills, but I'd rather sniff the shit up my nose. I liked the feeling it gave me.

As I snorted the first line, my cell began ringing next to me on the floor. I wanted to ignore it. I was busy, but when I glanced down at it, I decided to answer it, anyway.

"Hey, bitch." I sniffed into the phone. My nose was tingling, and I closed my eyes.

"Diamond, I know you're not over there getting high this fucking early in the morning!" Melanie snapped into the phone.

"Girl, mind your damn business. What the hell you calling so early for?"

"To see what the hell you were doing, but obviously, your ass is busy. You said you were done with that shit. How the hell—"

"Damn, I thought I was grown. I'm good, Melanie. I really don't need a lecture from you. Especially when just the other day, you were over here snorting that shit up your nose too. You must be around your little boyfriend or some shit. Acting brand new and shit."

"Girl, fuckin' bye." She laughed. "What you doing tonight, though? We should definitely go out. A bitch just got paid, so I'm ready to show the fuck out."

"Mhm," I said, snorting another line of the pills. "We can do that. I wanna get drunk tonight anyway."

"Cool. I'll be over later. Hopefully you still have some pills left when I get there. You know how you act when you—"

"Bye, Melanie." I ended the call before she could respond. She was my best friend, but sometimes, she talked too damn much. She was the type to lecture me about what I was doing then start doing the same shit as me. I didn't understand it, but I knew that shit was annoying.

My life didn't seem as bad as it actually was from the outside looking in. I kept my appearance up, but most of the time, I was letting the drugs take over.

After what happened when I was nine, I couldn't stand to even look at my mom. I didn't wanna be around her, and most of the time, I was telling her I didn't want her to be my mom. I still meant that shit, too. So I was able to move in with my Aunt Linda. I thought moving in with her would be better, but it turned out, it was actually worse... way worse.

My Aunt Linda was a few years older than my mom, so I thought she would know how to raise a child, but nope. She didn't even have any kids of her own, so why did I think she would know how to raise me?

Back when I first moved in with my aunt, she had a boyfriend who would always stare at me. I never said anything to my aunt about it, because he rarely said anything to me. That was until one night, my aunt had to work late, so she left me at home with him.

His name was David. He was tall and lanky and had an elongated face. His nose was strong, and his lips were thin and almost always cracked. Sometimes, he would let his facial hair grow out but usually, his face was clean-shaven. His hair was short and somehow always looked oily. I remember he had tattoos all over his calloused hands, and he had one gold tooth. I didn't know where the fuck my aunt found this nigga, but I wish she would've left his ass there.

That same night, he was trying to give me a bath. I was nine at the time, so I knew how to do almost everything by myself. My aunt made sure of that. The entire time I was in the shower, I just felt weird. Something wasn't right about how that man was trying to give me a bath. He never tried it while my aunt was here, so why is he trying it now?

I remember getting dressed in the bathroom that night because I was too afraid to walk out of the bathroom in just my towel. He was sitting on the couch with a beer in his hand when I was walking back to my room. I didn't say anything to him, and he didn't say anything to me.

When I finally made it back to my room, I got in bed and went to sleep. I didn't think nothing else about David. That was until I woke up to him sitting on the bed next to me. No words were exchanged as he quietly pulled my pants down and started messing with my lady parts. Flashbacks of what Christian did in the woods flooded my mind. I couldn't understand why this was happening to me again.

Of course I knew it was wrong, but I was afraid to yell and scream like I did with Christian because I didn't want him to put his hands on me. So I just laid there silently and let the tears fall. To make matters worse, he started begging me not to tell anyone.

First off, he was a grown ass man. He knew exactly what he was doing. He knew how old I was, and he damn sure knew what the hell would happen if I told anyone what he'd just done to me.

I already knew I was going to tell my aunt what he did. Why wouldn't I? But then, he started saying how he'd do anything I wanted as long as I kept my mouth shut. I didn't care about anything he was saying because I knew in the back of my mind that I was still going to tell my aunt.

But then, I started thinking to myself. What if I told my aunt and she got mad at me? What if she blamed the entire thing on me like my mom did? What if she didn't even believe me? I didn't want to go through that again, so instead, I told David to give me money. A hundred dollars, because at nine, that was a lot of money to me.

David looked at me like I was crazy, but sure enough, he gave me the money, and I made sure to keep my mouth shut.

He would come in my room at least once a week. He would play with my nine-year-old vagina, then give me a hundred dollars. It went on until my aunt died and I had to move in with my grandma, who didn't give a fuck about me.

The only reason my grandma took me in was because she thought she was gonna get paid for it. Once she found out she wasn't getting shit, she started treating me like shit. She didn't care if I ate, did my homework, or anything else. The only thing she did was yell at me and demand me to clean up after her grown, old ass.

I was never able to go on field trips in school because she refused to pay for them. I hated her with all my heart. I knew deep down it was bad, but I also knew the way she treated me was worse. It didn't even bother me when she fell down the stairs, broke her hip, then later died at the hospital.

I didn't cry, and I didn't care to be at the funeral. For four years, I lived with her evil ass. Those were the worst four years of my life, and I was beyond grateful when Melanie's mom let me live with them.

Melanie's mom had a boyfriend, too. His name was Clarence. He wasn't ugly, but he was creepy. After what happened between me and David when I was nine, I felt like every man that looked at me wanted to have sex with me. That was one of the reasons I made sure to stay away from him.

That was until I woke up one day and everyone in the apartment was gone expect Clarence. All I was wearing was a small pair of shorts and a tank top. He was eyeing my body like I was a piece of meat.

He made it awkward when he started talking to me, asking me if I had a boyfriend and shit. Then, when I told him I didn't have a boyfriend, he went on to ask if he could be my boyfriend.

That's when I realized men were disgusting. What did a forty-year-old want with a fourteen-year-old? There were so many other women out there who were older than me. Like his fucking girlfriend, for example. The only reason he was here was because of her.

At that moment, I felt like my nine-year-old self again. Only this time, I was in control. Being that I wasn't like most fourteen-year-olds, I asked him if he wanted to have sex with me. Of course, his nasty ass said yes. He was ready. Smiling big as fuck, licking his lips and shit. That's when I went on to tell him that I would only have sex with him if he paid me.

He did.

I willingly lost my virginity to him at fourteen. I didn't count what Christian did to me as losing my virginity. I tried to wipe that entire memory out of my mind.

Ever since then, I refused to have sex with a nigga for free. Men weren't shit anyway, so why not use them for money?

I never told Melanie what happened between me and her mom's boyfriend. I felt like it wasn't any of her business, and plus, I felt like she would've told on me. That was a secret I was planning on taking to the grave.

There was a knock on my door which caused me to roll my eyes. One thing I hated was people coming to my house unannounced. That shit was annoying as hell.

Wiping my nose with the back of my hand, I stood to my feet and made my way to the door. I looked out the peephole and smacked my lips once I saw who was standing there.

"What, nigga?" I asked, swinging the door open.

He held up a wad of rolled up money. "Let's make this shit quick. I got shit to do today."

Lawrence stepped past me and into the house, and I shut the door with a small chuckle.

He knew he wanted to fuck when he pulled up the first time. I didn't know why he was playing.

TWO

K ODA
  "Nigga, fuck you walking around with them flowers and shit for? What bitch you going to see?" Sani asked as I looked at myself in the mirror.

Skin pale as hell due to my albinism, eye lashes blond, eyebrows blond, and my dreads that were in a ball on the top of my head were blond too. A nigga was fine as hell. Didn't give a fuck if people stared because they acted like they never saw an albino person before. The shit used to bother me when I was a kid, but my mom made sure to let me know that I was "normal."

"I ain't got no bitch," I said, picking up the flowers that I laid on the table. "And if I did, I damn sure wouldn't be bringing her ass flowers. Fuck I look like?"

"And you wonder why you're single," he let out.

"Fuck you, nigga." I was single because bitches couldn't handle a nigga like me. I even had a bitch tell me if she wanted to date a white boy, she would've just gotten one. The fuck kinda shit was that?

Ain't no white in my blood. Mama was dark skinned, and my pops was brown skinned. I used to get teased all the time for being 'white.' Shit used to hurt my feelings when I was a little nigga. Why wasn't I normal like everyone else? Why would people treat me like I was some deadly disease just walking around?

Back when my pops was still around, he would get mad at me when I'd be crying over that shit. He would always tell me to man up and shit, so that's what the fuck I did.

I got into my first fist fight in fifth grade. Beat the brakes off that nigga for calling me a white boy. I got kicked out of school after that. I didn't care. That nigga needed his ass beat.

After that, the fighting continued. I'd fight any nigga that had something to say about my skin. And if a bitch had something to say, I'd just call her out her name and make her ass cry.

"I'll be back," I said as I made my way to the door. I didn't tell him what I planned on doing because he would've tried to talk me out of that shit.

"You need to chill, Koda. Why you be acting so reckless? What you gon' do when they lock yo' ass up?" It was always the same shit with him. Shit that I didn't listen to. This was my life and I did whatever the fuck I wanted to.

As soon as I was in the car, my phone started ringing. My sister had been begging me to be one of her models for her hair show, but I just wasn't feeling that shit.

"What up, Lay?" I answered.

"Nigga, you know what's up. You never gave me an answer about being in my hair show."

"I don't wanna be in yo' damn—"

"Pleaseee, Koda? I never ask you for anything. Just do this one thing for me," she begged.

Aight, so that was a lie. Layla was always calling me and asking for shit. Ever since her boyfriend, Kevin, bought her a salon, she was always calling me for shit.

"Man." I sighed. "I guess I'll be in the damn show." I wanted to say no, but she was my only sister. Half-sister.

"Great! Whenever you get some free time, come by the shop." She ended the call before I could say anything else.

There wasn't much in this world that I hated, but I hated going to that damn salon. Them bitches didn't know when to shut the fuck up. Always complaining about some shit. Always talking shit about their boyfriends and husbands. The shit was annoying.

I gently placed the flowers in the passenger seat, then pulled off. I knew exactly where I was going since I'd been going for the past week just watching shit.

It took me a good fifteen minutes to get to my destination. The house looked how it always did. No cars in the driveway because they parked in the garage, nicely groomed front yard, and two white chairs sitting on the porch. Nothing had changed since I'd last been here.

I grabbed the flowers, got out the car, then quickly made my way across the street. I didn't bother covering my face because I wanted them to see me.

I rang the doorbell, then waited for someone to answer the door. It took a little minute, but the door finally opened, and the woman looked at me. She was an older woman, at least in her sixties.

She smiled once she saw the flowers.

"Did someone get these for me?" she asked, reaching her old wrinkly hands for them.

"I believe so, ma'am," I said, forcing a smile. I slowly reached behind me and pulled out the pistol from the waist of my pants. "They got you this, too." I said aiming the gun at her head. "Where the fuck yo' bitch ass grandson at?"

She dropped the flowers and immediately put her hands up.

"Oh Lord Jesus! I don't know where he is! I haven't seen him in days!" Now, I knew she wasn't lying because I'd been watching that house. That nigga hadn't been home in days.

"Show me where the fuck his room is," I demanded, pressing the gun into her temple.

She didn't say anything as she started walking. I had her old ass about to shit on herself, but I wasn't going to kill her. I needed her to let her bitch ass grandson know that I'd stopped by.

Once we were in his room, I immediately started raiding his shit. You could tell what type of nigga he was just by the way his room was set up. Every chain he owned was laid out on the damn dresser.

I took every single last one of them bitches. He had a MacBook just sitting on his bed. I took that shit, too. Then I walked into his closet and he had a few shoe boxes sitting in the middle of the floor. I felt like I'd hit the jackpot when I opened them and saw nothing but money.

I took all the boxes. Fuck this nigga. He owed me money anyway. If he would've just paid my ass, I wouldn't be over here about to give his grandma a damn heart attack.

"Let ya grandson know that I was here," I said as I left the room.

"I'm gonna call the police!" she called after me. I didn't give a fuck. I was gonna be long gone by the time the police got here.

I ran to the car with all the shit that I took in both hands. I was excited to spend all this nigga's money. The shit was crazy. He had all this money just laying around, but he didn't wanna pay me? He could've avoided all this shit, but he was a dumb ass nigga.

I laughed as I sped off. I thought about stopping at the mall, but I decided to go to my sister's hair salon and see what the fuck she was talking about. Maybe I could find me a bitch to take home with me. Them bitches were always staring at me like they wanted to fuck anyway, so why the fuck not?

Before I got to the salon, I decided to stop by the crib first. I needed to get this shit out my car, just in case I got pulled over or some shit. I just didn't expect Sani's ass to be on the porch smoking a blunt.

His face was buried into his phone by the time I got to the porch with everything. I almost made it through the door, but his nosey ass just had to look at me.

"Whoa," he said standing up. "Where the fuck you get all that shit from?"

"Nowhere, nigga. Mind yo' damn business."

He came closer to me to examine everything I was holding, then smacked his lips.

"I know yo' ass didn't just hit a lick in broad daylight," he said, ready to start with his bullshit.

"Nah. I call it a warning. You don't give me my money? I run up in yo' shit and almost make ya grandma have a stroke."

"I thought I told yo' ass to calm down."

See. Here he goes with this shit. He was always trying to tell me what to do like I wasn't a grown ass man.

"I do what the fuck I want, nigga," I said. Clearly, he kept forgetting that shit.

"Don't call me when you end up in jail since you don't know how to act and shit."

I ignored his ass, then walked into the house. I didn't know what the fuck this nigga was being negative for, but I wasn't with that shit.

When I was finally done in the house, I walked back out without saying shit to Sani. The only reason he kept telling me to chill and shit was because his family was on his back about how he acted.

That nigga was a fucking hot head. He was always in jail for some dumb shit. His siblings were bailing his ass out like every two weeks. Shit was ridiculous. He got into it with his older brother last month, and he told Sani he was done bailing him out. Next time, his ass was gonna stay in jail.

I didn't give a fuck about any of that shit. I'd been to jail a couple of times, but not like Sani. I knew how to fuckin' act, unlike his ass.

When I walked into Layla's salon, all eyes immediately fell on me. All conversations stopped, and I made my way to the back where her office was.

I lifted my hand to knock.

"Come in!"

Every time I came to her office, I made sure to knock because I walked in on her and her nigga fucking once. Wasn't a sight I ever wanted to see again, so I made sure to avoid it at all costs.

"What's good, Lay?" I asked, once I pushed the door open.

"Not shit. I'm back here hiding because them bitches out there getting on my nerves."

"They always get on my nerves. I don't know how you deal with it."

"Because there's money to be made— Koda, what the fuck? When the last time you got your hair done? You just walking around with that fuzz on the top of your head like that shit cute."

I shrugged. "The shit ain't bothering me. I still pull bitches."

She rolled her eyes. "You need to find you a girlfriend who knows how to do hair."

"Hell nah. I don't need no damn girlfriend. Maybe a bitch who can do hair, but not a girlfriend. That comes with too much drama I don't feel like dealing with right now."

"Why? Because you're too busy being a hoe?"

"Hell yeah." I laughed. Fuck these bitches.

The door opened, and Kevin walked in with a bag from Walgreens.

"Aight, so I got a bunch of these shits. I didn't know the difference between them," he said, dumping the bag out on her desk. Nothing but tampons fell out. "What's good, nigga?" he asked, turning his attention to me.

"Not shit. Just another day."

"Hell yeah. I feel it."

"Kevin," Layla snapped, making us both turn our attention to her. "I said pick up a pregnancy test because I missed my damn period! Did you even read the message?"

"I mean, I skimmed it. The word that stuck out the most was period."

I felt uncomfortable as fuck. This was some shit they needed to talk about while I wasn't around.

"I'm about to put my hands on you, nigga," she said, gathering all the tampons and putting them back in the bag.

"My bad. I was driving when you sent the text. You wanted me to crash and die trying to read your message?"

"No, Kevin. I want you to crash and die right now."

"Damn." I laughed to myself. "I can step out if y'all want me to."

"No, it's fine. I'll just go get the shit myself when I get off later. Thank you, Kevin, for nothing."

Kevin scratched the back of his head, then looked at me. "Aye, your birthday coming up ain't it?"

"Yep. Tomorrow."

"What you got planned? You going out?"

I shrugged. "I don't know. Probably find some hoes to fuck with and shit."

He glanced at Layla who was mumbling shit under her breath. "Come outside with me right quick."

I followed behind his ass and watched as everyone stared at us. There was one girl who caught my attention. Light skinned bitch with long ass hair and thick ass thighs. She was sitting down so I couldn't see what her ass looked like. I made a mental note to come back and talk to her after I got done talking to Kevin.

"I didn't want nothing," Kevin said as we got to his car. "I just didn't wanna be in there with ya sister while she's mad and shit. She likes to tell my business and shit when she's mad, and I don't need you knowing what I do behind closed doors." He slid in the driver's seat, and I got in the passenger's.

"Nigga, what?" I asked as he lit the blunt that he had behind his ear. "You one of them niggas that be eating ass and shit?"

He glanced at me but didn't say shit, so I took that as a yes. I didn't even take the blunt when he offered it to me. No thank you, my nigga.

"But nah," he said. "I'ma get you some bitches for your birthday and shit. You can come by the club if you want. I'll let you and whoever you with in for free."

I nodded. Shit sounded like a plan to me.

"I don't have a problem getting my own bitches," I let him know just in case he thought I was a square ass nigga or some shit.

He laughed. "Never said you did, my nigga. Just be prepared for the ones I know."

"You fuck with them ratchet bird bitches?"

He shook his head. "Some of them be ratchet, but nah. I wouldn't hook you up with one of them."

I lifted a brow. "My sister know you be in contact with bitches that sell pussy?"

"Nah." He chuckled. "But what she doesn't know won't hurt her. Just think of it as an extra way for me to make money."

"Nigga, what? You a pimp? You out here pimpin'?"

"Something like that. Why? You gon' snitch or some shit?" He looked at me and blew out smoke, and I shook my head.

"Aye, what goes on in y'all relationship doesn't have shit to do with me. Shit gon' be ugly as fuck when she finds out, though. I don't know why the fuck you even tryna hide—"

"Chill, bruh. I got this shit. If she hasn't found out yet, then she isn't gonna find out at all. Even if she did find out, all I would have to do is explain to her I'm just making a little extra money. She probably wouldn't even think it's that big of a deal."

He nodded like he had everything figured out. I didn't say anything else to his ass because I already knew wasn't no good gonna come from this. I just hoped I wasn't around when Layla found out what her man was doing.

THREE

DIAMOND
      I woke up the next morning on the floor, right next to my bed. I couldn't remember shit. All I remember was Lawrence coming back over, and that was it.

"Shit," I muttered, pulling myself up from the floor. Passing out like that meant I'd missed some money. I looked around the room, searching for my phone, and when I didn't see it, I made my way out of the room and into the living room. Sure enough, my phone was on the coffee table, lighting up from an incoming call.

I wasn't shocked at all seeing Melanie's name popping up on the screen. She was probably mad that I didn't go out with her last night.

"Hello?" I answered, voice still full of sleep.

"Bitch, I thought you were dead or some shit. You had me nervous as shit," she said, causing me to roll my eyes. "I'm already in the car and everything, on the way to your house."

"You always doing the most, Melanie," I said, plopping down on the couch. I had a banging ass headache, and my mouth was dry as shit. I was being too lazy right now to go in the kitchen and actually get me something to drink.

"I'm not doing the most. I'm being a good friend. You know you would do the same to me."

"Probably not." I laughed to myself. I wasn't the type of person to just randomly pop up on people if they weren't answering their phones. I would just assume that they were busy, and I would go on with my life. With all the things that had happened in my life, I only worried about myself. I didn't know how to worry about other people. I just didn't have it in me.

"You ain't shit, Dime." She laughed. "But unlock your door, though. I'm pulling up."

I let out a breath and ended the call. I forced myself to get up off the couch and unlock the door. Moments later, Melanie was walking in with my mail in her hand.

"Hey, boo." She smiled, handing me my mail. "Looks like you got a letter."

"I appreciate you getting my mail for me, but damn. Don't be reading my shit."

She waved me off as she went to sit on the couch. "Girl, shut the hell up. You come to my house and open my mail. You don't see me complaining." She was right, but I didn't give a fuck. Don't be reading my mail and shit.

I looked at the letter and smiled to myself. I knew exactly who the letter was from, but I would open it later.

"It's from Mia, isn't it?" Melanie asked, causing me to look at her.

"Damn, you all up in my business, ain't you?"

"Is she gonna live here when she gets outta jail?"

I lifted a brow as I sat my mail down on the table. "What does that have to do with you? You got somewhere to live, don't you?"

"I mean yeah, but I just don't think it's a good idea for her to live here."

"Why?"

She sighed to herself, almost like she didn't want to tell me what was on her mind.

"You act different when she's around. You act like I'm not even there."

I tried my hardest to contain my laughter. Was she serious? We were all grown, and she was acting like a damn teenager.

"You dead ass right now, Mel?" I chuckled, watching her twist her mouth up.

"Yes, I'm dead ass. Ever since you met her, you treated me different. I'm your best friend, not that bitch. You've known me longer anyway."

"Hmm," I said, with a click of my tongue. "That doesn't mean shit, though. You've known me longer, but she's shown more loyalty than you ever have. You really need to stop with that jealous shit."

"I'm not being jealous. She's ratchet and almost got you killed. You've been putting money on her books and shit, for what? And when does she get out?"

"Melanie, what the fuck does that have to do with you or what the hell you got going on with your life? When you didn't have anywhere to go, I let you live here, right?"

"Yeah, but—"

"But nothing. Shut the hell up."

Mia was... I guess you could say an ex-girlfriend. I met her through one of my tricks. She acted like she wanted to fuck, acted like she was gonna pay me, but the whole time she was planning on robbing my ass. It didn't go down like that though.

When she went to the bathroom, I went through her purse to see what was in there. She didn't have any money, so how the fuck was she gonna pay me? So when she came out the bathroom, I said something about it. I swear to God; this bitch pulled a knife from her ass and was trying to cut me with it.

I had my handy dandy pepper spray on me, and I got that bitch right in the eyes. After that, I beat her ass, and was about to leave, but I didn't. I stayed at that hotel and started talking to her like we were the best of friends. She was talking to me like I didn't beat her ass.

After that night, we did become best friends. Then, we became girlfriends. Melanie couldn't stand it. She hated the thought of us being together. Me and Mia would even fuck tricks together. We were both getting paid, until we were out one day trying to get groceries and Mia saw a bitch she didn't like.

I didn't even know this bitch had her gun on her, but once them bitches got to arguing, Mia said fuck it, and started shooting. I think she shot the bitch in her stomach and in her foot. Long story short, she got locked up. It was all good, though. She would be getting out real soon, and I could tell it was bothering Melanie.

"I just don't feel comfortable with her here, Diamond," she let me know.

"You don't even live here. So honestly, the way you're feeling doesn't even matter." I swear, Melanie was always crying about something. She was talking like she would have to be here when Mia got out. She had a whole house of her own.

"Whatever, Diamond. I get a strange feeling whenever she's around. You know, you're the one who told me to always trust my gut feeling."

Damn, I was tired of having this conversation.

"You wanna get something to eat?" I asked, knowing her fat ass wouldn't pass up free food.

"You know I wanna get something to eat." She quickly stood to her feet, and I looked around for my keys. "You going like that? You're not gonna do anything to your hair?"

I smacked my lips as I snatched my keys from the table. "Damn, you worried about everything I got going on today. How about you worry about Melanie? Do you even know how to do that?"

"Girl, hush. Excuse the hell outta me for wanting my friends to look presentable when they leave the damn house. I won't say anything else about your appearance anymore," she lied.

I chuckled and walked out the door with her following right behind me. She knew she couldn't keep her thoughts to herself even if she wanted to. She didn't care whose feelings she hurt, until they tried to fight her. Then, she was looking at me for help.

"I'm going to McDonalds, so I don't wanna hear your mouth, Melanie," I said, once we were in the car. She smacked her lips but didn't say anything. She knew better. If she started complaining, I wouldn't get her a damn thing. Eat right in front of her ass with no regrets.

I reached into the glove compartment, hoping and praying there would some pills in there, but I was highly disappointed when the only thing I had in there was the title to my car and the car's manual.

"Fuck," I muttered, moving things around.

"What you looking for?"

I ignored Melanie and lifted the manual up. Low and behold, there was a single pill there waiting for me.

"Yes!" I yelled, wanting to jump for joy.

"Are you fuckin' serious?" Melanie snapped as I popped the pill in my mouth without a care in the world. "You need help, Diamond. Like, you're really addicted to—

"Girl, hush. I'm good. Mind ya business."

"You're good? Bitch, you're a borderline fiend."

"You wanna get dropped off in the middle of the street, Melanie? Because that's what it's sounding like to me." I didn't even look in her direction as I drove.

"Whatever, man. I'm just saying you need help. Maybe you should go to therapy. You need to find a better way to cope with what you're going through."

My phone ringing in my lap caused me not to reply to her. Not like I was going to reply anyway.

"The fuck this nigga want?" I muttered, looking at the screen. "Hello?"

"What's good, Diamond?" Kevin asked.

"Not shit, nigga. What you want?"

"Aight, so my nigga's birthday is today, and I need you and Mia to—

"Mia's locked up, Kevin."

"Word? For what?"

Damn, nigga. You nosey as hell.

"For trying to kill a bitch that was talkin' shit. Not that it's any of your business anyway."

He chuckled. "You right. I guess it's just gonna be you then. How much you charge for a night?"

"For your nigga?" I asked, with a brow raised.

"Yeah."

"A thousand." I held in my laughter because I knew Kevin had money. Nigga owned his own club, and then brought his bitch a salon. Yeah, nigga, pay up.

"Damn, Diamond." He sighed. "Aight, I'll hit you up tonight, so answer the damn phone."

"Mhm." I ended the call, then went back to focusing on driving.

"You're too pretty, Dime," Melanie said, causing me to sigh loudly. I knew she was about to start again with her bullshit. "You're too pretty to be out here prostituting."

I smacked my lips. "Who the fuck said I was ugly, first off." I was being serious. I never thought I was ugly. Even when I was younger.

I was dark skinned, my body used to be the shit, but my weight fluctuated since I was on drugs. My hair was a decent length, but I never wore that shit. I preferred wigs.

"You know what I'm getting at, Dime. Let's not mention the videos you be making and uploading them," Melanie said.

I chuckled lightly. "You see why I don't tell you shit, Melanie? You be judging the fuck outta me."

I was also a video girl. I recorded myself masturbating and uploaded it to porn sites. People were gonna talk shit, but I didn't give a damn. I was getting paid for that shit.

"I'm not judging you—

"Yes the fuck you are, bruh. It's all good, though. I'm gonna keep doing what the fuck I want. Soon enough, you're gonna realize I don't give a fuck about what you have to say."

"That's the thing! You don't give a fuck about what anyone has to say! We're only trying to help you! Even Lawrence and his girlfriend were trying to help you, and what did you do? Fucked him, in the house he lives at with her."

I snapped my head in her direction. "Oh, that's my fault? It's my fault that Lawrence ain't shit?"

"You could've said no, Diamond! Then she walked in on it!"

I shrugged. "He paid me."

She shook her head and sat back in her seat. "You know what, I'm not going to say anything else about it. Just hurry up and get something to eat because I have things to do today."

"Girl, hush. You don't have shit to do today. Stop playing."

"Uhh, yes the hell I do. It's my boyfriend's birthday, so I'm spending all day with him." She gushed, and I rolled my eyes.

Melanie had been talking about her boyfriend for the longest, but I'd never seen or met the man. Honestly, I didn't even know what his name was. Shit, she was probably lying about the nigga, or either he wasn't claiming her ass. She acted too weird about him.

After we got something to eat, we both ate like we hadn't eaten anything in years, then she took her ass home. Lawrence was calling me, but I didn't have anything to say to his ass. I only used him for dick, pills, and money. If he wasn't talking about that, then we didn't have anything to talk about at all.

I decided to just take my ass to sleep and wait for Kevin to call my phone with money. I didn't have shit else to do anyway.

KEVIN CALLED me late as fuck. It was almost two o'clock in the damn morning, but being that I'd slept all day, I wasn't even tired. Plus, I charged him another band, so I was real motivated to get my ass to the hotel now.

I threw on a dress because it was easy access. It was peach colored, short as fuck, and had spaghetti straps. You could clearly see my nipples through the thin ass material, but I didn't give a fuck. I hadn't heard anything from Melanie, so I guess she was still out with her boyfriend.

I got into my car, put the address in my GPS, then was on my way to the hotel. I was kinda hoping this nigga came fast so I wouldn't have to be there long. I just hadn't been in the mood lately for these niggas. I just wished I could get paid for sitting at home on my ass all day. That's the only thing I wanted to do.

The hotel wasn't anything special. It was run down, and I was almost certain this place had roaches. I didn't even wanna go in the nasty ass room, but there was money to be made.

I parked the car, looked at myself in the mirror, then got out. I looked good, felt good, and I was about to fuck the shit out of this nigga and get paid for it.

"Hope he's not one of the niggas who likes to talk a lot," I muttered to myself as I approached the door. "I'm not in the mood tonight." I lifted my hand to knock then waited patiently for this nigga to answer the door.

I stood there for at least two minutes before the door finally came open.

"My bad," he said stepping to the side to let me in. "I was in the bathroom when you knocked."

I didn't say anything as I stepped into the room and watched him close the door. It kinda threw me when I saw that he was albino. Now, I had fucked plenty of men in my life but never someone who was albino.

He was dressed in all black. Black shirt, black joggers, with the black and white Jordans to match. His blond dreads were in a ball on the top of his head, and his hazel eyes roamed all over my body, as mine roamed all over his.

"You ready or what?" I asked. "There's no need to just stand here looking at each other."

He raised his blond ass eyebrow. "Get yo' ass on the bed then. Fuck you doing?"

Shit, say less, nigga. I wasted no time coming out of my dress and let it hit the nasty ass floor. After that, I pulled a magnum from my purse.

"Can you fit this?" I asked.

He looked at the condom, then snatched it from me. "Nah, this shit too small for me." He laughed.

I rolled my eyes, then went to sit on the bed. He was kinda cute with his big nose and big lips. I thought it was cute how all the hair on him was blond. Even his damn eyelashes.

He threw the condom I had given him on the floor and I looked at him like he was crazy.

"Nigga, you better use that shit," I snapped.

"Man, shut the fuck up. I got my own shit."

I shook my head. "Nah, you need to use the one I gave you. I don't know what the fuck you did to your condoms before I got here."

"Man, what? You think I did some dumb shit that could risk my dick falling off? I don't know who the fuck been in yo' pussy, and I damn sure don't wanna get yo' ass pregnant."

"Good," I spat. "I don't wanna get pregnant by yo' white ass anyway." Why did I feel like I knew this nigga? And why the fuck were we arguing?

He didn't say anything as he came out of his pants. He stepped out of his boxers and made his way toward me. Dick swinging and all. He let out a small chuckle when he saw how I was staring at it.

He had the type of dick I dreamed about. Yeah, it was white like the rest of his skin, but it was also long. The thickness added so much to it and almost made me say fuck using the condom. How the hell was I in a daze over the dick and I hadn't even gotten it yet?

He slowly rolled the condom on, then spread my legs. I guess this nigga was just gonna skip foreplay, huh?

"You weren't expecting head, were you?" he asked.

"Nah. You probably suck at it anyway." I wasn't even trying to be funny. Most men that I came across sucked at giving head. They bragged about it, only to disappoint me.

He grinned at me. "You funny as fuck."

No, nigga. I was being serious.

He spread my legs even further, then brought his head down like he was about to lick my honey pot. He was so close; I could feel his breath on it.

I smiled to myself because I just knew I was about to get head from an albino boy. My smile quickly fell when I felt him spit on it. I glanced down at him as he took his fingers and played in it.

"You thought like shit." He laughed. "I'm not about to eat yo' ass out."

"You're doing too much talking," I said, catching an attitude. The shit was pissing me off. Just fuck me so I can get my money and get the hell out of this dirty ass hotel.

He slowly stuck a finger inside me. His hazel eyes bored into mine as he waited for me to twist my face up in pleasure. I knew that was all he wanted me to do. I refused, but the shit was hard. I could feel my eyes wanting to roll in the back of my head, but I wouldn't let them.

He slipped another finger inside me and a soft moan slipped from my lips. He gave me a smirk and I wanted to slap it right off his face.

"Don't fight it, baby," he said, using his thumb on my clit. "Let me make you feel good.

His deep voice was low, his eyes were low, and his bottom lip was tucked in. I swear it looked like this man was glowing right now.

A few moments passed, and this nigga had me moaning like I was getting the best dick of my life, and he was still only using his fingers. If his fingers could do this, I could only imagine what his dick was like.

He had me wanting to beg him to give me dick, but nah. He was getting enough satisfaction from my loud ass moans.

"What you say?" he questioned, making me look at him.

"I didn't—"

"You said you want me to fuck you?"

"No," I huffed. It was hard to talk in complete sentences with his fingers all inside me.

"No? So you don't?" He quickly took his fingers out of me, and I instantly caught an attitude.

"Huh? I didn't say that," I said, propping up on my elbows.

"So, you want it?" He lifted a brow.

"Yes, nigga."

"Say it." He smiled.

I couldn't stop the eye roll even if I wanted to. "You playing."

"Nah, I wanna hear you say it."

I smacked my lips and sighed. "I want you to fuck me." I didn't beg for dick from no nigga. I couldn't believe this nigga was making me do it.

He spread my legs again then positioned himself at my entrance. The anticipation was killing me. I felt another eye roll coming, but he caught me off guard when he gripped my neck.

Okay, so he was one of those niggas who liked to choke bitches? I didn't have a problem with that.

He slowly slid into me, and a tiny gasp escaped my throat. My eyes decided to close by themselves. I planned on looking him in the eyes the entire time, but it wasn't going down like that. He let out a small groan as the bed creaked beneath us.

"What the fuck?" he whispered to himself as he quickly pulled out. I slowly opened my eyes to look at him, but by that time, he was plunging into me again.

"Shit," I breathed as my arms clung to his back. He put his face in my neck and let out a long sigh. He came up then put my leg on his shoulder. I let my eyes roll back as he stuck one of

his fingers in my mouth. I could taste myself from where he was playing with my womanly goodness. Nasty niggas were my weakness.

"Fuck, girl. Say my fuckin' name." His voice was still low. I opened my eyes to look at him. His eyes were still low, and he was resting his tongue on his bottom lip. He was getting finer and finer with each stroke.

"I don't know—"

"Call me daddy." A small smile formed on his lips, and I shook my head.

"I'm not calling you daddy, nigga," I managed to choke out. He put my other leg on his shoulder and watched himself go in and out.

"Say that shit."

"Fuckk, wait!" I put my hand on his abs, hoping that would slow him down, but it didn't. He curled his hips just enough to make me choke on pleasure. My nails digging into his back with my mouth falling open, and him watching it all play out on my face.

"What's my fuckin' name?" he asked again.

"Daddy." It just rolled off my tongue without me even thinking about it. He had my entire body shaking. I'd never had a man make me feel like this before. Never had a man to make me scream out like this.

By the time he was actually done with me, I couldn't say shit. I could barely move, so I just laid there watching him get himself together.

"Aye," he said looking at me. "Get the fuck out."

Did I feel some type of way? Hell yeah. Nigga had me wanting to stay here forever and cuddle with his white ass. I didn't say anything, though. I got up, put my dress back on, and he handed me some money.

I wanted to snatch it from him, but I didn't want him to think I had an attitude, even though I did. I probably wouldn't ever see this nigga again in my life.

"What the fuck just happened?" I muttered once I got back in my car. Nigga took my soul right out of my body and put that shit in his damn pocket.

FOUR

M IA

"HOW DOES it feel to be free, little nigga?" My cousin Julian asked me as I rode in the front seat of his car.

"Nigga, great. I was tired of those dusty ass bitches. I ain't never going back to that bitch."

He let out a small laugh, and his bitch snorted. I guess she was mad because I made her ass get in the back, but I didn't give not one fuck. You thought I was really gonna sit in the back of my cousin's shit? Bitch better show some fuckin' respect.

"You need to chill, Mia. I don't need you getting locked up anymore."

I smacked my lips. "Don't tell me what to fuckin' do, Julian. It's my life."

"Girl," his bitch muttered from the back. I turned around to look at her.

"What was that? You got some shit to say?"

"Wasn't nobody talking to you. Chill out." I wasn't too fond of her attitude.

"Okay, then stay back there and shut the fuck up before I shut you up. Fucking with the right one today."

"Really, Julian? You're just gonna let her talk to me like that? You're not gonna say anything to her?" she whined.

Julian looked at her through the rear-view mirror. "You a grown ass woman, Ebony. You better learn how to take up for yourself."

She didn't respond. She sat back in the seat and folded her arms like a big ass baby.

"Dumb ass bitch." I laughed. "Aye, take me to Diamond's. She's expecting me," I let him know.

"Mann." He sighed. "Y'all still cool?"

"Hell yeah, nigga. That my bitch. She ain't going nowhere just like I ain't going nowhere."

"It's never good when y'all two get together."

I shrugged. "Mind your business, Julian."

He shook his head but didn't say anything else. Neither did his little bitch in the back. Words couldn't explain how happy I was to be out of jail. I didn't plan on going back, but who does? No nigga gets out of jail and says, "Yeah nigga, I can't wait to go back."

"Oh shit," Juice said as we pulled up to Diamond's house. "Dime riding clean, ain't she?"

"You already know my bitch ain't gonna be out here lackin'." I laughed, opening the door. I saw his little bitch behind me opening her door too, but I stopped that shit. "Nah, stay yo' ass back there," I said, looking at her.

"What?" she asked, with her ugly ass eyebrows coming together. See, it was one thing to fill in your damn eyebrows, but at least make that shit look good when you do it. I could still see her damn concealer because her dumb ass didn't blend right. Them shits were dark as fuck, too. It looked like she'd colored them bitches with a Sharpie. Shit was ridiculous.

"Bitch, you heard what the fuck I said. If you get up here, I'm gon' beat yo' ass."

She sighed, closed her door, then sat back in the seat. She had an attitude, but I didn't give a fuck about that shit. She wasn't gonna say shit to me.

"You hell, bruh." Julian laughed as I got out the car. That bitch was dumb as hell. I wish somebody would tell me where I could and couldn't sit.

"Whenever I get a phone, I'll call you," I let him know.

"Aight. Tell Dime I said what's up. She still single?"

"Yeah, and it's staying that way, nigga. Worry about that scary bitch in the back. Tell her to learn how to do her eyebrows too." I laughed and made my way to the front door. I couldn't wait to see Diamond. It'd been way too long.

I lifted my hand to knock, but quickly decided against it. Diamond never locked her doors, so I just walked in. That bitch Melanie was sitting on the couch reading a magazine. I saw the displeasure all over her face when she saw me.

I smiled at her. "What's up, Melody?"

She rolled her eyes so damn hard. "For the last time, it's Melanie. Who the fuck do you think you are just walking up in people's shit?"

Melanie never liked me, and I never gave a fuck. I bet if it came down to it, Diamond would choose me over her ass.

"I live here," I said, blowing her a kiss.

"Melanie, have you saw my grey dress that I told you not to wear?" Diamond asked as she came from one of the rooms. She was too busy looking at her phone to realize I was standing there.

Melanie didn't say anything back because she too busy staring at me.

"Girl, I know you hear me talking to—" Her sentence was cut short as soon as she saw me.

"I'm homeeee!" I sang.

"Why didn't you tell me you were getting out, bitch?" she yelled, running to jump on me.

"I didn't wanna ruin the surprise."

"How'd you get here?"

"Julian gave me a ride. Him and his little bitch that was scared of me." I could hear Melanie let out a loud sigh like our conversation was bothering her or some shit.

"That crazy ass nigga." She chuckled. "Come on. We got shit to handle." She grabbed my hand and started toward the door.

"But, you said we were hanging out today," Melanie said, sounding like the sad bitch she was.

"We can do that later," Diamond said as she picked up her car keys.

"When is later?"

"Whenever I feel like it, Melanie. Damn."

We walked out the house and to her car. I could already tell it was gonna be a problem for Melanie with me living here.

"I hope you don't expect me to be nice to that fake ass bitch," I said once we were in the car.

She sighed. "Please don't make this worse than it has to be. You could at least try to be nice. Just for me."

I rolled my eyes. "Fuck that girl. Something just ain't right about her. I don't care how long you've known her."

"You always say that, but she hasn't done anything to me." She shrugged as she started the car.

"That you know of. Just keep your eyes open. People change every day."

She ignored me, but I didn't care. I never trusted Melanie. I just had a feeling I was gonna put my hands on her at least once. Shit, probably more than that.

"You hungry?" she asked.

"Money hungry." I laughed.

"Bitch, I'm serious."

"Nah." I shook my head. "I'm good for now."

"Good. That wouldn't do anything but slow us down anyway.

You need a whole new wardrobe. You look like a bum right now." She laughed, but I didn't.

"Bitch, fuck you. Just for that, I'm making you pay for everything."

"You already know money ain't a thing, shawty," she said as she waved me off. "I planned on buying everything anyway."

FIVE

DIAMOND

"Diamond," I heard Melanie say. "Are you still coming with me to the hair show? Or are you gonna be too far up Mia's ass to do anything today?" I laid in bed with the covers pulled over my head, wishing she would get the fuck on.

I was so hungover, it didn't make any sense. I knew I shouldn't have started drinking with Mia last night. That bitch acted like she didn't have a liver.

"Melanie," I groaned, not even wanting to open my eyes. "Go awayyy."

She smacked her lips. "See, I knew this shit was gonna happen. Mia comes back, and you start acting different."

"Girl, shut uppp."

"No. You need to hear this. You promised that you would go to the hair show with me, and here you are backing out of it. That's real fucked up, Dime. I thought we were—"

I cut her sentence short by throwing a pillow at her.

"Shut the fuck up, Melanie! You always crying about some dumb ass shit, and I'm tired of it!" I gave her a dirty look as I sat all the way up in bed. Why the hell was she at my house so early to begin with? And how the hell did she get in?

"I'm not crying. You said you'd go with me, and—"

"What time does the shit start?" I snapped.

"Six." She smiled, picking the pillow up off the floor. "So you have more than enough time to get your shit together."

She left out the room before I could say anything back to her. I really didn't wanna go to that damn hair show. But I do remember telling her that I would go. Plus, I did blow her off yesterday for Mia, so it was only fair.

"What the fuck?" I groaned, laying back down. I was regretting everything I drank last night. I didn't think I'd ever been this hungover before.

By the time six o'clock rolled around, I was feeling a lot better. I had thrown up twice and got me something to eat. After that, I did my makeup, hair, and got dressed. Of course, I was looking good as hell. I had to be the best-looking bitch wherever I went.

"You know, you really didn't have to get dressed up for this. It's not formal or anything," Melanie said as we approached the building.

I looked down at my outfit. A body hugging, maroon dress that stopped right above my knees and a pair of black heels on. What the fuck was she talking about?

"I'm not dressed up. This is casual, boo."

"No," she said, shaking her head. "What I'm wearing is casual." She was right.

She was wearing a plain white shirt with a pair of regular denim jeans on, and some tennis shoes. Her hair was in a high bun on the top of her head. I did look like I was dressed up compared to her, but that wasn't what I was going for. I just liked to look good.

"You know I like looking good, Melanie." I shrugged.

"Extra," she muttered. "But my boyfriend in the show." She smiled as we walked through the doors.

"Yeah, you said that about three times on the way over here." Shit was annoying, but I was ready to see what her boyfriend looked like. She wouldn't even invite the man to the house.

"When I introduce you, could you please be nice? He's... different. Not like most people."

I lifted a brow. "What? Is he slow or something?"

"No," she said, smacking her lips. "You'll see when you meet him. I just need you to keep your comments to yourself."

I rolled my eyes. "I say what I wanna say. Ain't nobody gonna beat my ass."

She pressed her lips together and didn't say anything else. I didn't even know why she was wasting her breath. She knew how I was, and I wasn't about to change for anyone.

"This some low budget ass shit," I muttered as we found a seat up front.

The decorations looked like we were about to attend a high school party. I wasn't that good at decorating, but I could've done better than this.

"I don't think we're allowed to sit up here. It says VIP." Melanie said as I pulled out my phone and scrolled through it.

"VIP? Bitch, ain't nobody VIP up in this bitch. If they say something to us, then we'll move. Stop acting scary." She gave me an uncertain look. I didn't care, though. I didn't even wanna be here.

Another hour passed, and the show finally started. Of course, I'd been talking shit the whole time. This is how you know this shit was about to be ghetto. How you gonna start a whole hour late?

"I'm ready to go," I said, folding my arms.

"Shh," Melanie snapped, as the lights began to dim.

I rolled my eyes. Couldn't wait for this shit to be over.

The music started blasting, making me perk up just a little. Then this woman slowly made her way down the runway like she was Tyra Banks or something. She wasn't ugly. Far from it.

She had on this bomb ass dress that stopped mid-thigh. Her hair was laid to perfection, hanging down her back, and her brown skin was glowing. Shawty looked real good. She was just walking too damn slow, making me bored all over again.

I let out a sigh and leaned back in my seat.

"Stop it," Melanie whispered. "Act like you have some damn home training." Melanie was really feeling herself tonight. I was about two seconds away from popping her ass in the mouth like she was my child. I'd wait until we got to the car to tell her how I felt, though.

I'll admit, some of the models looked good. Then there were some that looked a damn mess. It was taking everything in me to keep a straight face. Some of these bitches needed to get slapped for their outfit alone.

They were wearing see through dresses, with big ass panties that everyone could see. Then the bad bodied bitches who were wearing tight ass clothes? This shit was a riot. A laugh riot.

The music stopped, and another set of models got ready to walk the runway. So many people had their phones out recording, but this shit wasn't even worth it. If I was the owner, I'd be embarrassed.

"I'm ready to go," I let Melanie know.

"Hush. We can leave after this set."

The music started again, and I threw my head back with a loud sigh. I was being dramatic, but I didn't give a damn. I was just ready to get the hell out of here.

Well... I thought I was ready to get out of here until I looked up and saw who was walking. There he was, looking beautiful and albino like he did a couple nights ago.

His blond dreads were in a nice braided style, his clothes were on point, but that was expected, and the way he walked... he just knew he was the shit. I didn't realize how hard I was smiling until my jaws started hurting. I was definitely talking to him before I left.

I watched him the entire time he walked. Ever came across an albino Adonis? I was staring at one right now. It hit me that I didn't know his name, but was that gonna stop me from approaching him? Hell nah.

"Melanie," I said, grabbing her arm. "That's him."

Her brows came together. "Who?"

"The albino nigga. I fucked him the other day, and his dick changed my life."

"You did? It did? You sure it was him? He paid you? You sure it was him?" She twisted her face up, but I didn't think anything of it. She was always judging me for something.

"Yep. I'm positive it was him. I need that nigga in my life."

She looked at me for a while before she sat back in her seat, folded her arms, and crossed her legs. I peeped her attitude, but I didn't care about it. The only thing I cared about right now was him. He was over there looking like the man of my dreams.

When the whole thing was over, I quickly stood up and looked around. I wasn't leaving until I talked to him.

"Come on. I'm hungry," Melanie said, trying to leave. Oh, so now she was in a rush?

"Give me a minute. I need to talk to someone before we go."

She gave me an ugly expression. "Who? You're not about to talk to that boy, are you?"

I chuckled. "Actually, that's exactly who I'm trying to talk to." I smiled at her.

"You're wasting your time. He probably won't even talk to you."

"What? Why?"

"Because, you're a prostitute, Diamond. Don't know if you know this or not, but niggas don't like prostitutes." She had a small smirk on her face, like she was satisfied with what she'd just said.

"If I fucked him once, I can fuck him twice." I smiled. "Take yo' ass to the car if you feel some type of way."

I walked away from her dumb ass to see if I could find him. I didn't know why Melanie was throwing shade all of a sudden, but what she failed to realize was, I didn't give a fuck about anyone's opinion except mine.

I spotted ole boy standing at the table with the snacks, talking to the owner of the shop. The closer I got to them, the more familiar the girl looked. I couldn't remember where or why I knew her, and it was starting to bother me.

"Did you see how all eyes were on me when I walked out, though? I stole the whole mothafuckin' show, bruh," he told her as I approached them.

"Boy, bye. You're so full of yourself." She chuckled, then looked at me. He noticed that something had her attention, so he turned to look at me too.

"Hey," I said, smiling at him.

"Umm... can we help you?" Off gate she had a damn attitude, and I wasn't feeling it. I didn't even know the bitch, so why the hell did she have an attitude with me? She needed to have an attitude with the fact that this hair show was ratchet as fuck.

"I was definitely talking to him, not you." I raised an eyebrow as I looked at her. Bitches had me fucked up today.

"Okay, well, you can move around because—"

"Layla, weren't you supposed to be looking for Kevin?" he asked, cutting her off.

"Oh yeah. You distracted me and shit." She gave me a dirty look before she walked off. Dumb bitch. I bet she couldn't see me with the hands, though.

"What's up, ma? Didn't think I'd ever see you again." He gave me a small smile.

"Oh, so you remember me?"

"Hell yeah. The shit happened like a night ago. You were the most exciting shit I did on my birthday. Plus, it's not every day that I fuck somebody, and I still be thinking about it a day later."

He eyed my body with a lick of his lips, and I was ready to risk it all for him.

"I don't even know your name." I giggled. I was giggling? Because of a nigga? Oh, hell no.

"Koda. I don't recall getting your name either, shawty."

"Diamond Carter. You should—"

"Here," he said, shoving his phone in my face. "Put your number in this bitch. No need to beat around the bush and shit."

I slowly took the phone from him.

"First off, who the hell said I wanted your number?"

"Stop playing. I could tell you wanted it the night at the hotel. You wouldn't be over here, all up in my personal space if you didn't want something."

This nigga was so right. I didn't have anything to say as I put my number in his phone.

"When I call, you better answer, shawty," he said, once I handed the phone back to him.

"You better call, nigga," I said, slowly turning to leave. "I'll be waiting." I could feel his eyes on my ass as I walked away.

Mission fuckin' accomplished. I couldn't wait for him to call me. I just hope he didn't keep me waiting too long.

"Took you long enough," Melanie said when I got in the car. "You didn't even talk to him, did you?"

"Yep." I laughed. "Nigga been thinking about me since that night. I gave him my number, so he should be calling soon."

"Yeah, whatever." She snorted. She could stay mad. Nothing could ruin my mood right now.

SIX

MELANIE

"What you about to do?" Diamond asked when we pulled into the driveway of her place.

I shrugged. "Don't know." I wasn't feeling her right now. I knew I should've went to that hair show by myself.

"Oh, aight. I'm about to go see if Mia wants to get into something."

I rolled my eyes extra hard, but she didn't see it. I was just glad she was out of my car. As soon as she closed the door, I sped off. I had some shit to handle.

"Can't even believe this shit," I muttered, as I pulled up to a stop light. I thought about texting this nigga and letting him know that I was on the way, but what fun would that be?

I sped the entire way to his house. The only thing that was on my mind was fighting. Someone was gonna get their ass beat today, and it wasn't me.

When I pulled up to his house, I didn't see his car in the driveway. I didn't let that bother me, though. I parked right in front of his mailbox. I was gonna sit in his house until he brought his stupid ass home.

"Aye," I heard Sani's voice as I approached the door. "That nigga Koda ain't here."

"I know he ain't. His car ain't even in the driveway. I'll wait for him."

"Nah... I don't think he's coming home tonight, ma." Me and Sani weren't too fond of each other, so I knew he was only saying this because he didn't want me here. Nigga had me fucked up, though. I wasn't going nowhere.

"Well call him." I folded my arms.

"What?"

"You heard me, Sani. Call that nigga and make him come home. Tell him he has a surprise waiting for him."

The look on his face let me know that he didn't want to call Koda, but he slowly reached in his pocket and retrieved his phone.

As soon as he slid his finger across the screen to unlock it, we were both blinded by headlights that were pulling into the driveway.

This was even better.

Sani let out a sigh of relief as I started toward Koda's beat up car. This nigga was about to hear my mouth tonight.

"Really!" I yelled as he got out the car. Hair still looking good as hell from the hair show. "You out here paying bitches for pussy? This what we doing?"

He let out a loud sigh. "Yo, what the fuck, Melanie? Fuck you over here for?"

"What the fuck is wrong with yo' ass? You always out here embarrassing me and shit! You act like you don't have a girlfriend!"

He pulled an angry, pale hand down his face. "That's the thing, Melanie! I do what the fuck I wanna do because I don't wanna be with you anymore! You won't leave! You're still here for what?"

"What, nigga? You don't wanna be with me anymore? After everything we've been through? You're just saying fuck it? So it's fuck me and my feelings? You're just gonna waste my time like that?"

He shrugged easily. "I been told yo' ass how I was feeling. You always wanna act like you don't hear what I'm saying, so fuck it. Hell yeah, I'm doing what the fuck I want. I been done with you, Mel."

I was quiet because honestly, I didn't know what to say. For the past two years, he had been my man. My everything. My best friend. Not to mention, I let that nigga take my virginity. How was it that easy for him to leave?

He acted like I didn't mean shit to him. Like what we had wasn't real. I could feel my tears building up, but I wouldn't let them fall. I refused.

Sani coughed, indicating that he was still standing over there listening to our conversation.

"So, whatchu gon' do, Mel? You just gon' stand there looking stupid?" he asked, making me look up at him.

"So, you like prostitutes now?" I asked, weakly. Koda just wasn't the type of nigga to pay for pussy. Well, at least, that's what I thought. I didn't even know this nigga anymore.

"What that gotta do with you?"

Why couldn't he just answer the question? Why was he being difficult? All I wanted was answers.

"All I want is you, Koda. No one else. What am I supposed to do?" I just couldn't imagine my life without him.

I had already planned on marrying this man, then having his kids. Our future was so bright, but here he was fucking shit up.

"It's time to move on, Melanie. This relationship was over before it started. Stop tryna force shit."

"I just don't understand why you're out here paying for pussy, though. I thought you were better than that, Koda."

He smacked his lips. "How'd you even know about that shit?"

"Because the bitch is my best friend! Imagine how I felt when I heard another bitch talking about how good my boyfriend's dick is!"

"Man, chill. It's not my fault you wouldn't have me around your friends and shit. You was hiding my ass like I was the side nigga or some shit. How the fuck am I supposed to know what them bitches look like?"

I rolled my eyes at his dumb ass. I really wanted to hit him dead in his face.

"That's not the fuckin' point, nigga! You shouldn't be fuckin' other bitches, let alone paying for it!"

He waved me off. "On some real shit, though. She said my dick was good?" He had a small smirk on his face, and at this point, I was disgusted with him.

"Fuck you, nigga." I walked to my car without waiting for him to respond. I couldn't believe this shit was happening to me.

Diamond had stolen every single boyfriend I'd had in the past. Once I would bring them home, and they would catch a glimpse of Diamond, that was it for me. My boyfriends would start throwing little hints about her, next thing I knew, they were having loud ass sex in her room while I laid in bed, wishing I was somewhere else.

One time, I'd even walked in on her and one of my boyfriend's having sex on the couch. All she did was apologize and tell me it wasn't that serious, and she was just making money.

I specifically kept Koda away from Diamond, and she still found a way to have sex with him.

"It's time to move on, Melanie," I mocked Koda in a deep voice. "Dumb ass nigga!"

As a matter of fact, Diamond and Koda were perfect for each other. He was a dumb ass nigga, and she was a dumb ass bitch. Secretly, I felt like Diamond wanted to be me. She just always had to have everything I had.

I HOPED she wasn't looking for a relationship with Koda. That nigga was gonna dog her ass out just like he did me.

By the time I got home, the tears were falling. I didn't even wanna walk in my house because I'd just be reminded of everything that had just happened. Sometimes Koda spent the night, but I guess that was over now.

As I made my way into the house, my phone rang in my hand. I scoffed when I saw it was Diamond calling. I wasn't going to answer that shit. I didn't have shit to say to her.

"Call Koda, bitch," I muttered, slamming the door behind me.

SEVEN

K ODA
"It's about time you dropped that bitch," Sani said once
we made it into the house. Nigga never liked Melanie.

"She acted like she didn't have common sense or some shit. Bitch
was mad annoying."

"Nah, you were leading her ass on. Ain't no way she just kept
popping up on your ass like that."

I shrugged. "She knew I was doing what the fuck I wanted. She
was just happy to have the girlfriend title. She was one of those
simple hoes."

I knew I was fucked up for leading Melanie on and shit, but I just
didn't give a fuck. I told her that relationship shit wasn't for me. Bitch
should've listened.

She never met my mom, and I didn't have her around the rest of
my family and shit. I didn't know why she thought this shit was a real
relationship. I had everyone around me thinking I was single, and
that's how I fucking acted.

"Order some pizza. I'm hungry as fuck," Sani said once I sat
down on the couch.

"Nigga, what you doing? You got a phone, right?"

He didn't say anything as he pulled his phone from his pocket. I wasn't even hungry because I'd ate at Layla's hair show and shit. The food wasn't really that great, but it was better than nothing.

"You have fun acting like America's Next Top Model?" he asked, once he was finished ordering the pizza.

"Fuck you, nigga." I laughed. "I stole the fuckin' show. Bitches couldn't keep their eyes off me."

"Yeah right. Them bitches weren't looking at you."

"Damn, nigga. You sounding like a hater right now."

There was a knock on the door, which caused me to look at Sani. I knew the pizza wasn't here that fast, so who the fuck was knocking on the door?

"Chill, bruh." He laughed as he got up to answer the door. "It's just Miracle."

Miracle was this bitch Sani had been fucking with for a little minute. She tried to fuck with me on a couple different occasions, but I wouldn't let that shit happen. She just wasn't attractive to me.

"Damn, nigga," she breathed as she stepped in the house. "You took your sweet little time coming to open the door, didn't you?" She already had an attitude for no reason. That's probably what turned me off the most about her. She was always bitching and complaining about shit. It was annoying as fuck, and I didn't understand how Sani put up with her ass.

"Girl, sit yo' ass down. You stood out there for thirty seconds."

"Hey, Koda," she said as she walked past me.

"Wassup?"

"You got that nigga Onyx mad as hell. He kept saying some shit about you tried to kill his grandma. I think he put a price on your head," she let me know.

I laughed to myself. "I don't give a fuck. That nigga knows where the fuck I'm at, and still ain't making no noise. Gotta get other niggas to do his dirty work." I didn't try to kill that nigga's grandma. I made sure to keep her old ass alive. Nigga was mad at the wrong thing.

"I don't know why you're even messing with that nigga. Do you not know what he's capable of, Koda? You can't keep walking around here like you're invincible."

"With all due respect, Miracle, shut the fuck up. I don't give a fuck about that nigga or what he can do. All I want is the money he owes me. Fuck I look like, walking around worried about another nigga? That's some faggot shit."

"I'm just saying. You don't know who you're fucking with. He kills niggas just for—"

"Ayo, Sani. Shut your girl up. She getting on my nerves."

Sani chuckled as he sat down next to Miracle who was smacking her lips. She was talking too damn much about shit I didn't give a fuck about.

"This is why you're still single, Koda. You don't listen to nobody. You're reckless as fuck, and you're a little boy. Don't no grown woman want a young minded nigga."

Bruhhhh, why was this bitch still talking to me? What the fuck?

"Yeah, but you want a relationship with a nigga who clearly doesn't want one with you. You over there doing wifey shit for that nigga while he's fucking other bitches and enjoying life. Mind ya bidness, Miracle," I said, standing up.

"Come on, bruh," Sani groaned.

"Fucking other bitches? Nigga, you broke my phone the other day because you thought I was texting another nigga, when I was only texting my brother!"

I walked out the house because I didn't wanna hear them arguing. Bitch was speaking on shit she didn't even fucking know about. Another reason I couldn't stand her ass. I pulled out a Black from the package that I had in my pocket and lit that bitch. I could still hear Miracle yelling at Sani. I almost felt bad for starting that shit, but if she would've just stopped talking to me, I wouldn't have said shit.

I saw the pizza deliverer pull up in front of the mailbox, and an idea popped in my head. I smiled to myself as I slowly stood up. I snuck around his car as he opened the door. Nigga had his back turned to me, so he didn't even know I was standing behind him.

Before he could turn around, I had my gun pressed to the back of his head.

"Get on the fuckin' ground, nigga," I demanded as his hands shot up.

"Please don't shoot me," he whimpered, like a pussy.

"I said get on the ground!"

He quickly laid on his stomach, as I ran through his pockets. He didn't have shit but his wallet.

"How much money you got on you?" I asked.

"All my money is in my wallet!" he let me know, but nah. That nigga was lying.

I hit him in the back of his head with the gun, then went to the passenger side to open the door. I checked in the glove compartment, and there was an envelope full of money. I guess that's where he kept all his tips and shit. I took it, put it in my pocket, and walked back to the other side of the car.

He was still laying on the ground, and I could hear his hoe ass crying. I opened the back door and took the pizza, too. I didn't give a fuck.

"Ayo, get the fuck outta here before I kill yo' ass," I said. He quickly stood to his feet, then got back in his car. The nigga sped off before he could even shut his door all the way. I smiled to myself as I walked back in the house with free pizza.

"Here," I said, sitting it down on the coffee table. "Eat up, niggas."

Sani gave me a weird look. "You paid for it?"

"Hell nah." I laughed. "Got that shit for free."

"How?" Miracle asked, getting up so she could get her a piece.

"Don't worry about all that. Just be happy it was free."

"You robbed the pizza guy, didn't you?" she asked, as her eyes widened.

I shrugged and slid my hands in my pockets. "Maybe."

"Bruh, you always doing some shit! Didn't we just talk about you chillin' out? Fuck you robbing—"

"Chill, nigga." I laughed. "It ain't even that serious."

"Yes, it is! You robbed him at your house! He knows where you live! What if he calls the police?" Miracle asked, making shit worse. I didn't say anything as I made my way out the house and to my car. I wasn't gonna be able to stay with them niggas tonight. I didn't know where the fuck I was gonna go, but staying here wasn't an option.

Once I was in my car, I sat there for a moment, thinking about what my next move was gonna be. That's when that fine ass dark skinned shawty from the hair show popped in my head. Diamond? Is that what her name was? Or was it Destiny?

Shit.

I scrolled through my phone until I landed on her contact. She let the phone ring three times before she answered it.

"You got sixty seconds to talk before I hang up on yo' ass," she answered, making me lift an eyebrow.

"Damn, that's it? What if it's an emergency?" I asked.

"Then you call 9 1 1, my nigga. Who is this, anyway?"

"The man of your dreams, shawty. I'm a little hurt you don't know my voice."

"Swear to God I will hang the fuck up," she snapped. Clearly, she wasn't in a good mood.

"Koda," I said with a light chuckle. You don't remember me already, Destiny?"

She smacked her lips. "It's Diamond. Don't know who the fuck Destiny is."

"Damn, ma. I was close. No need to catch an attitude." I swear I could feel her roll her eyes.

"You weren't. You tryna fuck though? Is that why you're calling me?"

Damn. I was tryna chill, and maybe it would lead to sex, but she didn't even let that shit happen. She was straight forward with her shit.

"What if I was just tryna chill?"

She laughed. "You just tryna chill? You sure?"

I nodded like she could see me. "Hell yeah. Lemme get to know Diamond before I finish learning her body."

"Oh shit, aight. I'll send you my address."

"Aight, cool."

"Oh, and Koda? Since you're just tryna chill, when you get here, don't even think about sex." She hung up before I could say anything back.

"What the fuck?" I muttered, looking down at my phone as the text message from her came through. See, I wasn't even trying to fuck, but now, that was the only thing on my mind. It was all good though. I bet I could make her change her mind about that.

When I got to her house, I didn't expect her to live in the neighborhood she did. I mean, I lived in the hood. I didn't know why I expected her ass to live in one of those nice ass neighborhoods that's full of snitching ass white people. She had a nice one-story house with an all-black BMW sitting out front.

I parked right behind it, then stepped out my car. I was feeling good about this. I couldn't wait to watch her act like she didn't wanna fuck me. It was gonna be harder for her than it was for me.

Well, that's what I was thinking until I got to her door step and she opened the door before I could even knock. She was wearing a baby pink bra and panty set, with a black silk robe on. She already wasn't playing fair, bruh.

"Hey." She smiled like she was innocent.

"Wassup?" I said as she stepped to the side to let me in. The house looked even better on the inside.

"You thirsty? Want anything to drink?" she asked, as she shut the door.

I followed her into the kitchen. "What you got?"

"Hmm...I have juice, water, liquor." She turned to look at me. "You look like you drink brown."

"Word? That's how I look?"

She nodded as she pulled an unopened bottle of Hennessy from her freezer. "All I got is brown anyway because a bitch like me doesn't drink white. Honestly, I barely drink period, but I'm feeling good tonight."

She was looking good too.

"I'm not gonna drink too much. You not ready for that side of me yet." I winked at her as she poured me a shot and slid it to me.

She gave me a small smile. "If you say so, Koda. If you say so."

DIAMOND

I knew what the fuck I was doing when I pulled that Hennessy bottle out. Shit, I knew what I was doing when I answered the door in my bra and panties. This nigga really thought he was gonna come over here just to chill? Nah. I had been thinking about fucking since I gave him my number. I didn't even expect him to call me so soon, but here we were on the couch. He was fighting the urge so hard. It was kinda cute, actually.

"Sooo, Koda," I slurred. "Where do you work?"

He was drunk. He was so damn drunk, and I had him exactly where I wanted him.

"Walmart." He chuckled. "I already know where you work, so I don't even gotta ask." He looked at me with one of his blond eyebrows raised.

"You said it like it bothers you." I chuckled, not really caring.

"Nah." He shook his head. "The only thing that's bothering me right now is trying not to look at you because you're over there looking like my next meal."

"You're so silly." I laughed. "I do look good, though, don't I?"

"You did that shit on purpose." He looked at me through those low hazel eyes. He didn't know how hard it was for me too, but I refused to crack first.

"I don't know what you're talkin' about."

He took my hand and put it on his zipper. I could feel his dick begging to be released. But nah. I wasn't going to be the one to do it.

"I'm talkin' about this," he let me know.

I didn't know what it was about him. I'd never invited any nigga over to my house like this. Never got drunk with a nigga unless we were in a shitty hotel and he was about to pay me for sex.

Every time his eyes landed on me, I felt my entire body getting hot. My honey pot was yelling at me because she wanted this nigga bad.

Before I could open my mouth to respond to him, he roughly grabbed me by my face, and stuck his tongue in my mouth. I felt him tugging at the rim of my underwear, and I slapped his hand away.

"Nigga, you came over here to chill. No sex, remember?"

"Either you show me where your room is, or I'll just fuck you right here on the couch. It really doesn't matter to me." He shrugged easily.

I slowly stood up and made my way to my room. I didn't know where Mia went, and Melanie hadn't come over today. That was perfect. I didn't need anyone interrupting anyway.

Once we were in my room, I closed and locked the door, then cut the light out. He stood in front of me as I dropped my robe.

"Get yo' ass on the bed. Fuck you waiting on?" he demanded, coming out of his shirt. I didn't say a word as I got on the bed and prepared myself. I swear that nigga came out of all his clothes in two seconds.

His pale ass looked so good walking to my bed naked. I enjoyed watching his dick swinging, just like I did the first time we had sex. I let him take control, just like he did the last time.

He ripped my underwear off and tossed them on the floor. I was loving how rough he was being. Like yes, nigga. Throw me against the wall and call me a bitch. He was gentle when he took the bra off.

"You got Hershey kiss nipples." He chuckled, as he pinched one of them.

"Put them in your mouth." I breathed. He did just that. I was having an out-of-body experience, and he hadn't even stuck the tip in yet.

About five minutes later, he had me on my hands and knees,

screaming his name like I wanted to wake the whole neighborhood. He was choking me, slapping my ass, and now pulling my hair. I glued my wig on, so that bitch was secured...

Well, that's what I thought. The harder he went, the harder he pulled, and the more my wig slid.

"Koda, wait—"

"Shut the fuck up." Nigga was in his zone and shit, but my fucking wig was about to come the fuck off.

"Koda!"

"Yeahhhhh, that's my mothafuckin' name, baby. Say that shit!"

His dick was in my ribcage. Literally. Toes were tingling, legs were shaking, but my fuckin' wig, nigga!

"Ko—"

It was too late. I felt it peel all the way off, and he froze. I didn't even wanna look at him, but I did. Nigga was looking at my wig like it was infested or some shit.

So, here I was, with my jail braids out, looking like Cleo from *Set It Off,* all for some dick.

"Oh shit." He laughed as he handed the wig back to me. "My bad... I ain't know that shit was about to happen." He was laughing so fucking hard, and it was pissing me off. I got off the bed and walked into the bathroom.

"You can leave now, nigga."

"What? Nah, I'm not done. You better put a scarf on and lemme finish blowing ya back out. Stop being childish."

Stop being childish. I rolled my eyes. Wasn't even in the mood for sex anymore. I wanted this nigga to go the fuck home.

"I'm not being childish, Koda. I tried to tell you my wig was about to come off, but you wouldn't listen." I folded my arms as I looked at him. He looked amused.

"Pussy shouldn't be so good. It wouldn't have happened if your shit was whack." He shrugged.

I quickly grabbed my silk scarf and tied it around my head. I had never been embarrassed like this before. I didn't even wanna finish having sex with this man, but the way he was looking at me let me know he wasn't about to take no for an answer.

After I was sure my scarf was secure and he agreed on no hair pulling, he fucked me until we both couldn't go anymore. The last thing I remember was watching him, with my eyes barely open as he got dressed to leave. I wanted to let him know he could spend the night, but fuck that. I already gave him special treatment by letting him have sex with me in my bed, so it was probably for the best he took his ass home.

EIGHT

MIA "Nah-uh, bitch." I laughed as Diamond sat in front of me with her face all twisted up and shit. "No that nigga didn't! The whole wig, though? That nigga saw your braids?"

She rolled her eyes and nodded. "Hell yeah. I was tryna tell that nigga my wig was fuckin' slippin', but he wouldn't listen. I'm still mad about it."

"You kicked his ass out, didn't you?"

Melanie walked into the kitchen with her nose in the air and shit. She came over early as fuck and has had an attitude like we did some shit to her ass. I just really couldn't stand that hoe. How you gonna walk into a house with people in it, but not speak? Rude ass bitch.

"Yeah." Diamond chuckled. "I told him to leave, but he wouldn't. He told me to throw on a scarf so he could finish. So, that's what the fuck I did." She shrugged and laughed some more.

"Dick must be bomb as fuck. What you say his name was?"

"Koda," she said, with her eyes lighting up. I'd never seen her ass this happy when she was talking about a nigga. Only time her eyes would light up was when she was getting money.

I heard Melanie snort, and I cut my eyes at her. Once she saw me looking at her, she rolled her eyes and turned around.

"You got a problem?" I asked, making her turn around again.

"Did I say that?" she snapped back.

"Oh my goshhh," Diamond groaned, throwing her head back. "Y'all, don't start this right now."

"Nah, she over there making noises and shit like she has a problem, so I wanna know what's good." I sat back in my seat and waited for her to answer.

"I wanna know why you always got something to say to me, Mia. I was really over here minding my damn business. You don't even have a real reason why you don't like me. You're jealous, but that's okay. I'd be jealous of me, too." She turned around and went back to whatever she was doing.

"Jealous? Bitch, if you don't shut yo' raggedy body built ass the fuck up. Fuck I look like being jealous over a duck? You got me real fucked up right now, Melanie. I'll beat you the fuck up, and you know I will."

"Stop it," Diamond demanded, looking down at her phone that was lighting up. "Oh shit, he's calling me." Her eyes shot back up at me.

"Bitch, answer the shit. What you looking at me for?"

"Hello?" she said, putting the phone on speaker.

"Wassup? You up?" he asked. Nigga had a deep ass voice. He sounded fine as fuck over the phone.

"I answered, didn't I?"

"Nah, shawty. I meant up like showered and dressed." Diamond was smiling hard as fuck. If she was light skinned, her cheeks would've been turning red.

"Oh. Yeah, I am."

"Cool. You tryna go get some breakfast?"

She looked at me like she wasn't sure what she should say. I didn't know why she was acting like she'd never had a conversation with a man before.

"Yeah," she finally said. "We can go. How long you think it's gonna take you to get here?"

"I'm already here, ma. Pussy was too good. I never left last night."

Her mouth fell open, and so did mine.

"Oh shit." I laughed. I ain't never had a nigga do some shit like that before.

Diamond hung up, then walked over to the door and opened it.

"Bruh, he's really sitting out here!"

Melanie smacked her lips and walked off. I ignored her as I went to stand next to Diamond. Bitch always had an attitude for no reason.

"So, that nigga really waited out here all night?" I asked. "Hell nah. That's some crazy shit."

Diamond grabbed her purse off the coffee table and shrugged. "I'll be back. I'm going to eat, bitchhh." She walked out the door, and I closed it behind her.

As soon as I started making my way to my room, my phone started ringing.

"Nigga, you ready? I'm on the way right now," Julian said.

"I'm about to get dressed now."

"Mia, you said you were getting dressed a whole hour ago." I could hear the attitude in his voice.

"Yeah." I chuckled. "I lied."

"Man, I'm not about to be waiting for you all day and shit. You need a car, not me."

I rolled my eyes. "Shut the hell up. I'll be ready when you get here. I won't even do my makeup. Does that make you happy, sis?"

"I'm not ya sis, bruh. Just hurry the fuck up." He hung up, and I walked into my room.

Julian insisted on buying me a car. I didn't ask for that shit. I wasn't gonna ask either. I was the type of bitch to go and get it on my own. Or I would just steal somebody's. Shit really didn't matter to me.

I loved my cousin to death, but that nigga was annoying as fuck. Yeah, he was doing good for himself, but he was always throwing his money around. He loved broadcasting that he had it. Then, he'd wonder why all these bitches would just use his dumb ass.

It didn't take me long to get dressed at all. I kept it simple with an orange shirt and a pair of jeans. I didn't feel like wearing a wig today, so I just put my hair up in a high bun on the top of my head. I didn't put on makeup because I didn't need it.

I looked at my fine ass in the mirror and smiled. Skin light and smooth, lips full and pink, and a small black heart that I had tattooed under my right eye. I looked good and felt good.

I could hear Julian blowing the horn from outside, and I took my sweet little time leaving the house. This nigga knew I was not the one to be rushed, yet, he was doing it anyway.

There was some nigga in the front seat, so I got in the back. There was a girl sitting back there, too.

"Told you I wasn't gonna take that long," I said, closing the door.

"You took forever, Mia. Yo' ass should've been ready." He pulled off, and I looked at the girl who was sitting next to me.

She was pretty. Brown skinned with a nice amount of hair. She had her mouth twisted as she scrolled through the phone she was holding.

"Who the fuck is Ciara, Montana?" she snapped, looking at ole boy in the front seat.

"Come on, son." He sighed. New York accent thick as fuck. "Give me my fuckin' phone back, Leah. I told you I wasn't cheating, right?"

"You think I'm fuckin' stupid, huh? You think— Nigga, you paid for her food?" At this point, she was taking off her seatbelt.

"Chill, yo. It's not that serious—"

"Not that serious? This bitch sucking your dick or something? Huh? Is that why you're out here buying other bitches food?"

"Leah—"

"Ayo," Julian said. "I wouldn't have brought y'all with me if I would've known y'all were gonna argue the whole time."

"Wait 'til we get out this car, nigga. I'm gonna beat your ass.

Swear to God." She ran a hand down her face, then looked at me. "You got a boyfriend?"

I gave her a weird look. Out of all the questions to ask, that's what she lets come out her mouth?

"Nah." I chuckled. "I'm too crazy for these niggas. Especially ones like him that don't know how to act." I pointed at her nigga, and he smacked his lips.

"You feel me? My last boyfriend used to cheat and put his hands on me, and he fuckin' knows that! You'd think he'd fuckin' act right, right?"

I shrugged. "You can't make a nigga act right, Leah? Is that your name?"

"Yeah."

"Okay, well like I was saying, you can't make these niggas act right. It's really up to them. If he wants to entertain other bitches like he doesn't have one of the baddest ones on his arm, leave his ass."

"Aye," Montana said, turning to look at me.

"Shut the fuck up, Montana. Ain't nobody talking to you."

"Nah, son. You talkin' about me, though. Don't tell her no—"

"Anyways," I said, interrupting him, and not giving a single fuck. "Don't argue with him. Don't fight his ass or any of that. Just leave. He'll see what he had once you're gone. All niggas do."

She nodded but didn't say anything else. Her boyfriend didn't say anything either. I was the wrong person to give relationship advice. I wasn't the type to do relationships, and I would just tell people to be a hoe.

Your nigga not acting right? Be a hoe. He keeps starting arguments for no reason? Leave his ass, and be a hoe. I promise, it'll make shit better.

Once we got to the damn dealership, I rolled my eyes because I didn't want any of these cars. I stepped out the car and went to stand next to Julian. Leah slowly got out the car, and so did her nigga. He had the nerve to look at her like he had a problem, and I chuckled to myself. I swear, niggas were dumb.

"You see anything you like?" Julian asked, as Leah came to stand next to me. She still had Montana's phone in her hand, going through it. I almost snatched it from her, but I didn't know her like that.

"Nope," I said looking at all the Mercedes. "I don't want any of these shits."

"Come on, Mia. Choose a damn car before I choose the shit for you,"

"Wow." Leah laughed beside me. "Wow. Okay. So, this is what you wanna do, nigga? Okay."

Montana let out a loud sigh, but before he could even open his mouth to say anything, she threw the phone at him, hitting his ass right in the side of his head.

"Bruh!" he yelled, holding the side of his face.

"You a bitch ass nigga, Montana! Swear to God, I'm about to beat —" She didn't finish her sentence because she started swinging at his ass. This was the funniest shit right now.

Leah was so mad, and from the sounds of her punches, it sounded like those shits were hurting his black ass.

"Aye!" Julian yelled. "Yo, I'm not taking y'all asses nowhere else, bruh! What the fuck?"

"Beat his ass, sis." I laughed. While they fought, I looked over at the other side of the road and saw the car lot that I'd rather be at.

"Chill, chill, chill!" Montana yelled, trying to grab her little ass hands, but she was too quick for him. He was really letting this little ass girl handle him.

Julian was able to pull Leah away from Montana, but she was still kicking and screaming.

"I wanna go home!" she hollered, pushing Julian away from her. "I don't wanna live in Atlanta! Take me back to fuckin' Charlotte!"

"Son, take yo' ass to the car!" Montana yelled back, holding his bottom lip that was now bleeding.

Julian flipped his dreads out of his face, then came back to stand next to me. "Pick a fuckin' car, Mia. I'm ready to go."

I looked at him with my brows coming together. "Don't be mad at me because your friends started fighting and shit."

"Pick a car, bruh."

"I want one from over there," I let him know while pointing toward the Nissan dealership. I didn't need anything fancy. I just needed a car. He was always so extra.

"Are you serious? You really want one of those bullshit—"

"A car is a car, Julian," I said, giving him a big smile. He gave me the ugliest expression, but he took me over there.

About an hour later, I was happy, driving off the lot with my 2012 red Nissan Altima. Julian talked shit the entire time, but I didn't give not one fuck. You think he'd be happy about it, being that the car he bought me was way cheaper than the ones he was trying to spend money on, but niggas were never happy. You could never satisfy them.

Leah was in the passenger seat of my car because she said she couldn't stand to look at Montana right now. I could tell she was on that weak bitch shit. That was one thing I couldn't stand. Nah, show a nigga that you can act just like him. Show that nigga how you're a reflection of him.

"I just don't understand," she said quietly. "Why would he—"

"Aye, shawty." I flipped, cutting her ass off. "If you're about to say some sap ass shit about yo' nigga, then I don't wanna hear it. If you're not gonna do anything about it, then don't say shit else."

She looked at me with a lifted brow. She was probably shocked at what I said, but I didn't give a fuck. I was dead ass serious.

"Well, what would you do? If you were in my shoes? I moved to an entirely new state for this nigga. Left my friends and family for him. And this is how he acts?"

"He cheating?"

She nodded. "He was sending dick pics to some bitch."

I let out a loud laugh without even meaning to. "And you didn't break his phone? Leah, you got so much to learn about these dog ass niggas."

"I suppose you're gonna be the one to help me? You're gonna—"

"Stop talking and listen. He thinks he can walk all over you, and you won't do shit about it. He thinks because your last nigga cheated, and you stayed, that he can do the same thing. Nah. We're not gonna let that nigga do that. Hell nah. Not while you're hanging out with me."

Her eyes lit up. "So, you're gonna help me?"

"Chill, ma. I'm only gonna help if you're willing to let me. If I tell you to do something, you do it, aight? I don't need you acting scary and shit. Keep that energy somewhere else."

She nodded. "I'm not scary."

"You better not be. I don't fuck with scary bitches."

She didn't say anything else and we fell into a comfortable silence. Well, that silence lasted for about two minutes.

"Where are we going?" she questioned, as she glanced around.

"My place. I want you to meet someone."

"What? Already? You don't even know me enough to—"

"Shut the hell up. That's all I need you to do right now." She twisted her mouth up and sat back in her seat. I could care less about her attitude. I didn't know her ass, so I wouldn't feel any kind of way by putting her out my car.

When I pulled up to the house, I saw Diamond and that nigga hugging like he was afraid she was gonna leave his ass or something.

"Who are they?" Leah asked as I blew the horn.

"That's my best friend. I don't know who the hell that nigga is she's with."

"Looks like they're in love."

Exactly. That's exactly what that shit looked like and it made me wanna throw the fuck up.

"Aye! Get ya ass in the car! We got somewhere to go!" I hollered out the window. Diamond gave me the finger as she gave that albino nigga a kiss. It wasn't one of those small pecks, I'll see you later kind of kisses either. Nah. I could see that nigga's tongue all down her throat.

"Shit, looks like he's about ready to get her pregnant. How long they been together?" I rolled my eyes.

"They're not together. She literally just met his ass."

I watched as they talked and laughed for another three minutes, then he kissed her one last time, smacked her hard as hell on her ass, and turned to do a light jog to his car. When I pulled up, I didn't even notice his car sitting right there, but now that I'm looking at it? I'm highly pissed off.

Diamond got in the car, all smiles, and I turned to grill her.

"What?" she asked, innocently.

"Really? So, you in love and shit?" I asked.

"What? No! I barely even know the nigga!"

"Clearly. I can't believe you let him drive you around in that. You weren't embarrassed?" I watched him as he drove off in the 1997 white Honda Accord.

She shrugged. "I mean, at least he has a car though. I think he's doing pretty well for himself. He has a job too. And no, he's not a drug dealer or anything. He works at Walmart—"

"Wow, I never thought I'd see the day." I chuckled, bitterly.

She gave me a confused look. "See what day?"

"That you fall for a broke nigga. All you used to talk about was how whenever you decided to get married, it would be with an old ass white nigga who was about to die. Then after he died, you'd take all his money and live happily ever after."

She smirked at me. "Fuck you, Mia. Who the hell is this in the front seat? And whose car we in? You didn't steal this shit, did you?"

"This is my new friend Leah. And no, I didn't steal this. Julian bought it for me."

"Oh shit. Julian is still in town and he hasn't came to see me? That nigga fake as hell." She flipped her weave off her shoulder and looked at Leah again. "So, why she here? Y'all fuckin'?"

I smacked my lips. "No, bitch. She's having relationship problems and needs our help. Well shit, I thought you could help, but you over there looking like you're in love and shit."

"Girl, shut the hell up. Just because I go on a date with that nigga doesn't mean I'm in love. I barely know him."

"Well, y'all look like y'all have been together for years," Leah chimed in.

"Well, no one fuckin' asked you, Lathea."

"It's Leah. And I was just saying. No need to catch an attitude."

Diamond let out a small laugh. "I can tell already that you let your nigga walk all over you, and I don't even know your ass."

"What? How? I don't—"

"You're too nice, girl. I wish a bitch I didn't know would snap at me like I just did. I would've hit a bitch straight in her mouth. Who the fuck you think you're talking to?"

Leah glanced at me and I gave her a light shrug. Didn't know what she was looking at me for.

"I can't help it. I've been like that my entire life," she said, looking down at her hands.

"It's all good, ma. Hanging out with us, you'll stop that shit real soon," I said, hearing Diamond let out a small chuckle.

"Who the fuck said I wanted to hang out with her? How you just gon—"

"Diamond, shut up. You need to learn how to be nice to people other than me."

"For what though? How is that gonna benefit me? How y'all two even meet? I know you're not out here just picking up random bitches off the street."

I sighed loudly. "No. I didn't find her on the street. She was with Julian when—"

"Oh, so she's fuckin' Julian? You fuckin' Julian, Leah?" She turned all her attention to Leah and Leah shook her head. Diamond always thought somebody was fucking. I swear.

"Hell no. I would never fuck that nigga. I'm shocked he even has a dick anymore because he fucks anyone with a—"

"Aye," I said. "It was a yes or no question. Don't be talkin' shit about my cousin either."

"I was just saying," she let me know in a soft tone.

"There you go with that shit. Girl, if you don't man the fuck up," Diamond let out.

"Okay, let's start with her cheating ass nigga that's sending dick pics to other bitches," I said, watching Diamond's facial expressions change.

"Nah–uh." She laughed. "You letting your nigga do shit like that?"

"I didn't know he was doing it until I went through his phone earlier. I really think I should just leave him." Leah sounded so sad, and it pissed me off.

"No, don't leave him," Diamond held. "Nah. Claim yo' nigga back. You want him, right?"

Leah nodded. "Of course I want him, but I just don't understand—"

"Okay, here's what I need you to do," I said, cutting her off. "Go home to him, acting like nothing's wrong. Don't have an attitude or anything."

"Then get sexy for that nigga," Diamond chimed in. "Cook if you have to. But after that, find something to put on that you know will get his attention." Diamond stopped talking because her phone vibrated on her lap. By the way she was smiling down at it, I knew it was that nigga texting her.

"Then what?" Leah asked, being that Diamond had just stopped talking.

"Oh." She giggled. "Sorry, Koda's being nasty."

"So, that's his name? Shit sounds gay as fuc—"

"Hello? Then what?" Leah pressed.

"Okay, so after you get all sexy for him, pull his dick out. Is it big?" Diamond finally put her phone down and looked at Leah as Leah blushed.

"Yes. Big and thick."

"I know it is. A little dick nigga wouldn't act like this if he was with someone that looks as good as you. But anyways, once you slowly get that nigga's dick out, you look at it like it's the best thing in the world. Look at that shit like you tryna marry it." Diamond gave Leah a small smirk.

"That's it? I just look at it?" Leah sounded so disappointed.

"Pepper spray it."

"Huh?"

"You heard me, Leah. Pepper spray his dick."

I lifted an eyebrow in amusement.

"Bitch." I snickered. "What kinda crazy shit?"

"I bet that nigga will act right! Don't look at me like that!" Diamond flipped her hair again, satisfied with what she'd just told Leah.

"I don't think all that is necessary," Leah said, sounding skeptical.

"Fine," Diamond said easily. "Stay with that cheating ass nigga and let him walk all over you. I told you what to do." She sat back in her seat and picked her phone up again.

"I don't even own pepper spray. Like, where would I even find any? They just sell it in stores?" Leah's phone started ringing, but I snatched it from her before she could touch it.

"Don't you dare pick up the phone for that nigga. Let him think you're out with another nigga. Shit is gonna drive him insane." I laughed.

"I got some pepper spray you can have," Diamond said, eyes not even coming up from her phone. "I got way too many anyway."

"So... I just spray it? Then what?"

"Beat his ass. While he's holding his dick and screaming like a little bitch, you beat that nigga like he stole something from you," I said, while nodding my head.

"Then after that, you take his phone from him. Take his phone and start recording. Shit, take some pictures too. Then upload them. Put all that shit online, and then let bitches know that you'll do the same shit to them if they text your man again." Diamond bobbed her head up and down like what she just said was good.

"Oh my God," Leah whispered.

"No. Don't do what she just said. You're gonna make that nigga leave her. We don't need him leaving."

"Don't know why the hell y'all are even listening to me about relationships. I've never even been in one." Diamond laughed. "I fuck these niggas, not love them. Fuck all that extra shit."

"So, you making that white nigga pay you for sex or what?" I asked, watching her twist her face up.

"He's not white. Stop saying that shit. And he paid the first time."

"Wait, you make niggas pay you to have sex?" Leah asked, as her phone started ringing again in my hand.

"Hell yeah. How you think I make money? Ain't nobody getting this shit for free," Diamond said confidently.

"Except that albino nigga." I chuckled. "How the hell that nigga even afford you if he works at Walmart?"

Diamond smacked her lips. "Kevin paid. Mind your damn business, Mia. Shit."

"Kevin? I forgot about that nigga. I'm shocked he still has your number. Ain't he married?"

Diamond shrugged. "I don't know. I don't talk to his ass unless he's sending tricks my way. Other than that, there's nothing to talk about."

She was right about that shit. I was shocked when I found out that Kevin was in a relationship because that nigga was one of the biggest hoes.

"We should go pay that nigga a visit. He still lives in that same house with his sister, right?" I asked, watching Diamond smile at her phone.

"Hell nah. That nigga been moved. I forgot he even had a sister. Them niggas didn't look anything alike."

"Because they're not really related. Shit, they were probably fuckin'."

"Probably." Diamond laughed. "Bitches out here nasty."

We stayed in the car for another hour talking shit before Leah decided she was ready to go fuck some shit up with her nigga. She was scared, I could tell, but she wasn't speaking on it. We exchanged numbers so she could tell me how it went, then me and Diamond pulled off. I was actually tired as hell, and the only thing on my mind was going to bed.

NINE

SANI

"How you even meet that bitch?" I asked Koda as we waited at a long ass red light. Ever since he got his happy ass in my car, he'd been talking about some bitch he was fucking with. Something about it being his ex-girlfriend's best friend.

"Kevin," he said, looking down at his phone.

"What? So, it was Kevin's bitch? Ain't he with your sister?"

"Nah, she wasn't Kevin's bitch. Let's just say he introduced us." He still hadn't looked up from his phone.

"When you meet her?"

"My birthday." He grinned, then finally put his damn phone down.

"So, y'all together or something? You over there acting like you never met a bitch with good pussy before."

"Damn, nigga. You over there sounding mad as fuck. I'm just feeling the girl, aight? That ain't a problem, is it?"

I shrugged. "That shit ain't none of my business. Long as you're happy, nigga. Just don't be surprised when she starts fucking other niggas or something."

"What?" he snapped, head turning in my direction. "Fuck you saying shit like that for? You know something that I don't?"

"Nah." I laughed. "I was just saying because you can't trust these bitches. Get ya panties out ya ass, yo."

"Nigga, fuck you. I know what I'm doin—"

"Move, bruh!" I heard someone yell from behind us. "Get yo' dumb ass out the fuckin' way!" I looked in the rearview mirror at the red Altima that was behind me. Yeah, the light was green, but since she wanted to be extra, and was blowing her horn like she was fucking stupid, I wasn't moving.

"Bruh," Koda let out as I put the car in park. "Don't do this shit. Let's go."

"Nah, fuck that bitch. She wants to play, then we fuckin' can. I don't give a fuck."

"I'm just tryna get home. I got shit to do!"

"Aye!" she yelled again. "Move this piece of shit before I move it for you!"

I rolled down my window, then poked my head out.

"Bitch, fuck you!"

"Oh my fuckin' God, yo." Koda said, pulling a hand down his face. I didn't give a fuck. I hated impatient ass people. I mean, yeah, I should've been paying attention, but she didn't have to be extra like she was.

Once I saw her door pop open, I just knew it was about to be some shit. I thought about waiting until she got to my window, then pulling off on her ass, but when I saw the way her body looked through my mirror, all that shit went out the window. I didn't even feel like I was mad anymore.

"Fuck y'all niggas doing, kissing and shit?" she spat as she got to my window.

She was light skinned, with long ass black hair, long ass eyelashes, and a tattoo of a heart under her eye. She looked dangerous. Nah, y'all ain't hearing me. She looked like the type of bitch to cut a nigga's dick off for cheating kinda dangerous. Everything in me was telling me not to even try this bitch, but fuck it.

"My bad, shawty. Ain't no need to yell, though."

"No need to yell? Bitch, you're parked at a fuckin' stop light! I got shit to fuckin' do! Now, if I was to hit your piece of shit ass car, it would be a fuckin' problem! Move!"

She was yelling, but I couldn't even be mad. Only thing I was thinking about right now was getting her pretty ass in my bed. Didn't know how the fuck I was going to do it, but I was gonna try.

"You that mad?" I asked with a light laugh.

"Am I that— Hell yeah, nigga! Get out the fuckin' way!"

"I will once you put your number in my phone."

"Bruhhhhh," Koda groaned, but I ignored his ass. Fuck him. What I was doing was more important.

"You serious, nigga?" she asked as she crossed her arms.

"Hell yeah. Until then, I'm not moving."

She looked at me, eyes squinted before she finally smacked her lips and held her hand out for my phone.

"B2K lookin' ass nigga. Give me the fuckin' phone."

I didn't say anything as I handed her my phone. I could hear Koda mumbling to himself, but I still didn't give a fuck. Ole girl was more important than him right now.

Once she was finished putting her number in my phone, she shoved it back in my face, and I gladly took it.

"Now get the fuck out my way, nigga. I'm not playing with you." She stormed back to her car, and I pulled off. The car was awkwardly silent, but I could feel Koda staring a hole in the side of my head.

"What, nigga?" I asked, glancing over at him.

"You really did all that for a bitch's number? When is it ever that serious?"

"Did you see her? You can't tell me that bitch didn't look like the woman of my dreams."

"Nah, she looks like she'd murder you in your sleep. You always pick the crazy bitches to fuck with."

"What? You don't even know if she's crazy or not," I defended.

"Niggaaa, she got all the way out the car to talk shit to your face! She has a whole tattoo under her eye, bruh. Any bitch that can get her face tatted is crazy."

"You're just talkin' shit. Probably mad because I got her number and you didn't."

"Nah, I like my bitches dark. She was too light for me."

I twisted my mouth up. "Your last bitch wasn't dark skinned. Or did you forget about her already?"

"Nah, I ain't forget about her. She was at Diamond's crib yesterday." He chuckled.

"Who the fuck is Diamond? That's your new girl?"

"Yep."

"You foul as fuck. I always knew you wasn't shit, but damn, nigga. You don't think Melanie is gonna find out?"

"She already found out. Remember the other day when she came over yelling and shit? Yeah, she was mad because she found out I was fuckin' her best friend and shit."

I looked at that nigga like he was crazy. "Hold the fuck on, nigga. That's the bitch you paid for? You out here fucking a prostitute?"

"Nah, nah, she ain't a prostitute," he tried to explain, but he couldn't. I remembered Melanie's annoying ass yelling about how he was paying for pussy and shit.

"Then what is she? Because it sounds like—"

"It sounds like you need to mind your damn business, bruh. Shit. Worry about your bitches, and let me worry about mine."

I nodded. "Aight, nigga. You got it. Sounds like she's everybody else's bitch, too."

"Fuck you."

I laughed but didn't say shit else as we pulled up to our place. Miracle's car was parked out front, and I remembered we were supposed to be chilling today. Now that I ran into the woman of my dreams, I didn't even wanna see her ass.

"Your girlfriend here." Koda laughed as he opened his door.

"Nigga, fuck you. Don't call her that shit." Miracle wanted to be my girlfriend so bad, but I didn't even like her ass like that. I couldn't understand why we couldn't just fuck and leave it at that. Women always wanted a whole lot of extra shit.

"It's about time you got here. I've been out here for a whole hour," she said as I approached her car.

"Whose fault is that? I told you to call me when you were about to be on your way, shawty."

She shrugged. "I wanted to surprise you, but I had no idea you were gonna take this long to get here." She flipped her hair off her shoulder, then looked at Koda who was walking past us. "Well hey, Koda. You always act like you're too good to speak to somebody."

He looked at her and chuckled. "You not my bitch, Miracle. I don't have to speak to you." He kept moving toward the house and she twisted her mouth up.

"Why don't you ever say anything to him when he's rude to me?"

I smacked my lips and made my way back to my car. Here she goes with that shit.

"Nah, you haven't seen that nigga be rude, Miracle. That's just the way he is. You should know this by now."

"He's such a child. I'm not even surprised that he's still single," she said, sliding into the passenger seat.

"That nigga is single because he wants to be. I don't see why you're worried anyway."

"I'm not worried about his ass! I was just saying that—"

"You're always just saying something about his ass. I'm starting to think you'd rather be fucking him instead of me."

"Nigga, are you serious? I would never fuck him. How many times have I told you I wanted to be in a relationship with you? Huh? You act like I'm not good enough to be your girlfriend."

I sighed and pulled out the driveway. Honestly, shawty wasn't my type. She was too needy, cried too damn much, and she was always complaining. That shit got on my nerves and we weren't even together, so I know I'd be ready to lose my mind if I actually decided to make things serious. Nah. Fuck that.

"Don't start this shit," I muttered, hearing her smack her lips.

"Don't start it? Why not? Why whenever I bring up relationships, you act like I'm speaking another language? You talking to other bitches? You telling them the same thing you tell me?"

"Where you wanna eat at, shawty?" I asked, completely ignoring everything she said to me.

"So, you're just gonna change the subject like I didn't just say anything to you? See, this is exactly why I don't like talking to you. You wanna act grown so bad, but your grown ass can't even communicate. Childish ass nigga."

I slammed on the breaks, causing her to hit her head on the dashboard. Dumb ass hoe wasn't wearing a seat belt, so that shit wasn't my problem.

"Sani—"

"Get out my car, ma," I said, easily hitting the locks on the door.

"What? In the middle of the road? You're really putting me out?"

I nodded. "Hell yeah. You annoying, bruh. All you do is complain. That's why I don't wanna be with you. I only enjoy fucking yo' ass, but that shit ain't even fun anymore because you act like you're too good to suck dick now! Get the fuck out my shit, and delete my number. I'm done with you, shawty."

She sat there looking at me with her mouth hanging open. She had about five seconds to get the hell out my car before I pushed her ass out.

"Wow. So that's it? It's that easy for you to be finished with me? Like I didn't mean anything to you?" Her voice was trembling, but that shit didn't bother me.

"You never meant shit to me, Miracle. Get the fuck out."

She opened the door and stepped out. She slammed the door, thinking that was gonna piss me off, but hell nah. I sped off and didn't look back. Honestly, the whole time she was in my car, I was thinking about that dangerous girl from earlier. Now that Miracle was out my car, I might as well call her.

I picked up my phone with one hand, trying my hardest to focus on the road without running over anything, then unlocked it. Her number popped right up.

Mia.

She damn sure didn't look like her name was Mia, but shit, that wasn't gonna stop me from calling her. She let the phone ring three times before she answered it.

"Who is this?" she answered.

"Damn. That's how you answer the phone? No hello or nothing?"

"Your number ain't saved, so clearly you not even important enough for me to—"

"You gave me your number earlier."

She smacked her lips. "Oh, the B2K looking ass nigga. I didn't expect you to call me so soon. You ain't one of those desperate ass niggas, are you?"

"Hell nah. Ain't never been desperate for some pussy," I scoffed.

"So, that's what you're calling me for? Some pussy?"

"Nah, nah. I was calling to see if you was hungry. We can go—"

"You paying?" she cut in.

"I mean... yeah. I planned on it—"

"I'm about to text you my address. Don't take forever to get here either. A bitch over here starving." She hung up before I could even respond. I wasn't too mad, because right after, I got the address to her crib.

I did a U-turn in the middle of the street and headed straight to her place. I ain't never been this excited to see a female. A nigga smiled the whole way there. Cheeks were hurting and everything, and I didn't give a single fuck as I called her ass back to tell her I was outside.

She'd changed clothes. She was wearing one of those bodysuit things that was burgundy, some sandals with her pretty ass toes out, and the way her hair was blowing in the wind and shit made her ass look like something straight out of a magazine.

"Hey," she said, as she slid in the passenger seat.

"What's up? You look good."

She chuckled. "I always look good. You won't ever catch me looking bogus."

"Where you wanna eat at?" I asked, backing out of the driveway.

She shrugged. "I don't care. Just make sure them mothafuckas don't have roaches."

I glanced over at her. "What? Why would—"

"Nigga, you'd be surprised. I used to work at Burger King before I got locked up, and they had roaches and rats crawling all around that bitch. Shit was crazy."

"Locked up for what? The hell you be out here doing?" I asked, lifting an eyebrow.

"Nothing major. Just tried to kill a bitch for running her damn mouth. Shit was crazy as fuck."

I glanced at her. "So, you just be going around tryna kill people and shit? That's what you like to do for fun?"

She chuckled. "I mean no, but sometimes, I just get pushed to that point. Don't worry. I'm not gonna do no crazy shit. You gotta push me to that point."

"I'm sure whatever it was that she was talking about you wasn't that serious. How'd you try to kill her? Running her over?"

She smacked her lips. "Not that serious? Well, you can't speak on what you don't know. And, hell no. When I saw her, she decided she wanted to start popping shit, so I got the strap out the car and started bussin' at her ass. I shot her in her fuckin' stomach and foot, yo. I was aiming for her head, but—"

"Sounds like your aim is off, ma." I chuckled.

She lifted a brow. "You testing me? You want me to shoot you and see if my aim is off or not?"

"What? Hell nah. I was just saying if you were aiming for her head, how the fuck you end up shooting her in the stomach? Was she running and shit when she saw you? What the fuck happened?"

"Alright, so I'm in the parking lot, and I see her walking out the store. That's when she decides she wants to walk up on me, trying to argue and shit, and I wasn't having it. So I started shooting. Once she heard the gunshots, she started running and ducking and shit. You know, usual scary bitch shit."

"Usual? I mean, I think it's normal for someone to start running for their life when they hear gunshots. Maybe, you missed because she was moving too much." I shrugged.

She shook her head. "Nah. Fuck that. If I catch that bitch out in public again, I'm not gonna miss. I'm waiting for that day." She smiled to herself.

I just nodded because I didn't know what to say. I knew she was a little crazy, but I didn't know she would prove that shit with the first five minutes of being in my damn car.

What the fuck was I getting myself into?

TEN

DIAMOND
"I'm actually glad you were able to make it over here," my mom, Tanya said, and I fought the urge to roll my eyes. "I've been planning this dinner for the longest, I'm just glad I can finally get all my kids together for once."

"Yep. I'm here," I replied in a dry tone. I really didn't even wanna come. Tanya blew up my phone so damn much, reminding me that she needed to talk to me, there was no way I could forget about it even if I wanted to.

"You look nice. From what your sister says about you, she describes you so... different."

I scoffed. I bet she did. When I realized my mom didn't give a damn about me, I was sad for a moment, but then I got over it. Why waste my time with a woman who got mad at me for getting raped?

So I started rebelling and not listening to my mom. My brother and sister started looking at me like I was one of the worst humans on earth.

Me and Apryl had a pretty decent relationship before that nasty ass nigga wanted to take my innocence in the woods. Like any other little sister, I looked up to Apryl. I wanted to be just like her. I would even get my hair styled just like hers. That's how bad it was.

It was like my entire family blamed me for getting raped. One day I heard my mom talking on the phone, telling one of her little friends that I probably asked for it. What nine-year-old asks to get raped? By someone who I trusted because my brother trusted his nasty ass.

"She told me that you lost a lot of weight, but you look fine to me," Tanya said.

"I'll be right back," I let out while standing to my feet. Before she could respond to me, I was out the front door. I didn't know what the hell I was thinking coming over here sober. I knew damn well I wouldn't be able to deal with them sober.

When I made it to my car, I pulled open the glove compartment, and retrieved the bag of pills that was getting smaller and smaller. My phone began ringing in the seat, and I just let it, after I seen it was only Koda calling me.

Koda was fun, and he had good dick, but good dick wasn't gonna pay my bills. I liked his company and how he would keep me laughing, but I just couldn't. He wasn't paying for my time, and I came with a price.

"Shit," I muttered, realizing I didn't have any water or anything to drink in my car.

As I examined the bag of pills, I saw Apryl's car pulling up. At that point, I just said fuck it and popped the pill in my mouth.

I decided to just wait in my car because I didn't wanna speak to Apryl, but once she saw me, she made sure to walk her happy ass over to me anyway.

"Oh wow," she said, flipping her stiff ass weave from her shoulder. "How did Mom get you to come over? Did she have to bribe you with drugs or something?"

I chuckled to myself. "Apryl, get the fuck away from me before I beat yo' ass. Don't even know why you even wasted your time coming over here."

"You know, it's really funny that you said that. Having that type of attitude won't get you a man, sis." She flashed her large diamond ring that I could care less about. "Yep," she continued when she caught me looking at her ring. "Lawrence proposed."

I dug into the bag of pills and grabbed another one. Then I quickly got out the car and brushed past her, while popping the pill in my mouth.

Yes. Apryl was Lawrence's girlfriend, or should I say fiancée that kicked me out when she caught us having sex. Lawrence wanted me, but when he realized he would never get me, he settled for Apryl. When I didn't have anywhere to go, he told me I could stay with them. Yeah, Apryl was living there too, but she wasn't paying any bills, so she didn't have a say so.

Everything was fine. I would ignore Apryl like we weren't even family, and I would also ignore Lawrence's advances. The only thing I was worried about was getting my money up so I could get my own place.

But one night, I came in drunk as hell, and Lawrence took advantage of that. He flashed money, pills, and weed, and I swear my clothes came off by themselves. After that, we were having sex damn near every night in the bed he was sleeping in with my sister.

I didn't feel bad when Apryl caught us having sex. I would always hear her running her mouth about me when she was on the phone with whoever. She also always had some smart shit to say when I came around, so I started fucking her nigga while I was sober. He was throwing me money too, so it was a win-win situation for me.

I could still remember the look of hurt that was on Apryl's face the day she walked in on her nigga drilling me from the back. She knew she wasn't gonna leave Lawrence because the money was too good. So to make herself feel better, she kicked me out. I didn't let that shit bother me, though. I got my own place right after they kicked me out, so I was good. Fuck the both of them.

"It was so romantic how he did it, though," she gushed as if I asked her or some shit.

"That's so sweet. His other bitch must've turned his proposal down, so he decided to just settle with you... again." I let out a shrill laugh and stepped back into Tanya's house. Words couldn't begin to explain how ready I was for this little get together to be over.

"Hi, baby." Tanya smiled at Apryl. "You look so good." They engaged in a hug and I sat down on the couch and pulled out my phone. I had a text message from Koda, and it caused me to smack my lips.

Koda: Damn you must be busy?

Duh, nigga! If I didn't answer the phone, that clearly means I'm busy.

Me: Yeah

I chuckled as I hit send. I thought about being petty and sending Lawrence a text, but I decided against it. I'd let Apryl be happy with her nigga that had community dick. He would be hitting my line soon, acting single as fuck anyway.

Koda: Hit me up when ur done.

I rolled my eyes. I enjoyed him, but it was time to cut his ass off. When he dropped me back off the other day, I couldn't stop thinking about him. I didn't like that feeling. I only felt like this over a man once, and what did he do? Took my heart and fucking ran away with it.

So, it was fuck these niggas, and fuck these relationships.

Me: Probably won't be able to do that

Koda: Damn it's like that? When am I gonna see you again?

Me: When you pay for it

He read my message but didn't reply. Honestly, I didn't care. All he did was give me good dick and take me to IHOP. It was time to get back to business.

"Finally," my mom damn near yelled. "Michael is finally here."

I couldn't keep my eyes from rolling even if I wanted to. I'd never understand why my mom treated my brother like he was a king. In her eyes, he could never do wrong. That was some of the dumbest shit I'd ever witnessed.

Michael walked through the door like he owned the place. Apryl and Tanya greeted him with hugs and kisses, and I just stayed there sitting on the couch because I wasn't impressed by this nigga.

When they were done greeting him, someone walked in behind him. Someone that I thought I'd never see again.

"What's good, fam bam?" Christian asked, giving Tanya and Apryl hugs. "You always got it smelling right in here, but that ain't nothing new."

Tanya playfully hit him in the chest, and I could literally feel my entire body shaking. It could've been because of the two pills I'd taken, but I really believed it was because I was staring in the face of my rapist.

He looked at me, probably because he could feel me glaring at him. He quickly looked away, though. We hadn't seen each other in years, but he knew that what he did would never be forgiven.

"Come eat," Tanya sang. For a moment, I was too stunned to move. My so-called family was really okay with this man? Tanya was acting like he was another one of her kids. "Come on, Diamond. We're about to pray."

Slowly, I pulled myself off the couch, and made my way into the kitchen where they were all sitting at the table. I took the seat at the end of the table and folded my arms. I was leaving as soon as I finished eating.

"Bow your heads and close your eyes," Tanya said. She began saying grace, and I just sat there with my arms folded, staring a hole in Christian.

He glanced over at me, but once again, he quickly looked away.

"Bitch ass nigga," I mumbled.

"Excuse me?" Apryl snapped, looking in my direction.

"Girl, nobody was even talking to you. Keep praying to your white Jesus, and leave me the hell alone.

"Diamond?" Tanya asked, now turning her attention to me. "Is there something wrong?"

"Is there something wrong? Yes! Y'all are all sitting at this table with a fucking rapist! Y'all acting like this man didn't take my innocence when I was a fucking kid!" I hollered, without even meaning to.

They all looked at me like I was crazy. Everyone except Christian.

"Well, Diamond, you went up in front of the church and told everyone that you forgave him. There's no need to dwell—"

"I did that because you made me! You forced me to do that shit! I never forgave this bitch ass nigga, and I never fucking will!"

"Well," Apryl chimed in. "From our understanding, you were wearing those itty-bitty shorts that Mom told you not to wear. You were asking for it. You've always been fast as a little girl—"

Her sentence was cut short because I slapped the shit out of her with the glass plate that was sitting in front of me. It shattered, and cut my hand a little bit, but I didn't care. She deserved it. To sit here and say that a nine-year-old deserved to get raped was unheard of.

She let out a blood curdling scream, and all hell broke loose from there. I started giving Christian an ass whoopin' that was well overdue. I smashed a glass in his face, and after that, I picked up my keys that had the pepper spray attached to it and got his ass right in the eyes. So now, him and Apryl were screaming at the top of their lungs.

I locked eyes with my brother who was looking like he'd been waiting for this to happen, and I casually made my way over to him. For him to still be friends with Christian said enough.

"Diamond, I—" He didn't get to finish his sentence because I pepper sprayed him too. No one was safe right now.

Looking around, I saw that my mom was nowhere in sight. I knew exactly what that meant. She was somewhere calling the damn police. I walked all over the house until I found her, in her room, sitting in the corner, with the phone glued to her ear.

I thought about leaving her alone. I should've just gathered my shit and left right then and there, but all the flashbacks started rolling through my head and I just snapped. I took her phone from her and threw it against the wall, then I started beating her ass like she'd stole something from me. As of now, she wasn't my mom anymore. I had already lost all respect for her after the rape happened, but now, I wouldn't even claim this woman as my mom.

"I hate you!" I yelled, throwing her head into the wall as hard as I could. The way I was feeling right now, I could kill her with my bare hands and not give a single fuck.

When I finally came back to reality, my mom was unconscious, her face was bloody, and I still pulled out my pepper spray. I opened each of her eyes and sprayed her with it. If she went blind, I wouldn't give a fuck.

I quickly turned to leave, but I was greeted on the steps by three police officers. They were talking to me, but I couldn't hear shit they were saying because I felt like I was in a daze. They slapped the handcuffs on my wrists and hauled my ass outside.

As they were walking me to my car, I could hear Apryl crying, and that caused me to smile. I smiled the whole time they put me into the back of the car. Fuck them. As of today, they were no longer my family.

ELEVEN

K ODA

"Nigga, I know you not over there in your feelings about a bitch you just met a week ago. Not hoe ass Koda." Sani laughed.

I cut my eyes at him. "Nigga, fuck you. I'm not in my feelings about no bitch. If her ass was to call me right now, I wouldn't even answer that shit. Fuck her. I can get bitches in my fucking sleep."

He laughed at me. "You caught feelings for a hoe? Mannn, that pussy must be immaculate, nigga. I'll be damned if—"

"Nigga, shut the fuck up. You been talking about that Mia chick since last night. You already in love, and you haven't even smelled the pussy."

He let out a small laugh. "You don't know what the hell I did. Don't speak on shit you don't know."

So yeah, I was pissed the fuck off at the message Diamond sent me. I mean, I guess I should've expected it because she was selling pussy, but I don't know. I guess I just felt like she would stop that shit once she saw that I was tryna fuck with her.

"Fuck these bitches," I said easily as my phone rang in my hand.

It was an unknown caller, and I thought about declining it, but decided against it. "Hello?"

"You have a collect call from...Diamond. Do you accept the charges?"

"Yeah."

"Hey." Diamond sighed into the phone. "I'm umm..."

"Locked up?" I chuckled.

"Yeah. I got the money to get out, I just need a ride. Could you—"

"I'm on the way." I ended the call before she could say anything else then stood to my feet.

"Where the hell you rushing off to?" Sani asked, watching me grab my car keys.

"Diamond's locked up, so—"

"Pussy whipped ass nigga." He laughed. "I thought it was fuck her, though."

"Nah, nigga. It's fuck you." I was out the door, not giving a fuck about his ass judging me. He was about to be the same way over Mia. I could tell.

"THANKS," Diamond said once she slid into the passenger seat. There was blood all over her shirt, and her hair looked a fucking mess.

"I shouldn't have, after that dumb shit you sent to my phone earlier."

"Dumb shit?" She flipped. "Nigga, that was some real shit. You think chillin' with you for free is gonna keep my fuckin' lights on?"

"I don't got nothing to do with that—"

"Exactly, so shut the fuck up. I need niggas that will pay for my time because this shit ain't free. Nothing comes for free—"

"Shut the fuck up before I put yo' black ass out my car. I'm not tryna hear that shit. If I wanna chill with you, then that's what the fuck I'm gonna do. I don't give a fuck about none of the shit you're talking."

Her mouth fell open. "Black ass!" she shrieked. "You have no room to call me black ass! At least I got melanin, white mothafucka. Goofy looking ass nigga. You can't even be in the sunlight for long periods of time! You're like a fuckin' vampire, bruh!"

"Man—"

"Ahhh-ha! I got Melanin," she sang. "Face ass nigga. Fuck you." She sat back in the seat and folded her arms and I let out a small laugh.

"You done?" I asked.

"You look like a fuckin' polar bear."

I lifted a brow. "Damn. Tell me how you really feel."

"I got talked about my entire life for being dark skinned—"

"And you think I didn't? I wasn't even supposed to be this color. Both my parents are black." She rolled her eyes and didn't respond. She just looked out the window. "What happened, though? Why your shirt so bloody."

"I had to beat some ass today. Nothing major." She said it so easily, like it was a sport to her or some shit.

"Yeah, obviously. Whose ass were you beating?"

"My sister, the nigga who raped me when I was younger, my brother, and my mom. Ouuu, I beat my mom's ass the worst, though. She deserved every second of that shit. It was crazy."

"Hold on, what? You got raped? When?"

She sighed. "I really don't wanna talk about that. Not right now."

I bit the inside of my cheek. That just wasn't some shit you brought up, then didn't explain.

"How you gonna be my girlfriend if you don't even wanna talk about the shit that's bothering you?"

She snapped her head in my direction. "Boy, who said I wanted to be your girlfriend. You don't even know me. You don't know nothing about me."

"I know that the pussy is good, and you can deep throat my—"

"I'm not even talking about that. I'm talking about actually knowing shit about me. You already know what I do for a living—"

"Yeah, and that shit's about to stop."

"So, you just gonna keep interrupting me today, huh? Ole goofy ass nigga." She folded her arms again and turned her attention back out the window.

"Nah, chill. I'm not gonna interrupt your crybaby ass anymore. Now tell me about your childhood."

She was quiet for a moment.

"I got raped when I was nine by my older brother's friend. He raped me in the woods, and when I told my mom what happened, she got mad at me." She let out a small chuckle. "She said it wouldn't have happened if I would've stayed with my brother. Then earlier, they told me I asked for it by what I was wearing."

"When you were nine?"

She nodded. "Yep. To make matters worse, my mom made me go up in front of the entire church and tell everyone that I forgave him, when I didn't. I'll never forgive that nigga. If I ever see him again, I'll probably kill him. That's what I wanted to do today."

"What happened? Why was he even around you?"

"Because my family are some fucking retards!" she yelled. "Okay, so my mom calls me over there because she wants to have dinner with all her kids and shit, and my brother walks in with that nasty ass nigga behind him. My family is hugging all over him like he didn't rape me. Like he didn't stick his dick inside me. Mannn, that shit was crazy."

I kinda didn't even know what to say back. I didn't expect for her story to be this fucking crazy. This shit sounded unreal.

"So, what happened after that? Did y'all eat dinner together like y'all were a big happy family?" I hesitantly asked.

"No, we didn't make it that far. My mom was praying over the food, and I was staring at that nigga because I was mentally stabbing him in his fucking throat. After that, I called him a bitch ass nigga, and my hoe ass sister had something to say about it. Long story short, my entire family says it's my fault, so I got up, started beating ass and started pepper spraying everybody. My mom called the police on me, but I made sure to beat her ass before they even showed up. I straight knocked her ass out." She chuckled, and I was still shocked.

"So, you just carry pepper spray with you?"

"Yeah, but this one was on my keychain. It really came in handy today. It felt so good putting my hands on them. If I had to do it all over again, I would've. Like, I just don't understand how you blame a nine-year-old for getting raped. That nigga was like seven years older than me too. I'm not understanding."

I nodded. "That's a nasty ass nigga. There's no telling how many more bitches he's raped in his lifetime. That's some nasty shit right there."

"Exactly. I hadn't even started my period yet. But after that, I moved in with my fuckin' aunt and her boyfriend. He used to come in my room and molest me, too. Then afterward, he would be crying and begging me not to tell anybody." She rolled her eyes, and once again, I was shocked. What the hell was wrong with these niggas that's in her life? This some of the craziest shit.

"What happened with him? Did you tell?"

"Nope. I made his ass start paying me. Nigga would give me a hundred dollars for—"

"What? So that nigga was paying you to touch you and shit? How old were you?"

She shrugged. "About ten or eleven. I don't really remember."

"So, you started this shit at a young age? You were making niggas pay for the pussy and you weren't even a teenager yet? Man, this some of the craziest shit I've ever heard."

"Exactly," she huffed. "That's why I don't tell people about my past. I just let them judge me from what they think they know. Could you take me to my mom's place, please? I need to get my car."

I glanced at her. "You sure that's a good idea?"

"Nigga, I'm not about to leave my car over there. There's no telling what they'd try to do to it. No thanks."

"I mean, I just don't want you to be fighting and shit while you just—"

"Boy, shut yo' goofy ass up. I'm not gonna be fighting. Just going to get my car, and nothing else."

"You got one more time to talk to me like you crazy, and I'm putting yo' ass out my fucking car. Stop playing with me, Diamond."

She didn't say anything else. She sat in the seat with her arms folded and just stared out the window. I let out a small laugh because it was way too easy for me to get under her skin.

"So, you gonna tell me where ya moms live or what? If not, I'ma just go back to my crib."

She told me where her mom lived, then was quiet for the rest of the ride. I didn't know why she was over there feeling some type of way. I didn't give a fuck who you were, you weren't about to talk to me like I was crazy. I felt like she was gonna have to learn the hard way, though.

"Look at these bitches," she spat as we pulled up to her mom's crib. "Standing outside like they're just the perfect family. I hate them, bruh." She sat in the seat glaring at them for a moment before she popped the door open and got out.

I felt like I should've gotten out the car with her, but I didn't. From the looks of it, she had things under control. I rolled down my window, so I could hear what they were saying.

"I just came for my keys!" Diamond yelled at the tall chick that looked just like her. I could see that her face was fucked up from my car. Diamond did a number on her ass.

"Why? So you can pepper spray the entire family again?!" she shot back. "Hell no. If you wanted your keys so damn bad, you shouldn't have left without them!"

They stared at each other for a minute before Diamond pushed her ass out the way and walked her ass right up in the house. After that, she came right back out with her keys in one hand, and some nigga following her.

"Nigga, leave me the fuck alone! Go tend to your fiancée that's standing over there with her face all cut up. I don't got shit to say to you, bruh!"

"I'm just tryna see if you good, though. I ain't have shit to do with what went on in there," he pleaded as Diamond walked to her car.

I let out a small chuckle as I reached in the glove compartment and pulled out the strap. I was waiting on the day I ran into this nigga, but I didn't think it would be today. It was all good, though. This made it easier for me.

Slowly, I got out my car as Diamond's sister approached them.

"First off, why the hell you all up in her face?" she screamed at Onyx. "I told you to never talk to her again, right? And you're gonna just do it like I'm not standing here?"

Diamond laughed. "Girl, your fiancé talks to me damn near every day. He's in love with the chocolate. Can't leave it alone."

See, that shit bothered me. I didn't know what the fuck it was about Diamond, but knowing she fucked this nigga made me wanna kill him even more.

"Nah, man. I don't talk to her at all," he said, but even I knew his ass was lying. "I was just making sure she was good because from the story y'all told me—"

"So, we're lying now?" Diamond shrieked. "You weren't just over my house, Lawrence?" The fact that she was calling him by his first name let me know them fucking around wasn't a one-time thing.

I'd had enough of this conversation. I didn't wait for that nigga to respond when I made my presence known.

"What's good, nigga?" I asked, watching him turn around and look at me. He had a mug on his face at first, but he quickly wiped that shit away when he saw it was me. I aimed my gun at his head because, honestly, I didn't give a damn about what he had to say to me. That shit didn't matter. All I wanted was my damn money.

"What you doing here, bruh?" he questioned, sounding like a bitch. His girl who was standing next to him was looking at me through wide eyes. Diamond looked unbothered, which let me know she didn't give a fuck about this nigga.

"You know like I know that shit doesn't matter. You got my money, though?"

He didn't say shit, which let me know the answer. I let out a small laugh. He was parading around town like he was that nigga, but he still owed me money? Nah. It didn't work like that.

"Aye," Diamond said, getting my attention. "I know it's rude to interrupt right now, but I really don't think it's a good idea for you to shoot this man right here in front of my mom's crib. She already called the police on me once today, and I know for a fact she'll do it again and get my entire family to blame me for the shooting."

I glanced to the porch, and the woman I'm guessing was her moms was standing there, staring at me. She looked like the type of woman to call the police too.

"Fuck," I muttered, lowering the gun. "Aight, nigga. I'ma see you," I let him know.

Diamond opened her car door and said, "I'm going to your house."

Shit, say less.

I kept my eyes on Onyx's bitch ass as I backed up to my car. I had so much shit I wanted to ask about what Diamond and Onyx had going on, but that shit was gonna have to wait.

Once I was in my car, I sped off, and Diamond followed right behind me. I didn't wanna bring her ass back to my crib because Sani was there, and there was no telling what his ass might say to her. I mean, it was nothing for me to beat his ass, but I was hoping it didn't even get to that point.

The whole ride back to my crib, I couldn't stop myself from glancing in the mirror to make sure Diamond was following me. I just had a feeling she was gonna dip on my ass, especially after the message she sent me today about paying her ass. I wasn't paying for shit. Fuck I look like paying for pussy in the first place? Nah, that shit didn't even sound right.

I was even a little surprised that Sani was sitting on the porch when we pulled up. He was talking to the nosey ass neighbor, Slim, and smoking a blunt. I didn't have a problem with Slim, he just was always loud as hell. Nigga was always yelling for no damn reason, like we all couldn't hear his ass.

"Nah, nah!" he yelled, as I got out the car. "The shit ain't gon' be nothing like that! I already told mothafuckas to leave that drama shit at their crib. I'm not—"

"Nigga, that don't mean shit," Sani countered as Diamond walked over to me.

"Yes it does, bruh! We just gon' have a little get together. It ain't gon' be a party or nun like that."

"I can't feel my hand," Diamond said, holding her hand up, showing me how cut up it was. "I might need to go to the hospital because—"

"Nah, you good," I let her know, walking toward the house.

"How you gonna tell me what I am? I don't think not being able to feel my hand is a good thing. I'm just saying that a doctor will—"

"Damn!" Slim yelled, making me let out a small sigh. "Who is this? I ain't never seen her pretty chocolate ass over here."

"Mind ya bidness, nigga. She ain't for you," I said as he came to dap me up.

"I'll never understand how a nigga that looks like you can pull bitches that look like this."

Diamond raised a brow. She didn't seem mad though. She was more amused than anything.

"Just ask ya wife." I chuckled, grabbing Diamond's hand that wasn't cut and leading her into the house.

"That nigga loud as fuck." She laughed, walking into my room.

"He always yelling for no damn reason. I swear he's half deaf or some shit. He be across the street in his own crib and I can hear his ass talking. That shit be annoying as fuck."

She plopped down on my bed. "I don't know why I expected your room to be junky. I should've known better because your car is clean as fuck." She was holding her hand up like she was afraid to rest it like she was doing the other one.

"Nah. I'll lose my mind if my shit is a mess. That nigga out there be living like that. I don't know how he does it."

She didn't respond to me because she was too busy looking at her hand. The shit did look pretty bad, but I think that was because all the dried-up blood that was on it.

"I really think I should go to the—"

"Nah," I said, interrupting her. "Come on."

"What? Why didn't you ask before I sat down and got comfortable?"

"Come on, Diamond. Not gonna say the shit again."

TWELVE

D IAMOND

I sighed loudly to myself as I got off the bed and followed Koda into the bathroom. Now that I was thinking about it, it wasn't such a good idea to hit Apryl in the face with that plate because now I was paying for it.

"What are you about to do?" I asked, watching him turn on the water. The bathroom was small as hell. I mean, there was nothing wrong with it, but I could tell that two men lived here.

"What you think I'm about to do? Drown yo' ass in this small ass sink?"

"Shit, you might. I just watched you try to blow a nigga's brains out in front of me, so you're some type of crazy."

He gave me a weird look as he gently grabbed my hand and placed it under the water. That shit didn't feel good, but it was my own fault. I should've just beat Apryl's ass instead of hitting her with the damn plate.

"How long you been fucking that nigga?" he asked as he looked down at my hand. I fought the urge to roll my eyes. Now he was worried about who I was fucking? Not once had I asked him about the bitches he dealt with, and I wasn't going to. It was none of my damn business.

I shrugged. "I don't know. He be paying me, so I really don't be thinking about shit like that."

"Dead that shit."

"Huh?" My brows came together as I looked at him, but all his attention was still on my hand. It didn't hurt that bad now that I was used to the water hitting it.

"Why do you do that? You know damn well you heard what the fuck I said, but you still act like you didn't. You like hearing me repeat myself or some shit?"

I shook my head. "No, nigga. You just let some crazy ass shit fly out of your mouth, and I'm trying to make sure I heard you right."

"You heard me right. Dead that shit. I don't want you fucking with that nigga anymore."

I looked at him through the mirror. Hazel eyes fixed on my hand, and his brows knitted together, with the look of concentration on his face. How was he even keeping himself in this serious state like he didn't just say some off the wall shit to me? What the hell was this?

"Okay, Koda," I started, jabbing a finger into his hard chest. "First off, you're not about to tell me who I can and can't fuck with. Not once have I asked you who you were fucking. Not once have I—"

"I was fuckin' your best friend," he said easily, eyes finally meeting mine. "Melanie. Shit, I guess you could say we were in a relationship, but I wasn't feeling it."

What the fuck?

Honestly, I didn't know what to say. It explained everything, though. Melanie was mad as fuck when we left that ghetto ass hair show. She kept telling me I didn't have a chance with Koda because of how I made my money. She tried her hardest to talk shit to make me feel some type of way about going to talk to him, but all she had to do was tell me that was her nigga. I wouldn't have even approached him.

"So, you were her boyfriend that she would never let me meet?

You knew that we were friends, but you're just now telling me? You don't think that was something I needed to know?"

"Honestly." He laughed. "That shit don't even matter, shawty. I mean, yeah, I should've told you, but what was the point? By that time, we'd already fucked. I wasn't feeling her anyway. Broke up with her the day you gave me your number." He finally cut the water off, then softly covered my hand with a rag.

"Damn..." I muttered. "I feel like a bad friend. She hasn't really talked to me since then. Usually, she's always at my house, and in my business, but not this time."

"I don't know why she didn't tell you. If you ask me, she brought all this shit on herself." He led me back to his room.

I mean, I guess he was a little right. Melanie couldn't really be mad at me because I was just now finding out. If she would've opened her mouth instead of acting like a little bitch, I probably would've left Koda alone... maybe.

I sat back down on the bed and watched Koda pull out a first-aid kit. I didn't expect him to have it, but he was a hood nigga. They always came with hella surprises.

"This might burn a little bit," he said while opening a small alcohol wipe.

I shrugged. "Do what you gotta do, Dr. Koda."

He sat down on the bed next to me and started wiping my hand with the wipe. It stung a little, but it wasn't too much. I could handle it.

"How do you know Lawrence?" I asked because I couldn't take the awkward silence.

He scoffed. "Fuck that nigga."

"That's not telling me what he did, though. You're acting like you didn't try to kill him in front of me less than thirty minutes ago."

"He owes me money, but he's not tryna come up off it. I don't play about my money. Gave him more than enough time to get me my shit, and he still hasn't, so next time I see him, it's lights out for his ass. You see how scared he was when he saw me."

"Yeah. He's a hoe ass nigga."

"So you were fucking him knowing he was engaged to your sister? You don't think that's just a little fucked up?"

I looked at him with the sickest scowl on my face. "Hell no. My sister is just like my mom. Shit, maybe even worse. She blames me for getting raped, always talking shit, and she thinks she's better than me. Whenever I say something, she always has some slick shit to say right after it. I'm tired of that shit. Plus, her nigga came on to me. I ignored it at first, but then I just said fuck it. He probably got caught cheating again. That's the only reason he gave her ass a ring."

Thinking about Lawrence and Apryl pissed me off. First off, why the hell was he trying to talk to me when I walked back into my mom's house to get my keys? Then he tried to lie and say he doesn't talk to me anymore, when we literally just had sex not too long ago.

"He be hitting you up a lot?"

"I guess you could say that. I mean it's nothing but money to me. I don't give a fuck about the nigga."

He looked at me like he wanted to say something but decided against it. After he was finished cleaning my hand with the alcohol wipe, he pulled out something that looked like a roll of tape.

"Nigga, I know you're not about to tape my hand," I said, snatching my hand away from him.

"Nah." He laughed. "It's a Band-Aid." He grabbed my hand again and started wrapping it like he knew what he was doing.

"I really wanna ask why you know how to do this."

He shot me a grin. "Don't worry about all that, ma. Just know that you always gon' be good over here."

"Boyyy, bye," I said, while rolling my eyes. "If my hand gets infected, I'm beating yo' ass."

"It ain't gon' get infected. I know what the fuck I'm doing."

"Yeah, well I don't know that."

He didn't respond to me as he finished wrapping my hand with the Band-Aid. It was really hard to move it now, but it felt better now that there was something on it.

We fell into another awkward silence. I didn't know what to say. Shit like this didn't usually happen to me. I didn't just chill with niggas that I was fucking like this, and I damn sure didn't feel nervous around them, like I was now.

He glanced up at me, and for a moment, we just stared at each other. After the stupid ass day I'd had, I just needed something to get my mind off of it. I didn't wanna think about my family at all, so without saying anything, I pressed my lips against his.

I guess he was having the same thoughts as me because he willingly plunged his tongue into my mouth, while aggressively grabbing my face. My lady parts instantly woke up because I loved that aggressive shit. I wanted to moan into his mouth, but I felt like it was too soon. He hadn't even done anything yet.

"Take this shit off," he commanded in a low voice, with his lips still against mine.

I gave him a small smirk as I pulled away from him and quickly came out of my shirt. It was a little hard to do everything that I wanted because of my injured hand, but I managed. When he saw how much I was struggling, he decided to help me with my pants.

Once my pants were off, he ran his pale hand down my lace underwear, then came back up and took over my mouth again. He removed my panties all while still kissing me, then tossed them to the floor. Meanwhile, my body was on fire just because he was touching me.

He gently laid me down and pinned my hands over my head. He kept his eyes on mine as he slowly slid in with his hands still having mine pinned above my head. I could feel my eyes trying to close as I tried to calm myself down.

"Nah," he whispered. "Keep them eyes open, baby."

I'll admit. It was a little hard because each time he slowly entered me, I wanted to let out the loudest scream.

"Kodaaa," I moaned softly, wishing he would let go of my hands so I could hug his body closer to mine. He came for my neck and let out a small grunt.

"Fuck," he said, coming back up to look at me. "This shit mine now." His dreads were hitting me in the face, but I couldn't move them. "You hear me, Diamond?" he asked, with his brows coming together and his tongue resting on his lip.

I nodded because talking right now wasn't an option. You'd think he'd know by now that talking during sex wasn't something I was good at.

He smiled at me. "I can't hear you."

"I heard youuu," I let out with my eyes closing.

"Eyes on me, mama," he said against my mouth harshly. The bed was creaking so loud, and my moans were louder. I was sure the two niggas outside could hear me, but right now, at this moment, none of that mattered.

In my whole entire life, I had never had dick like this. Lawrence didn't even have good dick like this. I swear I could feel him rearranging my organs.

He pressed his forehead against mine. "I'm not pulling out," he said with a small smile forming on his face.

"Nigga, you better pull out."

"Mmmm, nah."

That nigga was serious about not pulling out, and it pissed me the fuck off. I wasn't too pissed though, because after he did it, he finally let go of my hands, and fell on the bed next to me. He pulled my body closer to his and I couldn't understand why the hell I liked this pale ass nigga.

"So," I started. "I think albino dick is the best dick ever."

He let out a small laugh. "Nah, it's just *my* dick that's the best dick ever."

THE NEXT DAY

"So, you're in love with that nigga or something?" Mia asked as soon as I stepped through the door.

"Girl, what?" I laughed. I had been in the best mood since yesterday. Spending the night with Koda made everything so much better.

"You saw me calling you last night. You were probably too busy having that white boy's dick all in your mouth."

I plopped down on the couch next to her. "It wasn't in my mouth, first of all. Yesterday was crazy, though. I ended up in jail, and yo' bitch ass ain't answer the fuckin' phone." I crossed my arms and looked at her.

"What? I didn't get no damn call for you. You already know I would've been down there ready to beat any bitch that looked at me the wrong way. What the fuck happened?"

"My mom and her kids had me fucked up." Mia didn't know about what happened to me as a kid. I let her know about getting molested, then getting paid for it, and I let her know about Melanie's mom's boyfriend, but she didn't know that I was raped when I was nine. I didn't like talking about it. Honestly, I wished it would've never happened.

I sighed to myself and began telling her what happened when I was nine, then I told her about everything that happened yesterday. When I was finished, she was mad as fuck like I knew she would be.

"So... your mom is really okay with that nigga being all up and through her house like he didn't rape you?" she asked.

"Yep. She sure is."

"She deserved that ass whoopin' you gave her. I can't believe you pepper sprayed everyone in that damn house."

I shrugged. As of now, they were all dead to me. They better not hit me up for anything ever again.

"Fuck them," I spat. "But I found out Koda was with Melanie..." I let my voice trail off because honestly, I still didn't know what to say about it.

She let out the ugliest laugh. "That's why she's been acting like a little bitch lately? I'm so shocked she hasn't been over here like she lives here and shit. Damn, you really fuck all her niggas."

I rolled my eyes. Yeah, I had fucked a few of her niggas in the past, but that's only because they paid me for it. Was I supposed to just let free money get away? Man, hell nah.

"She's such a child for not speaking up about the shit. I think I'm gonna go talk to her." I nodded to myself and she gave me the ugliest expression.

"For what? It's her fault that she acted like she couldn't open her mouth and speak the fuck up. You don't owe her shit."

I waved her off. "I know I don't owe her shit. I just wanna know why the hell she didn't tell me."

"Fuck that little ass girl."

I chuckled to myself. "I'm still gonna go."

She sat there for a second before she gave me a small smile and said, "I'm coming with you. She might try to fight and shit. I just wanna make sure I'm there when—"

"You know damn well she's not gonna try to fight me. She's not stupid."

"Yeah, you right, but I'm still going. Don't give a fuck how you feel about it."

Mia was only going to make things worse, but I wasn't going over there to try to rekindle our friendship. I just wanted to talk.

So about two hours later, I had brushed my teeth, took a shower, fixed my hair, and I was ready to go to Melanie's house.

"So where you say you were going?" Koda asked. We'd been on the phone for the last ten minutes since he was on his break. Mia was taking her sweet little time getting dressed like she always did, and she was about to get left.

"I'm going to talk to Melanie. I just want her to know that I didn't know you were her nigga and she should've spoken up instead of—"

"What the hell you about to do that shit for? Leave it alone. It ain't that serious. You making it out to be—"

"I'm going to her house, Koda. I don't care what you got to say about it. I'm not going over there to fight that girl."

"Man, you can call her ass and have that conversation. She's gonna think you came over there to fight her."

I smacked my lips. "No she's not. If I tell her I'm not tryna fight her then she's not gonna have anything to worry about. What would I want to fight her for, anyway? She hasn't done shit to me."

"If you say so, Dime. Shit's gonna get ugly if you go over there. You know Melanie just like I know her." I twisted my face up because I really didn't like the way that shit sounded. "But I gotta get back to work. I'll call you when I get off, baby."

"Mhm," I said, ending the call. I felt like everyone was against me going to Melanie's house, but I didn't care. This was some shit I wanted to do, so that's what the hell was gonna happen.

About ten more minutes passed, and Mia finally brought her ass into the living room.

"You ready?" she had the nerve to ask.

"Bitch, I've been ready. You the one that was taking a whole thirty hours just to go talk to a bitch. Damn." I stood up and tossed my hair over my shoulder.

"Girl, hush. Melanie ain't going nowhere. I didn't even take that damn long. You're being dramatic." I ignored her as I grabbed my keys and headed for the door. She followed right behind me still talking shit. "You should probably just leave the shit alone, anyway. Ain't nobody that pressed over that albino dick."

I smiled to myself as I thought about sex with Koda. I had never had a nigga fuck me like he did yesterday. I was so okay with the dick, I was fine with saying this was his now. I was okay with being in a relationship, I think.

"We're kinda together now," I said quietly, waiting for Mia to cuss me out.

"What?" she asked, stopping in her tracks. "What the fuck did you just say to me?"

I let out a small laugh as I opened the door to my car. "Girl, get your crazy ass in the car before I leave you."

She glared at me the entire way to my car, then got in and slammed the door.

"So, you're really in a relationship with that nigga? You barely even know him."

I shrugged. "I know him enough. Clearly, he has the same feelings for me—"

"This shit is crazy. Never thought I'd see the day you get a boyfriend. I didn't even think you knew how to be in a relationship."

I started the car and looked at her. "Honestly, I don't. I'll see how this works, though. Doesn't seem like it would be too hard."

"I'm just too shocked for words right now. I don't even know what to say about the shit. I wonder how Melanie is gonna take it. She might try to fight you for real."

I didn't say anything as I backed out of my driveway. I didn't feel like Melanie was gonna try to fight me. What was there to fight about? Her not opening her damn mouth? That shit just didn't make sense to me.

My phone began ringing on my lap, and I smacked my lips when I saw it was Lawrence calling. I wasn't running low on pills, so honestly, me and him didn't have anything to talk about.

"I know you hear your damn phone ringing. You should answer it, it's probably your little albino calling."

I smacked my lips. "Girl, fuck you. Koda hasn't done anything to you for you not to like him."

"He's albino. Albino people scare me." She shrugged like what she said was okay.

"He's normal just like the rest of us. The only difference is his skin. We have melanin and he doesn't."

"Whatever," she said, trying to dismiss me. "I don't like the nigga. And now that you're in a relationship with his white ass, I don't like him even more."

I didn't bother responding to her. I knew the only reason she was mad was because she was jealous. She probably felt like I was gonna spend all my time with Koda, but I was determined not to be that person. I wasn't gonna start ignoring my friends just because I had a boyfriend now. Shit, why couldn't we all hang out together?

My phone began ringing again on my lap, and I let out an

annoyed breath. I slid my thumb across the screen and aggressively put it to my ear.

"What, nigga?" I snapped at Lawrence. "What the fuck you calling me for?"

"Hey... uhhh... I know you probably don't wanna hear from me right now, but your sister was in a real bad car accident and—"

"I don't give a fuck!" I yelled before I even realized it. "Fuck her. What the fuck you calling and letting me know for? She's not my family no more. I don't give a fuck about her or her fuckin' wellbeing! Get the fuck off my phone with that shit."

"I mean, I just thought you'd wanna know. It's real bad. She's in a coma now... I just thought you'd want—"

"She deserved it." I laughed. "She deserved all that shit. Bye, Lawrence. Don't call my phone no more." I hung up on him before he even had a chance to respond. What the hell was he calling and telling me for? Especially after everything that happened yesterday? Shit sounded like karma to me. I didn't give not one fuck.

"What happened?" Mia asked, as I gripped the steering wheel.

"Apryl was in a car crash, and her nigga thought it was a good idea to call and tell me about it. I don't give a fuck about none of that. Bitch in a coma now and everything."

"Damn. That's kinda fucked up. You don't even care a little bit?"

My brows came together in confusion as I looked at her. "Am I supposed to care? After she told me with a straight face that I deserved to get raped at nine? Nine years old, and I deserved it? That shit doesn't even sound right. So just like I deserved to get raped, she deserved being in that car crash. Get the fuck outta here with that shit."

She looked at me like she had something else to say, but she decided against it. I was glad because there was no changing my mind about how I felt about the situation. Lawrence should've known out of all people not to call me. I'm no longer a part of that family.

It took us about fifteen minutes to get to Melanie's place. Her car was parked outside, so I knew she was home.

"You might as well tie your hair up because you know she's gonna pull that wig right the fuck off when you tell her you're in a relationship with her nigga." Mia laughed, popping her door open.

"Shut the hell up. She's not gonna try to fight me. Especially since the nigga broke up with her that night he gave me his number. So either way, they weren't going to be together anymore."

She just shook her head as I got out the car and made my way to her door. I could hear her laughing, so I lifted my hand to knock then patiently waited. I almost got pissed off and started banging on the door because she took damn near five whole minutes to open the door. Then when she did, she had the nerve to look at me like I'd done something to her.

"What?" she asked, folding her arms.

"Bitch, that ain't how you fuckin' greet somebody," I said, trying not to get mad because if I got mad, I already knew I would end up hitting her ass.

"First of all, why you here? Secondly, why you bring her with you if you know I don't like her?"

I lifted a brow in amusement. "Fuck all that shit you're tryna talk. I just came over here to ask why you didn't tell me you were with Koda."

She twisted her face up so bad when I said his name.

"Because it was none of your damn business, Diamond. You fuck all my niggas anyway for money, so this one was no different. Even if I would've told you, you still wouldn't have given a fuck because that's the type of nasty bitch you are. Niggas would rather fuck a prostitute for a night than actually be in a relationship."

"Not that nigga." Mia snickered. "That nigga is okay with being in a relationship with Diamond. He moved on pretty fast, don't you think?"

"What?" Melanie questioned. "What the fuck are you even talking about?"

"Diamond and your albino nigga are together. In a whole relationship. He broke up with you so he could get with her. That shit could've all been avoided if you would've opened your mouth like an adult instead of being a little cry baby bitch about it. Crazy how life comes at you, right?"

For a moment, Melanie just stood there staring at me, not knowing what to say. I could see her eyes watering up, but she was trying to blink them away.

"So you knew that he was my nigga, and you still agreed to be with him?" Her voice cracked, and I tried my hardest not to laugh in her face.

"I just found out yesterday. I mean, I would've been knew if you would've told me. But here we are." I shrugged.

"What the fuck was your point of even coming over here? I don't care that you're with that nigga! He's gonna cheat on you just like he was cheating on me! You ain't special, bitch! Why would he want to be with someone who has sex for money? Why would he want to be with a pill head? Why would he want to—"

"You wanna fight?" I asked, before my brain could even register what I was saying. I didn't come over here to fight, but she was pissing me off with all this shit she was talking. "You mad because that nigga doesn't want you? How you gonna stand here and call me a pill head when you be popping them bitches, too?"

"You came over here to fight?" She ignored everything else I'd just said to her. No, I didn't come over here to fight, but shit. Now, I felt like fighting.

Without saying anything else, I punched her ass right in the mouth. I didn't give her time to recuperate before I started wailing on her ass. Honestly, I felt like this ass whoopin' was long overdue. Melanie was always throwing shade about me having sex for money. She was always telling me no nigga would ever want to be with me because of how I made my money, but now look. I got a boyfriend.

Melanie wasn't even trying to fight back. Well, I didn't think she was. I wasn't getting hit at all from her ass. When I got tired of hitting her, I slung her to the ground by her hair, then stood over here, waiting for her to get back up and try to fight some more. Instead, she just sat on the ground with tears streaming down her face.

"Fuck you, Diamond," she cried. "You were never my friend. Friends don't do the shit you did to me! My mom gave you a place to stay when you didn't have anywhere to go! Bitch, we were damn near sisters!"

"And your mom's nasty ass boyfriend was fucking me." I laughed, watching her mouth fall open. "That nasty ass nigga was fucking a fourteen-year-old and paying me for it. You always think you know what you're talking about when it comes to my life, but bitch, you don't. I've been fucking niggas for money since I was damn near ten. You think that shit bothers me when you say something about it?"

She didn't say anything else. She just sat there looking at me like she was in shock. No one knew what I went through in my life, yet, they were always trying to judge me about the shit I did. They were always trying to make me feel bad about the shit that I did. Especially when it was about the drugs that I did because my life wasn't normal like everyone else's.

"Let's go," Mia said. "This bitch clearly doesn't want these problems." I nodded then made my way to my car. Mia didn't know about my childhood and what I went through, and she still never said anything about my pill addiction.

Speaking of pills, I needed some right now. As soon as I got in my car, I sped off to find the nearest gas station.

"Told you y'all were gonna fight. I mean, it wasn't really much of a fight because that bitch didn't even try, but—"

"Please hush," I said, running my fingers through my hair. I really didn't go over there to fight. I kinda felt bad that it happened, but Melanie shouldn't have been running her damn mouth like that.

As soon as I pulled into the gas station, I barely parked the car before I hopped out. All I needed was a bottle of water so I could take some pills, because taking them dry like I did yesterday was not the move.

I was in and out of the store within a minute. Mia was looking at me like I was crazy when I got back in the car.

"What the hell you got going on, Diamond?" she asked, as I pulled the glove compartment open.

"Minding my business." I chuckled, pulling the bag of pills out. Yesterday, I'd taken two and I liked the effects it had on me, so today, I was gonna take three. Shit, after what just happened, I think I deserved it.

I popped three pills in my mouth, then drank my water like I hadn't had anything to drink in years.

"I wanna smoke," I said.

"Shit, I can call Julian if you want...You know he stays with—"

"Call that nigga," I demanded. I couldn't wait for these pills to start taking their effects on me.

THIRTEEN

K ODA

"The fuck?" I muttered, as I called Diamond for the third time. Her phone was just ringing, then going straight to voicemail. It was pissing me the hell off because what the hell was she doing? I told her ass I would call her as soon as I got off, and now she wasn't answering?

I thought about just going home, then trying to call her later, but the crazy in me wouldn't let that shit happen. So I hopped in my car and sped all the way to her crib. I hoped for her sake she was just sleep or some shit because I really didn't wanna walk in on her and some other nigga. I hope she didn't think I was playing when I told her that shit was mine now.

I broke all types of traffic laws trying to get to her crib. I was already thinking the worst. I knew I was about to bust up in Diamond's crib with the strap out and everything. I was the type of nigga to shoot first, then ask questions last. Hopefully, I wouldn't have to do no shit like that, though.

When I pulled up and saw Diamond's car parked out front, I let out a sigh of relief. At least I knew she was home. Now, I was hoping, for her sake that she didn't have anyone in there that didn't have no business being here.

I quickly parked the car and damn near ran to the door. I had my gun out because I was ready for whatever at this point.

I banged on the door with the gun, then waited patiently for someone to open the door. When the door swung open, that bitch that Sani was so pressed over was standing there with a mug on her face.

"What the fuck yo' white ass banging on the door like you're crazy for?" she hollered. Any other time, I would've checked her ass for talking to me like she was crazy, but there was too much other shit I was worried about right now.

"Where's Diamond?" I asked, ignoring her and her stank ass attitude.

"In her damn room. Maybe you should've called her before you came, nigga."

I brushed past her and headed straight for Diamond's room. When I got in there, she was passed out on the floor right next to her bed. I instantly started to panic.

"Aye," I said, rushing over to her. I shook her a little bit, but she didn't budge. She didn't even move a little bit. She was breathing, so that made me feel a little better.

I set the gun down on the floor, then picked her up and gently laid her on the bed. She let out a small groan, and I shook her a little bit more, still trying to get her to open her eyes.

"Nooo," she groaned in a soft voice. "Stop it, Koda."

"Wake your crazy ass up, yo," I said, causing her eyes to fly open. She sat straight up and looked around the room like she didn't know where she was at.

"What the fuck?" she muttered. "What are you doing here?"

"You weren't answering your phone, so I thought—"

She quickly jumped off the bed and ran into the bathroom before I could even finish my sentence. When I heard her throwing up, I made my way into the bathroom with her.

"You good?" I asked, automatically thinking she was sick.

"Get out, Koda."

I chuckled to myself because that shit definitely wasn't about to happen. I had to look away from her because watching people throw up made me want to fucking throw up.

When she was finished, she flushed the toilet, then brushed her teeth. Her hair was all over the place from how she was just sleeping, but she still looked good enough to eat. Shawty looked like my next meal, honestly.

She finished brushing her teeth, then rinsed her mouth out with mouthwash. After that, she looked at me and gave me a small smile.

"Hey," she said, falling into my arms. "I feel terrible."

"You sick?"

She shook her head. "No. It happens sometimes."

"What? So, you just randomly throw up? This shit normal to you?"

"Yep." She walked back into her room, then turned her light on. I followed behind her, and that's when I saw the bag of pills on the dresser, and lines of cocaine. Well, that's what the shit looked like to me.

"What the fuck is this?" I questioned, walking over to the dresser. "You a coke head?"

"No. It's pills that I crushed up," she said it like that made it any better.

"What? So, you crushing up pills to snort that shit?"

She looked at me as she sat down on the bed. "Is that a problem, Koda?"

"Hell yeah. You said this shit is normal to you. So, that means you do this often. You got a drug problem, ma."

I sat down on the bed next to her, and she gave me a light shrug.

"I've been through a lot in my life. Being raped at such a young age really fucks with me. Then, the fact that my family still fucks with my rapist makes—"

"I get that, shawty, but there's people out here going through shit worse than that, and they're not out here doing drugs."

She gave me a small smile, obviously still high off whatever the fuck was in those pills.

"Well, they're not me, are they?" She laid back on the bed and I glanced at her. She had her eyes closed and was smiling.

"You need to go back to sleep," I let her know.

"I'm not even tired. Did you come over here to fuck, though? Because I honestly don't think my vagina can handle that right now."

"Nah, I didn't come over here to fuck. I came to see what the fuck you were doing because you weren't answering your phone. Had to make sure you weren't out here fucking some other nigga."

She opened her eyes to see if I was being serious, then let out a small laugh.

"You serious? You're so funny."

I kicked my shoes off so I could get comfortable on the bed with her.

"I'm dead ass. I came prepared to kill you and that nigga. Shit, your friend out there probably would've been dead, too. She had too much mouth when I opened the door, and I wouldn't leave any witnesses."

"You're crazy." She smiled. "Never had a nigga crazy over me before. Ohhh shittt."

"Pussy was too good for me not to be. Don't even know how you were still single."

"Because niggas out here stupid, and they don't make me no money. Then y'all be cheating on the bitches that really be down for y'all, and—"

"Whoa," I interrupted. "Don't put us all in the same category."

"You were cheating on Melanie, weren't you?"

"I mean, yeah, but I had already told her that I wasn't fucking with her like that anymore."

"But did you break up with her?" She propped up on her elbows to look at me. Her eyes were low and red like she hadn't been getting any sleep.

"Nah—"

"So, you were cheating?" Shit, in my head, me and Melanie weren't together, so I was able to do whatever the hell I wanted.

"I guess you could say that."

"Exactly. Today, she told me you were gonna do the same shit that you did to her, to me."

"So, you went over there?" I asked, with a lifted brow.

"I sure did."

"Y'all didn't fight?"

"Yeah." She laughed. "I mean, I fought her. She didn't really do too much fighting back. The fight was really a waste of time if you ask me."

"Going over there was a waste of time, period. You should've left that shit alone."

She shrugged. "Don't really care at this point. She got her ass beat because she was talking shit. I really just wanted to have an innocent conversation with her."

I was shocked that Melanie hadn't called me or popped up on me to bitch and complain and shit. She was probably too embarrassed to show her face.

"Did you get what you went over there for?" I asked as she cuddled under me.

"No, I didn't. She found out that her mom's boyfriend was paying me for sex when I was fourteen."

The thought of that shit really bothered me. How could a grown ass man be okay with having sex with a fourteen-year-old, and paying them for that shit? It didn't even sound right. Those were the types of niggas that needed to be thrown in jail for life.

"What else happened today?" I asked, changing the subject because I didn't wanna talk about this shit.

"Uhh... Oh yeah, Lawrence called me today. He was talking—"

"What? The fuck that nigga want?"

"Well, if you wouldn't have interrupted me, I would've told you, impatient ass nigga." She rolled her eyes. "Anyways, he was talking about how my sister had gotten into a real bad car accident and how she's in a coma. Just a bunch of shit I didn't care about."

"Damn," I said. "Is she gonna be good?"

"The hell if I know. I didn't know why the fuck he called me in the first place."

"Because that nigga wanted to talk to you. I'ma handle that shit, though. That nigga thinks I'm playing with his ass."

"Fuck him. He really ain't important, anyway," she let me know.

"I know, shawty."

THE NEXT DAY

I ended up falling asleep with Diamond. I didn't realize how tired I was until I actually laid down. Diamond had woke me up because she was in the bathroom throwing up, and the sound of it was making me sick.

"Oh God," she groaned as she flushed the toilet. I laid in the bed waiting patiently for her to come back in the room. She brushed her teeth, rinsed her mouth out, then stepped out of the bathroom looking sick as hell.

"See?" I said, as she got back in the bed. "This is exactly why you need to stop with that pill shit. It's making you sick as fuck."

She sighed loudly. "I'll stop when I'm finished with this bag that I got."

"Nah, you need to stop now. There's other ways that you can cope with your childhood traumas."

She smacked her lips. "Don't tell me how to cope with something if you've never even been through the shit. That's like me telling you to stop smoking weed because—"

"Nah, that's two different things."

"How? Weed is a drug, right? That shit makes you feel good, right?"

"Yeah, but smoking doesn't make me throw up. I can smoke as

much as I want, and it still wouldn't make me throw up. I can wake up from smoking weed and be fine. You on the other hand—"

"I just said I'd stop after I finish with the bag I got now, right? Why you still pressing the issue?"

"Damn, ma. What you got an attitude for? I'm just trying to look out for my shawty."

"Mhm." She closed her eyes as I kissed her on her face. "Everyone always has a problem with what I do."

"That's because they care about you, Dime. You can't be too mad at that."

"Mmmmm," she said, grinding her ass against my dick, making that shit spring to life. "I want some dick," she let out in a soft voice. "Can I have it?"

I didn't plan on having sex with her because I had some shit to do, but I knew me passing on sex wasn't about to happen.

"You sure you can handle it?" I asked, placing kisses on her neck. "I'm not tryna hurt you."

"I think I'm good," she said, coming out of her shirt. "I'll feel a lot better after I get some dick."

So after I dicked Diamond down, she went right back to sleep, and I left her crib. I didn't see her friend as I was leaving her house, and that was some shit I was happy about. I didn't feel like hearing her mouth anyway.

When I pulled up to my place, I wasn't even surprised seeing Melanie's car parked in front of my mailbox. I knew I would be hearing from her ass sooner or later.

Melanie stepped out her car right as I stepped out of mine. I blew out a breath because I already knew she was about to be on some bullshit.

"Really?" she shrieked. "You're really in a relationship with a hoe?"

"Who I get in a relationship with doesn't have shit to do with you. Why you even over here, Melanie?"

She walked up on me, and I could see that her lip was busted. At least Diamond didn't beat her ass too bad.

"You're right, but out of all people, her? A girl who gets paid for sex? A girl who my mom let live with us, and to pay us back, she has sex with my mom's boyfriend and get him to pay her for it?"

"Nah," I said, closing my car door. "That nigga was raping her. He was well over thirty fucking a fourteen-year-old. Rape."

"What? She's probably the one who came on to him! Just like she did with you and all my other niggas! You were dumb enough to actually wife her hoe ass up."

I let out a laugh. Melanie was trying her hardest to make me feel some type of way about Diamond, but that shit wasn't about to happen. Everyone had a past, and now that I knew what went on in Diamond's life as a child, I didn't blame her for being the way she was now.

"Why you here, Melanie? I know you didn't drive all the way over here to talk about another grown ass woman," I said, watching her twist her mouth up.

"You really left me for her? A prostitute? When you were the main one saying how you would never pay for pussy?"

I shot her a small smile. "I'm not paying for it."

"Okay, but you did! Does she even know the real you? Does she know where you really work, or what you really do for a living? Does she know how you're not really broke—"

"Get the fuck outta here, Melanie. We don't have anything else to talk about. Diamond is who I wanna be with. At least I know she not gonna hide my ass like I'm a side nigga." I walked away before she could even respond to me. I didn't know why she brought her stupid ass over here to begin with.

I stepped into the house mad as fuck. I should've never wasted my time with Melanie, but I thought she would've turned out to be a different bitch.

"Why you over there looking like you 'bout to beat a nigga's ass?" Sani laughed, pausing the basketball game he was playing.

"Because I am." I quickly moved to my room so I could find some shit to wear, then shower. I meant to do this shit last night, but I got distracted fucking with Diamond's pill head ass.

I took a quick shower, threw on some clothes, then made my way back into the living room. Sani was still in the same spot playing the game, and I sat down on the couch across from him.

"What's up? What you got going on?" he asked.

"I got some shit I need to handle. I need for you to ride with me."

"Nah. I'm not getting involved in none of the dumb shit you got planned today. I've actually been enjoying my freedom. Shit, I'd like to keep it that way, too."

"It ain't even gon' be on no crazy shit."

He gave me a look because his ass knew better. He could see through my bullshit, but I didn't give a fuck either way. I was gonna do the shit regardless.

He smacked his lips as he turned his game off. "If I get into some shit because of yo' ass, I swear to God—"

"Nigga, shut the fuck up. When do you ever get in trouble because of me? You be doing that dumb shit by yourself." He didn't say anything back as he put on his shoes. He knew I was right. Every time that nigga got locked up was because he decided to go out here and act like he didn't have any sense.

"This got something to do with that Onyx nigga, doesn't it?" he asked, once we were both in the car.

"Why you think that? What if I was going to see my sister? See, you always think you know some shit."

"If you were going to see your sister, you wouldn't have asked me to come with yo' ass. That's some shit you can do by yourself. You tryna stake out or some shit? In the day time?"

"Nah, I'm just about to see if he's at his crib. I'm not even gonna get out the car."

He scoffed, but he didn't say anything else. Shit, if that nigga was standing outside, I was damn sure gonna put two bullets in his head, no questions asked. I knew this nigga was running from me, so he was probably really about to go into hiding like the little bitch he was.

"You're really doing this over two hundred dollars?" Sani asked, after a while of not saying shit.

"Hell yeah. Don't say shit to me when you were the one who was about to kill a nigga over twenty dollars."

"It wasn't twenty. It was nineteen. But that shit was different—"

"No the fuck it wasn't. If it hadn't have been for your sister, you would've killed that nigga over nineteen dollars. Don't say shit to me about what I'm doing."

"Aight, bruh. You got it."

The rest of the ride was quiet. I low key wished Sani would go back to the reckless nigga he used to be because now, he was always trying to preach about something like he wasn't out here doing the same shit. It was crazy to me, but I guess it was a good thing that his ass wasn't in and out of jail anymore.

"That his car?" Sani asked when we pulled up to his crib. I parked on the other side of the street, but if he would've came outside, I'm sure he would've known it was me.

"Hell yeah. I should go knock on the door and end his life right then and there."

Sani glanced at me. "Nah, man. I don't think that's a good—"

"Shut up, nigga. The door's opening."

That bitch ass nigga stepped on to the porch, not even paying attention to his surroundings. He was too focused on his phone to even notice me and Sani sitting right across the street from his house.

I quickly pulled out the strap and rolled Sani's window down.

"Aye, bruh? What you doing?" he asked in a hushed tone. I ignored him, though. Right now, I was feeling like it was now or never. "You not about to shoot this nigga in broad daylight—"

"Lawrence!" I yelled, causing him to look up at us with his brows coming together. He was probably wondering who the fuck it was, and why they were calling him by his government name.

I pulled the trigger, hitting him once in his stomach, then again, hitting him in his chest. He fell to the ground and I sped off.

"The fuck, nigga?!" Sani snapped as I laughed. "You said you weren't about to do no crazy shit! You said—"

"Chill. I didn't kill his ass. This shit is just another warning. Get ya panties outta ya ass, bruh."

"A warning? See, man, hell nah. I ain't doing this shit with you no more, so don't even ask."

At this point, I didn't give a fuck. I did what I came for. Sani talking shit wasn't even bothering me right now.

FOURTEEN

D IAMOND

3 MONTHS LATER

"This is so stupid," I muttered to myself as I read the text message again that Koda had sent me.

KODA: GET DRESSED. TAKING U TO MEET MY SIS AFTER WORK

He didn't even ask if I wanted to meet her. He was just demanding me to do the shit, and I wasn't feeling it. I remember that attitude his sister had with me when we were at her ratchet ass hair show, and I was trying to talk to her brother. She acted like she had a problem with me, so no, I didn't want to meet her.

"I don't understand what you have an attitude for," Mia said, as I cut my eyes at her. "You should be happy your white boy wants you to meet some of his family."

"I already met her, and she was a bitch. She didn't even know me, but she was acting like she had a problem. I don't be doing anything to these bitches."

"Did you fuck her nigga?"

I twisted my face up. "Kevin?"

"Oh shit, Kevin is his sister's boyfriend? Yo, I never knew that. You learn something new every day, for real."

I rolled my eyes. "I really don't wanna meet her. I don't wanna get dressed, so I'm not. You know what, I'm actually about to call him and tell him that I don't wanna meet his sister. He can't make me do what I don't wanna do right? It doesn't work like that."

She gave me a look like she had something to say but decided against it. I was glad because I didn't give a fuck about anything she had to say right now. I was gonna do what the hell I wanted.

I let another thirty minutes go by before I finally called Koda. I was actually hoping he wouldn't answer since he was at work, then I would just text him that I didn't feel comfortable meeting his sister because she—

"What's up, baby?" he answered in a low voice. It didn't sound like that nigga was at work to me.

"Hey... I'm not gonna be able to meet your sister because I'm just not—"

"Stop playing." He laughed.

"I'm being serious, Koda! The first time I ever met her, she had an attitude with me. She didn't like me for no reason then, so what makes you think she's gonna like me now?"

"You trippin'. She didn't have no damn attitude with you."

"Yes, she did! How you gonna tell me?"

"Because I know my sister, Dime. You dressed yet? I'm leaving work right now." What the fuck? Was this nigga not hearing what I was saying to him or something?

"No, I'm not dressed. I'm not going."

I heard him let out a small sigh. "Diamond, please don't make this shit more difficult than it has to be. We've been doing everything you wanted to do this entire week. Why can't you just do this one thing for me?"

I smacked my lips because I knew he was gonna make me feel bad for not wanting to go. I still didn't understand why I had to meet his sister. Why just her? Why was she so special? Why couldn't I meet his mom or something?

"Fine." I sighed. "I'll go get dressed now."

"See? Was that so hard? You over there overthinking and—"

"I was not overthinking, Koda. I'm wearing whatever the hell I wanna wear, so when you get here, don't try to make me change."

"Dress like you got some damn sense, and we're not even gonna have to worry about that shit."

I rolled my eyes. I already had it planned out in my head that I was gonna wear some off the wall shit.

"Yeah, whateva, nigga. See you when you get here." I ended the call before he could respond.

"Sounds like you're going to me." Mia chuckled. I cut my eyes at her. She had been smiling at her phone for the last hour.

"Who the fuck you texting over there?"

"Bitch, who said I was texting? I'm over here minding my business." I didn't believe shit that had just came from her mouth, though. She was trying to hide it from me.

"You're texting a nigga, aren't you? Lemme find out Mia is liking dick again."

She let out a small laugh. "You're like three months late," she muttered.

"What? So, you've been messing with a nigga for three whole months, and you're just now telling me?"

"I mean, you've been too far up Koda's ass to pay attention to anything else. Have you even talked to your mom?"

I swear, I almost smacked the taste out of her mouth. What the hell did I need to talk to her for? We didn't have shit to talk about.

"Talk to her for what?" I asked, already tired of this conversation.

"Shit, I don't know. Is your sister good? What about Lawrence?"

I laughed as I started to walk away. "You real funny, Mia. Don't try to change the subject because you don't wanna talk about the little nigga you've been messing with. It's all good, though. As soon as I get back from this nigga's sister's house, you better believe I'm gonna be all up in your business."

"I'm not gonna be here!" she called after me. Now that I think about it, Koda had been spending all his time here, and Mia was always gone. I just never thought anything of it because I thought she was with her cousin or something.

Once I was in my room, I stood in my closet trying to decide on what I was going to wear. I had so many short dresses that Koda hated, and I think that's exactly what I was going to put on. It was starting to get cold outside, so I knew Koda was going to come in here running his damn mouth. I'd be okay, though. I'd just throw a jacket on.

I decided on a baby pink dress that stopped right below my ass. I loved the way pink looked against my skin. That's probably why it was one of my favorite colors. I laid the dress out on the bed, then went inside the bathroom so I could take a quick shower.

What I thought was going to be a quick shower turned into a twenty-minute shower. I was just loving the way the water was feeling against my body. I honestly didn't want to get out, but I knew I had—

"Aye!" Koda yelled, busting through the door. "Why you still in the shower, bruh?" I covered my body like he hadn't saw me naked before.

"I'm almost finished. Get out."

"You should've been finished! You should've been dressed and ready to go as soon as I pulled up, Diamond. What the fuckkk?"

I smiled at him because I knew it would piss him off. He hated when I would laugh while he's trying to be serious.

"The fuck you smiling at, Diamond?"

"You," I said, letting the water run all over my body to rinse the rest of my body wash off. "You fine as fuck, nigga."

"Get yo' ass out the shower, yo. We're gonna be late as fuck."

I ignored him and took my sweet little time rinsing off. What he wasn't about to do was come in here and rush me. He knew I hated being rushed, so I couldn't understand why the hell he was doing it.

"It's just a dinner, Koda. The worst that can happen is them eating without us. I wasn't going to be in there eating anyway because I don't eat everybody's cooking." I shrugged as I stood up and dropped my towel. Maybe if I got some dick before we left, it would put me in a better mood.

I grabbed the body oil off my dresser and handed it to him.

"What you giving me this shit for? You really need to hurry your slow ass—"

"I need you to put it on me, Koda. Don't try to act brand new like you don't be begging me to oil my body down. Come onnnn."

He stood there, biting the inside of his cheek, because he knew exactly what I was doing. He didn't wanna do it *right now*, but he couldn't resist.

"You really doing too much, Dime." He sighed, as he came closer to me.

"What are you talking about? I'm just trying to be oiled. You want me to meet your sister as an ashy bitch? You want me to give her a reason to talk about me, because you know she's going to."

He slapped me hard on the ass, making a small gasp escape my throat.

"I know what you're doing, shawty," he said in a low voice, squeezing oil on to his hands. "You ain't finna get me, though."

"Finna?" I chuckled. "Nigga, that ain't even a—"

"I'm not giving you dick right now, Diamond. You think I give a fuck that you're standing in front of me, butt naked, looking all choco-latey and shit?" I looked at him and he had his blonde ass eyebrow raised.

"Boy, bye." I laughed, finally feeling his hands on my body. "You know you give a fuck. Dick hard as fuck right now—"

"No it ain't."

"I bet it is." His hands came to my breasts, and from the look that he was wearing, I knew he had an erection. He was trying to front like he didn't, but nah.

He gave me a small smirk. "Turn around."

I slowly turned around, knowing he was letting his eyes travel all over me, and felt his hands rubbing on my back.

"I think I deserve dick for this actually," I countered. "Every time we did something that I wanted to do, we always came back and—"

"I'm not giving you dick, Diamond. You're not about to make us later than we already are. Get dressed so we can go." His voice was stern, so I knew he was serious. In effect, I rolled my eyes because I didn't get my way. Now, I was really about to have an attitude. He didn't even know what he was getting himself into.

I walked away from him while he was still trying to oil me down. Since he wanted to hold out on me, I was going to do the same when we got back to his place later. I was just gonna take my ass right to sleep. Get butt naked, rub all on his dick like I wanted it, then go to sleep.

"You really got an attitude?" he asked as I slipped into my dress.

"Nope." My tone was dry, so he knew damn well I had an attitude, but to avoid talking about it, I just simply told him no. I didn't wanna talk to him, period.

"You can get some dick as soon as we get back, I just—"

"Don't care. Let's go." I ran my fingers through my hair, then slid some flip flops on because I didn't care about looking cute right now. I didn't care about going to this damn dinner, and I didn't care about the fact that Koda was trying to make me feel better about the entire dick-getting conversation.

"Mannnn," he groaned, following out my room behind me. "You're about to have an attitude for the rest of the night?"

Silence.

Why was he asking stupid ass questions? Of course I was gonna have an attitude all night. I wouldn't be me if I didn't.

"Mia," I said, getting her attention. "Keep your phone on just in case I have to beat a bitch's ass tonight."

"Aight." She laughed, and Koda smacked his lips behind me.

"We're taking my car," I said, trying to walk toward it.

"Nah. You know damn well we ain't doing that." He gently grabbed my arm and pulled me toward his car. I hated riding in his damn car. Mine was better, so why not just take mine?

"Whatever," I snapped, snatching away from him.

He let out a loud sigh when we were both in the car, and I didn't care.

"Aye," he said, backing out of my driveway. "Lose the fuckin' attitude. I'm not about to take you in here and you're acting like—"

"Shut the fuck up, Koda. Why won't you just stop talking to me? Why you keep pressing the issue? You want me to be mad, huh? You want me to—"

"Lose the attitude, Diamond. I'm not gonna say that shit again."

"Fuck you." I crossed my arms and glared out the window. He wasn't about to sit here and tell me what to do.

"You're really this mad over not getting dick, bruh? You're really sitting here pouting like a little ass kid because—"

I cut off his sentence by turning the radio all the way up. What he had to say didn't matter. All I wanted to do now was get to his sister's place, act like I was better than every mothafucka in there and go on with my evening. Koda trying to talk was only making things worse.

He didn't bother saying anything else to me as we drove, and I was glad. I had time to think about how petty I was going to be when we got back home. I smiled to myself thinking about it.

I wasn't even a little bit surprised when we pulled up to his sister's house. It was huge. It looked like something straight out of a magazine. I knew she wasn't going to be living in some dump because Kevin was her man. That nigga had more money than he knew what to do with.

"Come on," Koda said, after he came around to my side of the car and opened the door for me.

I stepped out of the car without saying anything to him. I just knew I needed to get to the bathroom. After that, I'd be good.

Koda put his hand on my lower back as we both moved toward the front door. Just from looking at the immaculately groomed yard, I knew they had money. Their yard put mine to shame. I barely even had grass anymore because I stopped caring about it. I wasn't about to go out there and cut the grass myself, and I damn sure wasn't paying anyone else to do it. Fuck all that.

"Hey!" Layla said as she pulled the door open. She was happy to see her brother, of course, but when her eyes landed on me, I could damn near feel the displeasure radiating from her.

Koda pulled her in for a hug, and I kept my face stale. No need to be fake just because she was my boyfriend's sister. If she wanted to be nice, then I'd play that part. But if she wanted to be a bitch, then we could play those games too. The shit honestly didn't even matter to me.

"What's up?" he asked when they finally pulled away from each other.

"It's about time you got here. I thought you were gonna— Koda, look at your fuckin' hair!" I knew she was talking about the new growth sticking out from the top of his dreads because I had been telling him to go get his shit re twisted, but he wouldn't listen to me.

"Man, my hair ain't what I'm worried about right now."

"You act like I don't have a whole shop," she huffed as we both stepped into her house. "You act like you can't come and get that shit done for free! A real girlfriend wouldn't let her boyfriend walk around looking like that." She cut her eyes at me and I gave her a small smirk.

Let the games begin, bitch.

"I need to use the bathroom," I said, flipping my hair from my shoulder.

"Say hey before you start asking to go places in *her* crib, shawty," Koda said, making me want to slap the white off his ass.

"Hey." I flipped. "Could you please show me where *your* bathroom is, in *your* house so I could use it?"

"Down there to the left," she said, pointing in the direction of it. I fought the urge to roll my eyes as I made my way down the hall. I wanted to run into the bathroom, but I didn't want them to look at me like I was crazy.

I passed through the kitchen and spotted Kevin standing at the counter. I gave him a small wave as he looked at me like he'd saw a ghost. I thought he would've known I was coming over, but maybe Layla didn't tell him. I don't understand why she wouldn't do that, though.

When I finally made it to the bathroom, I shut and locked the door, then stood in front of the mirror staring at my reflection. I was losing weight, but it wasn't too noticeable right now. Well, at least not in my face.

I quickly dug in my purse and pulled out the small baggie, and my wallet. See, I told myself I wasn't going to get addicted to this. I told myself I was going to quit the pills, and just try to live a normal life. I *wanted* to do it. Especially after Koda found out about my little pill habit.

It didn't work that way, though.

Once I had finished that bag of pills, I started going through withdrawals. Like, bad withdrawals. I would wake up in a pool of sweat, then right afterward, I would get the chills to the point I was shaking like a wet little puppy, my anxiety was eating me alive, I would feel nauseous, but never throw up, and irritable as fuck. I was going off on everyone, especially Koda.

After the third day of feeling that terrible abdominal pain, I knew something had to give. I knew I wasn't going to be able do that shit. Lawrence wasn't answering the phone when I called, so I had to find something else. Another drug that I knew I could get from Julian easily.

White.

Nose candy.

Yayo.

I told myself I wasn't going to get too addicted to it, but once I felt that high, everything went out the window. I needed it. I desired it. I craved it.

So here I was, in my boyfriend's sister's bathroom, forming a line of cocaine with an old Victoria's Secret gift card that I still had in my wallet. I only did one line because I knew that would be enough to get me through the night.

"Fuck," I whispered, after snorting it up one of my nostrils. I started rubbing my nose like crazy because it was tingling. After that, I sneezed twice, and flushed the toilet as if I really used the bathroom.

I quickly cleaned up the mess I made and put everything back in my purse. There was little bit left on the sink, so I dabbed my finger in it, and rubbed it on the top of my gums. The taste was terrible, but it was worth it.

I checked my appearance in the mirror again, ran my fingers through my hair, and stepped out of the bathroom. I heard Koda's voice, so that's where I went. He was sitting on a couch across from his sister, and I went to sit next to him.

"Hell, yeah," he said, in the middle of a conversation that him and Layla were having. "Had a long ass day at work. Tired as hell now, but you know I wasn't about to pass up your good as cooking." He smiled at her as I caressed his face.

The high was kicking in already, and honestly, the thoughts in my head about what I wanted to do to him right now were screaming at me.

"Honestly," his sister said. "I thought you would've been coming over by yourself. I had no idea you were bringing your *friend* with you."

I slipped off my flip flops and put both legs over his lap. I put my hands on the sides of his face, pulling himself closer to me. I heard what his stupid ass sister said about me being his friend. She knew I wasn't, and the shit bothered her.

"What you doing, ma?" he asked, quietly, with a small smile tugging at his lips.

I didn't say anything as I pressed my lips against his. I thought I was going to just give him a small peck, but once our lips touched, I eagerly slipped my tongue in his mouth, letting him know what I wanted, all while showing his sister that I wasn't just a little friend of his.

I felt his hands moving up my thigh and a small moan escaped my lips. I needed him to move his hands up just a little bit more and claim what was waiting for him. I wasn't wearing panties, and I knew it was a mess down there.

His mess.

That's when he quickly pulled away, probably because he remembered where the hell he was at. The look of lust in his eyes was apparent. He bit down on his lip and squeezed my thigh telling me to chill until we got home. Little did he know, he wasn't getting any ass when we got there.

Layla uncomfortably cleared her throat and I smiled at her. Kevin came to join her on the couch, trying his hardest not to look at me. Shit didn't have to be awkward between me and him, but that's what he was doing.

"So," Layla said, not knowing what to say next. "How have you been? You talked to Dad lately?"

Koda scoffed. "Nah. Don't plan on it either."

"You can't keep taking your anger out on him."

"Why the fuck not?" he snapped. I laid my head down on his shoulder. I loved the way he smelled. I would wear his clothes just for his scent. I mean, his clothes were much more comfortable, too, but the smell of them was enough to get me wet.

I ran my hand up his chest as I inhaled deeply. He smelled like weed, because I was sure he'd smoked on the way to my place, Dove, and his natural scent.

Kevin's eyes were on me. I could feel them, but I wasn't going to look at him. He was making shit weird.

"Well..." Layla started, reluctantly. "I kinda invited him over here. Him and my mom."

Koda had briefly told me the story about his dad. He said his dad was in his life up until he was about three, then he left his mom and went and got married to another woman. Layla's mom. Layla and Koda met a few years ago, and Koda still didn't fuck with his dad. He hadn't talked to him since he was younger, and he was okay with that.

"I'ma leave before he gets here," Koda let her know, causing me to smile at her. This was great news because I didn't wanna be over here in the first place.

"Why? I know you're mad about what he did to your mom, but—"

"You don't know shit, Layla," he said, easily running a pale hand up my thigh again.

"Could you stay for me? Please?" she damn near begged. I had to keep myself from smacking my lips. Koda seeing his dad tonight was gonna end badly. I could feel it.

"Nah. You should've told me that nigga was coming when you invited me. I damn sure wouldn't have brought my girl over here—"

"So, y'all together?" Kevin asked, finally saying something since he'd been in the same room as us.

"Yep," I gushed, kissing him on his cheek.

"Why you care?" Layla spat, like there was a problem going on between them that we didn't know about.

"I was just asking a question," he replied with his brows coming together.

"Why? Huh? You want her to be your girlfriend or something?"

"What? Bruh, you trippin'. I was just joining in on the conversation."

She glared at him. I could see it all over her face that she wanted to punch that nigga straight in his mouth, but she wasn't about that life. She wasn't the type to do it.

As they were having a stare off, there was a knock on the door, and I felt Koda's body stiffen up. He really didn't want to see his dad. But I honestly wanted to know what the nigga looked like.

Layla muttered something under her breath as she got up from the couch to go get the door.

"Nah, we gotta go," Koda said, standing up. "We gotta get the fuck outta here." But, before I could even stand up, Layla was appearing with a woman who looked exactly like her, and a big broad man who I instantly knew was Koda's dad.

They didn't look alike, but they were built the same. Tall and broad. Actually, his dad looked very well to be his age.

"Aight, we're about to get up outta here," Koda announced as him and his dad locked eyes. I could tell that his dad wanted to talk to his son, but Koda wasn't going for it.

"Already?" Layla asked, acting like she didn't know he didn't wanna see their dad. "Y'all just got here."

"I'll come back another time. If I stay, ain't no telling what might happen." I grabbed his hand as I stood next to him. I wasn't going to attempt to talk him out of this because I had been ready to go.

"Can you please just stay?" she begged. "For me?"

He let out a small sigh, and right then, I could tell that Koda had a soft spot for his sister.

"Aight, yo."

DAMN! I JUST WANNA LEAVE!

"I thought you'd be happy to see your old man," his dad said with a small smirk on his face. He turned his attention to me. "This your girlfriend? Pretty chocolate thang, huh? I always knew you would never have a problem getting a woman. I'm Sylvester, by the way." He held his hand out, and I looked at it for a moment before I reluctantly put my hand in his.

I didn't expect him to take my hand and kiss the back of it like Koda does sometimes. Nigga got all his charm from his damn daddy.

"Diamond," I said, pulling my hand away from him.

He flashed me a smile, and I saw nothing but Koda. These niggas looked alike, but they didn't. Did that even make sense?

"Hi, Koda," Layla's mom said with her arms out. Koda just looked at her though. I mean, why would he get along with the woman that basically ruined his family?

"Nah." Koda laughed. "I'm good. Don't touch me." I bit my lip to suppress a laugh. I didn't know why, but I loved when Koda was rude to people. If I was wearing panties right now, I would've taken them off and threw them right at his ass.

Layla's mom cleared her throat, then glanced at me. "Hi, I'm Anita."

"Diamond," I repeated.

"Son," Sylvester started, "I'm glad you decided to stay. I've been wanting to talk to you for some time, but—"

"Don't call me that shit. Not your son, bruh. If you wanted to talk to me, then you would've. Don't stand here and lie. You too old for that now."

"Just because you grown don't mean you can talk to me anyway you want to. I'm still your father, *boy*."

"Nigga, fuck you," Koda spat. "You ain't shit to me. Never will be shit to me. You know it like I know it—"

"I ain't gonna tell you again, Koda."

Koda let out a bitter laugh. "Nah. If I stay here, I'ma beat this nigga's ass. I'll hit you up later, Lay." He didn't wait for anyone to respond to him as he began walking out, pulling me with him.

Once we were outside, I couldn't contain the smile.

"If y'all would've fought, I would've beat the fuck outta his wife," I let him know as he opened the door for me.

He pulled me closer to him and gave me a quick peck.

"I wouldn't have let it get that far. You don't need to be out here fighting anyway."

I ignored what he said and slid into the passenger's seat. Words couldn't even describe the happiness I felt because we were leaving. I just knew I was gonna say something to his dumb ass sister if she kept looking at me like she had a problem. She was Koda's family. Not mine. I would've beat that little ass girl like she stole something.

"She did that shit on purpose," Koda let me know. "She invited that nigga over there because she know I'm not gonna take time out my day to talk to his ass. Fuck I look like?"

"Why does she want you to talk to him so bad?"

He shrugged. "I don't fuckin' know. She's been trying to get us together for the past couple of months. I don't have shit to say to that man. Where the fuck was he at when I was younger and was still willing to talk? Somewhere being a husband and father to someone else. Nah. Not talking to his ass."

"Fuck him. I never even knew my dad. Nigga got my mom pregnant and dipped. I don't even know what he looks like. If I saw him on the streets, I wouldn't even know it was him."

He glanced at me as he drove down the dark road, surrounded by trees.

"Yeah, I'm not gonna be that type of parent when we have kids."

He rested a pale hand on my thigh, and I lifted a brow.

"Well, who said I wanted to have kids? What if I don't want any? Would that bother you?"

"Nah." He said as I started to move his hand closer and closer to what had been begging for him since he showed up to my place to pick me up earlier. "If you didn't wanna have kids, that shit wouldn't bother me."

He started pulling over and I looked at him like he was crazy. Why was he pulling over on this dark ass road?

"What are you doing?" I asked, watching him take off his seatbelt.

"About to get some pussy since you wanna be nasty." I just looked at him because I honestly didn't know what to say back to that. I wasn't about to tell him no, though.

I unbuckled my seatbelt, popped the door open, and got in the backseat where Koda was already waiting on me. He was undoing his pants and quickly sliding them down. Being that I was just wearing this short ass dress with no underwear, I pulled it up, and straddled him. He was already standing at attention, and I was already leaking, so I easily slid down on to him.

"Fuck," he grunted, grabbing handfuls of my ass and pressing himself into me as far as he could.

My entire body tingled with pleasure. I thought since he was on the bottom, I was gonna be the one controlling this, but he held on to my hips and started thrusting himself in me.

"Ahh!" I shrieked, while he showed no mercy on me. "Kodaaa!"

"Take this dick," he said, grabbing my face with one hand so we were now looking directly at each other. His hazel eyes were boring into mine that I was trying to keep from rolling back.

Every time I would moan his name, he would moan mine right back. My legs were shaking so bad, so I knew the climax was coming next. I guess he could see it all over my face because he said, "Nah. Don't cum yet. You can't cum until I do." He stuck his tongue in my mouth as he finally released my face and gripped my ass again. He took his other hand and found my clit, and I swallowed a moan that probably would've came out as a scream. "Yeah," he said, looking at me through low eyes. The look on his face looked like he was getting even more pleasure just from touching me like this.

His strokes were getting deeper and deeper, and it was getting harder for me to hold mine in.

"Koda," I whimpered while my entire body shook. "Please."

I saw the small smile that spread across his face, and I couldn't hold it in anymore. He had a look of satisfaction as he watched everything he was doing play out on my face.

"What I tell you, ma?" he asked, after kissing me like he would never see me again. At this point, I couldn't even talk anymore. My eyes were closed, head was thrown back, and my mouth was hanging open.

He pumped into me three hard times, before he let a long groan escape his lips. I slumped into his chest, and I closed my eyes. The plan to not let him get any tonight flew straight out the window.

Gahhh damn, Koda.

FIFTEEN

K ODA

"I'm just saying, Koda," Layla said as she retwisted my hair. "You didn't have to be rude to him like that. He was actually really excited to see you. All he wants to do is apologize to you for—"

"Lay, that was a damn week ago. Why you still talking about it and shit? I don't give a damn what he wants to do. That apology doesn't mean shit to me. Fuck him."

She smacked her lips. "Stop acting like that. You know he's sick, right? He's sick. He's dying, and all he wants to do is make peace with his kids before he goes. For you to be rude to him really hurt his feelings."

"He didn't give a fuck about mine or my mom's feelings when he left us for your mom. How you think I felt as a young nigga when I found out my dad had a whole new family, but that nigga wouldn't even answer the phone when I called him? Now that he knows he's dying, I'm supposed to willingly let that nigga back in my life? Hell nah. It doesn't work like that."

After I left Layla's crib that night, I wasn't really feeling going back over there. She had been calling, but I didn't have shit to say to her because that was some dumb shit she did with trying to get me to talk to Sylvester. She out of all people knew how I felt about him. I still couldn't understand why she wanted me to talk to him so bad.

She was quiet for a moment as she did my hair. She wanted me to come to the shop to do it, but I wasn't feeling all that. She had a place in that big ass house where she could do my hair, so I told her that was the only way I was going to let her do it.

"He's sick, Koda," she said, after a while.

"Not my problem, Lay."

She blew out a breath. "Whatever, Koda. I just don't want you to be like one of those people who realize they should've given someone a second chance, but it's too late because the person is already dead. I'm just saying, you should forgive him. You two don't have to be close or anything because I know that ship has sailed, but at least accept his apology."

"Aye, I'm not trying to be rude or anything, but can you shut the hell up about that nigga? I don't wanna talk about him. I don't even wanna think about him. Change the subject."

"Whatever, Koda." She sighed. "But since you're making me change the subject, let's talk about that girl you brought over to my house last week. Desiree? Yeah, I don't like her."

I let out a small chuckle. "Stop playing. You know her name is Diamond. And she hasn't done a damn thing to you, so you don't really have a reason not to like her."

"What?" She flipped. "She's rude as hell! She thinks she better than everybody, her attitude is terrible, and from the outfit she was wearing, I know she doesn't have respect for herself."

"How is she rude when she barely said four words to you? How can you tell she thinks she's better than everybody when you haven't even had an intellectual conversation with her? And because she was wearing a dress, she doesn't respect herself? Do you hear yourself? You hear how stupid you sound?"

She stopped twisting my hair so she could look at me. Her brows came together in confusion.

"So, you really like her? Like, she's really your girlfriend?" she asked, like it was so hard for her to believe it.

"Hell yeah. You think I would've brought her over here if I wasn't serious about her? You think I let random hoes just meet my family?"

She bit the inside of her cheek. "I just can't understand what it is about her. Out of all the girls you could've chosen, you choose her? She just seems so... hood. Maybe even ghetto. If I were you, I would be embarrassed to be seen in public with her."

I looked at her like she was crazy. It was crazy as hell how she didn't know shit about Diamond but had so much to say about her. She was judging Diamond before she even got to know her.

"Don't speak on what you don't know," I said as she started back with my hair.

"I'm just letting you know how I feel, Koda. She's not your type."

"And how the fuck do you even know what my type is? When have you ever met any of my girlfriends?"

"I haven't, but I can tell she's just with you for your money. I can tell she had ulterior motives. She's gonna—"

"Like I said, don't speak on what you don't know. You don't know her like I do, so honestly, you can't tell me shit about her." I shrugged lightly as she shook her head.

"Don't say I didn't warn you, Koda. I just have the feeling that you two aren't going to last. She seems great for you now, but give it a couple of months. If you're not cheating on her already, you will be later."

I didn't bother saying anything else to her. She wasn't saying all this shit because she thought it was true. She was just saying it because she had her own personal reasons she didn't like Diamond. She didn't like Diamond the first day she met her. I wanted to ask what was the real reason she didn't like Diamond, but I knew she wouldn't tell me.

"How's the wedding planning coming?" I asked after a while of silence.

"It's coming. It would be nice if I could get some real help from Kevin. All he does is agree with everything."

"What's wrong with that?"

"I don't need him to agree with everything. I want him to be a part of the wedding too. Like damn. Tell me what you like. He doesn't care though. He keeps saying as long as I'm happy. Of course I'm gonna be happy, but that's not the point."

I lifted a blonde eyebrow. "Damn. Women are so complex. Why not just have a small ass wedding? Wouldn't that shit be easier?"

"I don't want a small wedding, Koda. My dream was to always have a big wedding. Now since I just found out dad is sick, I feel like I need to hurry up and do it because I don't want him to miss it, and I need him to walk me down the aisle."

Damn. How long did the nigga have to live?

"He could do that in your backyard, though."

"I'm not having a small wedding. I don't want one. Maybe whenever you find the girl of your dreams, you can get married too. But, until then—"

"I already found the girl of my dreams," I let her know with a small smile forming. "Stop tryna downplay my girl like that."

"Koda, you can't possibly think she's the girl for you? She doesn't even look like the type who knows how to be a wife. I'm telling you, she's only in it for your money. Hasn't all the other ones just been in it for the money?"

"Yeah. That's why I haven't told her about it. She thinks I work at Walmart."

She let out a small laugh. "You can't be serious right now." She shook her head. "So this is the girl of your dreams, but you're lying to her?"

"Nah, I'm not lying, I'm just trying to make sure she's really in it before—"

"Lying, Koda. It's going to be a mess when she finds out. You should know this, but it doesn't surprise me that you don't. You're a man."

"What the fuck is that supposed to mean? That I'm dumb or some shit?" She giggled and didn't say anything back. "I'll cross the bridge when we get to it. I'm gonna tell her, but—"

"How long have y'all been together?"

"About three months, I think. I didn't really write down the day we got together."

"Are her feelings like really invested? Is she telling you she loves you yet?"

I thought about it for a moment before I shook my head. I'd never said it to her and she'd never said it to me either. I'd been thinking about it.

"Nah. We ain't never said it."

"Hmmm... well that's kinda a good thing. Maybe she won't be *too* mad when she finds out, but she'll be mad. But you know, I wanna talk to her again. This time, without all the attitudes. Tell her to leave that shit at the door, Koda."

"She probably ain't gonna wanna come back over here, Lay. She didn't wanna come the first time," I said, watching her roll her eyes.

"Why? Ain't like she knows me or anything."

"Because you had an attitude at your hair show, and she felt like you were gonna have an attitude when I brought her over... and you did."

"What? I did not have an attitude with her. She came into my house with an attitude. Didn't even greet me before she started asking for shit."

"Promise me you won't have an attitude when I bring her back."

She looked at me through narrowed eyes. "Okay, I promise. But if she has one, I'm gonna check her about it."

Good luck with that shit.

I didn't know who Layla thought Diamond was, but she was always ready to go off on a bitch. That's what I didn't want to happen, though. I didn't need my girl and my sister arguing or fighting.

"WHAT?" Diamond asked as she looked at me like I had two heads. "You want me to go back? *You're* going back? After she tried to—"

"Chill. She said she wants to talk to you. She wants a do over. *Without* the attitudes and shit."

She rolled her eyes and let out a loud sigh. "She had an attitude as soon as she saw me. Tell her not to have no got damn attitude. Especially since I haven't done a damn thing to her."

"So, you'll go?"

She gave me the ugliest expression as she looked at me. "I guess so. But if she starts saying some off the wall shit, I'm gonna hit her ass straight in the mouth. Not playing with you or her." She pointed a finger in my face.

"I know that, mama. She's not—"

"I don't do too well with being disrespected. That shit is the quickest way to catch an ass whoopin'."

"Alright, Diamond. Just get dressed so we can go."

She looked down at what she was wearing, then turned her attention back to me. "What's wrong with what I'm wearing?"

She had on a white belly shirt with some grey sweatpants. Yeah, there was nothing wrong with the outfit, but I felt like she would rather put on some real clothes rather than just wearing "chill in the house clothes."

"Nothing, but you don't wanna—"

"This is what I'm wearing. It's just a fake ass dinner with your sister that doesn't like me. I'm not about to get dressed up for no shit like that."

She didn't wait for me to respond as she stepped into the bathroom and closed the door behind her. The only thing I was worried about now was them two getting through this shit. I didn't know why Layla had a change of heart all of a sudden, but I hoped she wasn't on no sneaky shit again.

"Your hair looks really nice," she let me know once she was out the bathroom.

"Thanks. Your wig looks nice, too." Today, her wig was burgundy. At first, I thought the wearing wigs things was a little crazy. I wasn't used to no shit like that, but now I didn't have a problem with it. It was like she had a wig for every damn personality she had.

"You think so? I glued this one real good since you like to pull my hair like you ain't got no damn sense."

"Stop playing, Diamond. That ain't your hair. Plus, I be too into it, and I forget you're even wearing a wig. Pussy shouldn't be that good."

She waved me off as she put her shoes on. "Shut up, Koda."

I followed behind her as we left out of her room, then out of her crib all together.

"Can your sister even cook? If I try her food and it's nasty, I'm going to tell her. I don't just go around eating everyone's cooking."

"I know, Diamond. You told me."

"I'm just letting you know, Koda. I don't want you to be surprised when I start talking shit."

"You won't talk shit because Layla can throw down in the kitchen. That's a fact."

"Mhmmm," she said, obviously not wanting to believe me. I was gonna let her find out on her own, though.

When we finally pulled up to Layla's house, Diamond let out a breath. I knew she didn't wanna do this shit, but I was just hoping she didn't act up. I put my hand on her thigh to get her attention.

"Don't put your hand right there unless you're trying to have sex right here, right now."

"I mean, I'm down with that, but I'm not tryna walk up in here smelling like I just got some good ass pussy."

She smiled at me, then popped her door open. I did the same, then when we met at the front of my car, I grabbed her hand.

"So I was thinking about this earlier when I was in the shower—"

"What? How much you were missing a nigga?" I interrupted.

"No," she said looking up at me. "I don't usually do shit like this. Well, I've actually *never* done shit like this... relationships, I mean. I've never been in one. I was actually afraid to get in this one because I didn't know how they worked. I thought you'd be tired of my ass by now."

"Nah," I let her know. "Don't think that shit will ever happ—"

"I love you," she said, making me close my mouth. I looked at her because for some reason, I thought she was joking. For some reason, I thought she was about to start laughing, and telling me she didn't mean that shit. But her face remained serious. She was just staring at me, waiting for me to respond to her.

I pulled her closer to me and watched as she smiled before kissing her. She stuck her tongue down my throat, and I felt my dick pressing at the zipper of my pants.

"I love you, too," I said, after I pulled away. I knocked on the door still while holding her close to me. In the three months we'd been together, I had never felt like this before. Shit, me and Melanie were together for years, and I didn't feel this way about her. Not in the beginning either.

Layla opened the door with a smile on her face. "Hey," she said, stepping to the side so that we could step in. "I didn't expect y'all to get here so early."

Diamond had a smile on her face, but I knew it was because of me and not because she was just being nice to Layla. The way she was squeezing my hand let me know that this was about to be hard for her.

"I didn't see the point of waiting to come over, when we were both ready," I said, stepping past Layla and into the house.

"I'm glad you decided to come back, Diamond."

"Thanks," Diamond said. I didn't think that word went there, but I wasn't going to say anything about it. I didn't want to say anything that could cause an argument. I needed everyone to stay in a good mood.

"The food is just about finished. I think the chicken will be ready in about five minutes. Everyone likes chicken, right?"

"Yeah." I laughed.

"Good. I made sure to cook something that everyone likes." She led us into the kitchen then we sat at the table. "Hold on, let me go get Kevin so we can all eat."

"This food better be good," Diamond said once Layla was gone.

"It is. I promise. You're gonna be eating it like you ain't ate shit in years. Watch."

She rolled her eyes. "You don't know what I'm about to do," she muttered.

About five minutes passed, and Layla returned with annoyance written all over her face. She didn't say anything as she got the rest of the food out the oven, then started setting the table. Kevin casually walked into the kitchen and gave me a small nod.

"What's up, bruh?" he asked, sitting in the chair in front of me.

"Not shit. Just another day." He dapped me up, then shot a quick glance at Diamond who was busy scrolling through her phone.

"So," Layla said finally coming to the table. "How did you and my brother meet?" Her attention was on Diamond.

"His birthday," she said, dropping her phone in her purse. "I had sex with him on his birthday, fell in love with the dick, then he kinda just didn't go away. Now, here we are. In a relationship."

"Oh... well, that's nice. Have you met his mom yet? You know it's *really* official when you meet the parents." I looked at Layla through wide eyes, but she didn't notice.

"No. I haven't met his mom, but he hasn't met my parents either, so I guess we're even." Diamond shrugged because meeting my parents wasn't a big deal to her. Not once had she said anything about meeting my mom. Shit, she didn't wanna meet my sister. I made her ass do it anyway.

"Oh. Well, don't you think you two should plan that?"

"No," Diamond said, flipping her hair off her shoulder. "It's not really bothering me. I'm dating Koda, not his parents."

"But meeting his parents are—"

"How long were you and Kevin together before you met his parents?" Diamond interrupted. "Oh wait, you didn't meet his parents, did you? Because he was a foster child, right?"

Layla pressed her lips together because she was trying to hold back whatever it was she wanted to say.

"Okay," Layla said, after she let out a breath. "Let's change the subject. What do you do for a living?"

"You serious right now? You really wanna know what I do for a living? Or do you already know, and you just want me to say it out loud?"

"I'm just asking a question, Diamond. Why would I know what you do for a living? I didn't even know you existed until my brother brought you over here the other—"

"Bitch, cut it out. You knew I existed. You knew exactly who I was when Koda brought me over here last week, too. Don't sit here and act like you're not pressed over me."

I put my hand on Diamond's thigh indicating that she needed to calm that shit down. Honestly, I didn't even think she could help it. I didn't think she knew how defensive she was coming off.

"Definitely not pressed." Layla laughed.

"I fuck niggas for money," Diamond let out. "I fucked your brother, and got paid for it, and I damn sure don't regret shit."

"You look like the type." Layla laughed.

"The type? What type? A hoe?"

Layla nodded, and I lifted an eyebrow. Shit was about to go all the way left.

"I mean, that's what you are. Any woman that fucks men for money is a hoe. There's no other word to describe it."

Diamond shrugged. "Okay? You think that hurts my feelings? Ask me who put me on. Go ahead, *Lay*. Ask me."

Layla bit at her bottom lip, then her eyes shot to Kevin. It was like she already knew the answer, but she still fixed her lips to say, "Who? Who was it?"

"Kevin." Diamond's smile was big as fuck. "Kevin found me because I was just standing on the street one day, then he told me how I could get better with my shit because I was sloppy with it. He told me he would let me know everything I needed to know, and he did."

"But you told me you didn't know her," Layla snapped at Kevin. "When I found pictures of her in your phone, you tried to make it seem like I was crazy. Everything I do is always crazy to you!"

"Come on, bruh," Kevin groaned, not in the mood to argue. "You're really about to do this shit in front of company?"

"Company? My brother and his hoe ass girlfriend?"

"Hoe ass?" Diamond laughed. "Girl, you better chill out before you get your ass beat."

"No one was talking to you, Diamond! You're nothing but a gold digger, anyway! I know you're only with my brother for his money!"

Diamonds eyebrows came together in confusion. "Bitch, are you retarded? That nigga doesn't have money! I was making more money than he was when out here fucking niggas to get paid. You think I'm with him for his Walmart check? Girl, get the fuck outta here."

Layla let out a shrill laugh. "The fact that you don't know about your own nigga lets me know that you two aren't going to last."

Diamond still had that confused look on her face as she turned to look at me.

"What is she talking about, Koda?"

Damn.

I didn't want her to find out like this. I wanted to be able to tell her when the time was right. Layla was a real asshole for this one.

"I... Umm..."

"He has his own clothing line! That nigga is making hella money just from sitting on his ass, and you didn't even know!" She laughed some more, and I felt Diamond's eyes on me. I didn't even know what to say.

"So, you've been lying to me?" she asked in a low voice.

"Yeah, but I have a logical reason—"

She stood up from the table, then stormed out before I could even finish my sentence. I cut my eyes at Layla who was also standing up with her arms folded.

"Thanks, bruh. I would've never came back over here if I would've known you were gonna be running your mouth like this." I got up from the table to follow behind Diamond.

"She was gonna find out anyway!" Layla called from behind me. I didn't care about none of that shit right now. It wasn't her place to tell Diamond what it was that I did for a living. That was a talk I planned on having with her later on.

"Aye," I said to Diamond once I was outside. She was standing at the end of the driveway scrolling through her phone. "You gonna let me explain myself or what?" I asked, stuffing my hands in my pockets. She ignored me, though. I expected it. "Look. I didn't lie to you on no little boy shit. Most bitches I come across know what I do for a living, so that's the only thing they want me for. My money. I wanted to make sure you weren't like those other bitches, so I—"

"You lied to me? Do I look like the type of bitch to want a nigga just for his money? I know how to make my own money, Koda! You not telling me makes me think you feel like I'm just a gold digger. Is that what you and your sister talked about? Me being a gold digger?"

I shook my head. "Nah. It was never no shit like that. I never talked about you like that. I just needed to know you were genuine."

"What else are you lying about, Koda?" she questioned, staring directly into my eyes.

"I'm not lying about anything else, Diamond."

She shook her head with a light laugh. "See, now I don't believe you. What's the name of your clothing line?"

I looked down at my feet and said, "Ink Apparel."

"Excuse me?" she shrieked. "Ink Apparel? That's yours? All that is you?"

I nodded because I knew what she was getting at. My shit was one of the most successful clothing lines. Successful enough to have famous people wearing it.

"I was gonna tell you," I said as she shook her head.

"I just don't believe you," she let out. "What's the real reason you didn't tell me? I know it's something else."

I pulled my bottom lip between my teeth. I hated how she could see right through my ass. Why couldn't we just move past this? I'm a millionaire. That's nothing to be too mad about.

"That was the real reason." I said, trying to convince her, but she wasn't having it.

"I can tell you're lying." She laughed. "What's the reason, Koda? I'm a big girl. I can handle it."

I let out a small sigh. "Because... I didn't want anyone to know we were dating. If the media found out I was dating a prostitute, I wouldn't hear the end of it."

She didn't say anything as she stared at me. I thought I saw her eyes welling up with tears, but she quickly blinked them away.

"So, you're embarrassed of me?" she asked with her voice cracking.

"No, but—"

"Take me home," she said, walking over to my car.

"Diamond, it's not what you're thinking. I'm not embarrassed—"

"Fuck it," she snapped. "I'll just walk. Don't call me no more. I'm done. I'll just find me a nigga that's not embarrassed of me." Diamond took off walking down the street, and I let her. There was no way I was going to be able to get her to talk to me right now.

"Shit," I muttered watching her walk and put her phone to her ear. I fucked up bad with this one.

SIXTEEN

D IAMOND
    "This is what I get," I muttered to myself as I stood at the
gas station and waited for Mia to show up. I confessed my feelings for
a nigga only to find out he's embarrassed of me. I knew I should've
kept my thoughts and feelings to myself.

It took about ten minutes, but Mia finally showed up in her red
Altima, and I stormed to her car. I was fighting the tears that were
threatening to fall. The fact that I was about to cry over this nigga
pissed me off even more.

"You good? What happened?" Mia asked, like I knew she would.

"Niggas are stupid, and I don't know why I even wasted my time.
I could still be out here fucking niggas and making money for it."

"You could, but instead, you wanted to get with a broke
ass nigga—"

"He's not broke," I cut in. "He lied about being broke."

She glanced at me as she pulled out of the gas station.

"What you mean? I never met a rich person who works at
Walmart."

"That's the thing, Mia. He doesn't work at Walmart. He lied about all of that."

"Well, what does he do then? Sell drugs like every other nigga?"

"No," I said, shaking my head. "He has his own clothing line. A whole clothing line, Mia!"

"Are you serious? What clothing line is it? Have I ever heard of it?"

"Ink Apparel," I said, gritting my teeth thinking about it.

"Nah." She laughed. "No he doesn't. I'm not about to believe that shit."

"He said he didn't tell me because he didn't want anyone to find out that he was dating a prostitute. He didn't want the media to find out."

Mia was quiet for a moment. She didn't know what to say, but I didn't blame her. I felt the same way she did when he told me that shit.

I just couldn't understand why he would continue to date me if he was embarrassed. What was the point of that? Why string me along? Why not just tell me how he felt from the beginning?

"Damn, Dime." She sighed. "I don't even know what to say back to that. Fuck that nigga. He doesn't know what the fuck he's missing out on."

"That doesn't make me feel better, Mia. I told him I loved him right before I found out he was a liar and embarrassed of me. I should've just kept my feeling and everything else to myself."

"You what!" she yelled, damn near swerving off the road. "So, now you're telling this nigga you love him? Do you even know what that feels like?"

I smacked my lips. "Fuck you, Mia. I know what I'm feeling. Now, I'm just wishing that I didn't. I wish I didn't have feelings. I wish that nigga would've never came into my life, gave me that bomb ass dick, and made me fall for his stupid ass."

"Aww," she gushed. "You're going through your first break up. It's okay, baby. You'll get through it. You wanna drink tonight? We can drink, and you forget all about that nigga."

I nodded. "Yes. That's exactly what I wanna do."

When we finally got home, I turned my phone off, went straight into my room, and locked the door. I didn't want Koda to call me because I knew he was about to start blowing me up soon. I didn't wanna hear his voice at all. I didn't even wanna think about him, so I pulled out the small bag of cocaine that I had in my purse, cleared everything off my dresser, and formed three lines.

One for my feelings for Koda.

One for him lying to me.

One for forgetting about everything that had happened just moments ago.

After I was finished, I laid in the middle of my bed and just stared up at the ceiling. I couldn't believe this was happening to me. I couldn't believe I was laying here with my feelings hurt all because of a nigga.

I still wanted to cry, and it pissed me off.

"What the FUCK?" I screamed, throwing the lamp across the room, and watched it shatter when it hit the wall.

"Open the door, Dime," Mia said, jiggling the door knob. "I got your favoriteee."

I didn't wanna open the door, but I had to remember that Mia didn't do anything to me. I couldn't take my anger out on her.

I sighed to myself and opened the door. She was standing there with a bottle of Patrón in her hand.

"Come on," she said, leading me out my room. "You're just gonna keep thinking about him if you stay in that room by yourself."

She was right.

"Gimme this," I said, snatching the bottle out of her hand, twisting the top off, and taking it straight to the head. I knew if I drank too much, I was going to black out, and that's exactly what I wanted to happen.

"It's still a little weird for me," Mia said as we sat on the couch.

"Seeing you actually caring about a man. Seeing your feelings hurt over someone."

"I thought the point of drinking right now was for me to forget about that stupid ass nigga, but here you are bringing it up."

"Sorry, it's just not normal for me. We can talk about something else, though."

"Yeah," I said, turning the bottle up again. "Let's talk about you and whatever nigga that's keeping your attention. Don't think I don't know."

She let out a small laugh. "I mean, me and him aren't official, so I really don't think it's anything to talk about."

I lifted an eyebrow. "Are y'all fucking?"

"Of course we are. I'm not about to just be chillin' with a nigga if he's not giving me any dick. What's the point?"

"I mean, you could chill with him because you actually like him as a person. There's nothing wrong with that."

"Nah, I'm good." She laughed. In a way, Mia was like me. She didn't like showing feelings, or getting her feelings involved with men. Now that she saw what I was going through, she was probably really nervous about investing her feelings. I didn't blame her though. We all see where investing our feelings got me.

"It's not that bad," I said, watching her roll her eyes.

"Girl, bye. I don't want a man right now. I'm good with being single and just having fun when I feel like it. I'm not committed to him, and he's not committed to me. That's how I like it, and that's how it's going to stay."

"That's what you think." I laughed as Mia's phone began ringing. She looked at the screen before she swiped her finger across it to answer, then put it on speaker.

"Hello?" she said.

"Mia!" Leah huffed into the phone. "I did it! I pepper sprayed his dick!" Damn, it had been so long since we told her to do that shit, I'd forgotten about it. I honestly had forgotten about her ass all together.

"What? Okay, so then what happened?"

"He started screaming and yelling and holding his dick. Then while I was at it, I pepper sprayed his dog, too. Now I'm in my car driving away, but I don't know where I'm going. I feel bad. I shouldn't have did that!"

"Well, what did he do?" Mia asked. "What did he do to make you pepper spray him?"

"I caught him out on a date with another woman. I was there with a friend, and imagine my surprise when I saw him walk in holding hands with another bitch."

"Damn," I said, shaking my head. "Niggas really ain't shit. He deserved to get pepper sprayed in the dick."

"I don't know what to do! How am I supposed to go home? What if he beats my ass when I come back?"

"You plan on going back?" Mia asked with her face twisting up in disgust. "He's cheating on you, Leah. Leave that dumb ass boy alone."

"There's no way he could change his ways, though? I mean, we have been together for—"

"None of that shit matters, Leah. Come to our house so we can talk to you, because right now you're sounding like a dumb bitch," Mia let her know.

"Okay." Mia ended the call and looked at me. I took another shot and smiled. I was already feeling the liquor. I knew it wouldn't be long until I was feeling good and not thinking about Koda.

"That's crazy," she said, looking at me. "I wonder why it took her so long to actually do it. We told her to do that shit months ago. She hasn't talked to us since, but now she needs our help because she wanted to be a dumb ass."

"I can't believe we told her to do some reckless shit like that, though. What's wrong with us?" I let out a small laugh and she did too.

"Right. If she doesn't be done with this nigga after this, I'm gonna block her number."

"I don't think I have her number to begin with. I'm not up to making new friends. You're the one who decided to bring her ass over here, trying to play Captain Save a Hoe."

She shrugged. "There's nothing wrong with being nice to people. The universe likes that shit."

I rolled my eyes. "Girl, don't even start with your universe shit. I don't wanna hear it." I could feel my nose beginning to run, so I tried to sniff it back up, but nothing happened. I could still feel it running, about to hit the top of my lip.

"Uhh... Dime, your nose is bleeding," Mia let me know.

Fuck.

I didn't say anything as I got up from the couch and hurried into the bathroom. Once I was in there, I got all the tissue I could and pressed it to my nose. I needed this shit to stop. I didn't want Mia asking me why my nose was bleeding either. I couldn't lie to her because she *always* knew when I was lying.

A few minutes passed, and my nose was still bleeding. It didn't seem like it was letting up or anything. That's when the door slowly opened, and Mia stood there with her arms folded.

"So, you're a coke head now?" she asked, as I looked at her. I really didn't want to tell her. I wanted this to be my only secret. I wanted to shake my head so bad and tell her I had just got too hot or something, but she knew. The look on her face let me know that she knew.

"I quit the pills," I said, voice barely above a whisper.

"Okay? You quit the pills, and picked up coke? You think that's better?" She had a brow raised like she was amused. I was fighting the urge to roll my eyes because I didn't like the way she was questioning me.

"I needed something." I shrugged. "Koda made me quit the pills. Plus, Lawrence hadn't been answering the phone when I called, so I decided to do something else. Something I knew would be easy to get. How did you know anyway?"

"Julian." She chuckled. "He asked me about it, but I kinda downplayed it because I really didn't want to believe it. I didn't wanna believe that my friend was becoming a coke head, so I didn't say shit about it. I mean, I saw the signs, but I still didn't wanna believe it. This was the icing on the cake, though. Nose just starts bleeding after you wouldn't stop twitching, and messing with it? Nahhh, I know what a coke head looks like. I know a lot of them."

I smacked my lips. "Signs? What signs?" I wasn't showing any signs about the drugs I was using. I still acted regular as hell. I didn't know what Mia was talking about.

"When you wake up in the morning, your nose is stopped up, then the shit is always running, and I don't know if you notice it or not, but you're always fucking with your nose now. Like, you can't go five minutes without touching the shit. But right now? Your pupils are dilated."

I didn't respond to her as I looked at myself in the mirror. Honestly, I couldn't say anything because she had just called me out. I didn't even know all those things were happening to me. I just thought it was normal.

"I'm not your mom, so I'm not about to be down your back about it because at the end of the day, it's your life," she said. "But just be careful. I don't want you to be like one of those strung out crackheads we see on MLK."

"I'm not a crackhead, Mia." I said with more attitude in my voice than it should've been.

"Keep it that way." The doorbell rang, and I let out a sigh of relief because I was tired of having this conversation. She went to open the door, and I finished up in the bathroom. I could hear Leah in there panicking, and it caused me to roll my eyes.

What the hell was she so scared for? She had every right to do what she did because she'd caught her man cheating. The nigga was caught! It wasn't like she pepper sprayed him for no reason.

My nose finally stopped bleeding, so I washed my hands, and stepped out of the bathroom. Leah was pacing back and forth like she'd lost her damn mind. She looked stressed the hell out.

"I don't know what to do," she said once I sat back down on the couch. "I wanna leave, but I don't know…"

"The fuck?" I said, causing her to look in my direction. "Fuck that nigga. He was cheating the last time we talked, and clearly, he's still cheating because you caught his ass. It's not a hard decision, Leah. Stop being such a weak ass stupid ass bitch."

She looked at me through wide eyes because she didn't expect me to say that, but that's how you had to talk to them when they were being dumb over a nigga. Otherwise, they wouldn't hear shit you had to say.

"I'm not being weak…" she said, sounding *just* like a weak bitch.

"You are. Taking him back shouldn't even be on your mind. That should be the last thing you're thinking about. But instead? You're pacing my fuckin' floor saying you don't know what to do. Nah. Leave. It's over. It's obvious that nigga ain't gonna act right. You take him back after this, and he's definitely gonna keep doing the same shit. That's how these niggas work. If women actually left a man after he cheated, would niggas still cheat?"

She stared at me for a moment while what I said processed.

"Sorry about her attitude," Mia said. "She just broke up with her boyfriend earlier. She's mad at the world right now."

I cut my eyes at her. Why the fuck was she telling my business for?

"He cheated?" Leah asked, looking at me with pity filled eyes.

"No," I spat. "He's a liar, though. Just like every other nigga I come across." I was supposed to be forgetting about this nigga, but here we were *still* talking about him. I picked up the bottle again and turned it up.

"What did he lie about, though? I'm sure it wasn't that bad to the point you had to break up with him," she said, sounding weak once again.

"What?" I yelled. "So, you're okay with your nigga lying to you? It doesn't matter how big or small the lie is, it's still a damn lie! You lie to me once, that only means you're gonna keep lying to me! What the fuck is wrong with you, Leah? Your nigga was lying *and* cheating! There was no way you were believing shit that come out of his mouth!"

"All men are liars, Diamond. You just kinda have to deal—"

"No! I'm not dealing with no damn liar! Either you're gonna act right or get beat the fuck up and left! Do you have standards? Huh?"

"Standards?" she asked, like I had offended her. "Do *you* have standards? You're the one who has sex with men for money. How could someone even be okay with being with you? I hope to Jesus you're not having sex with these men raw."

"Bitch, mind your damn business!" I screamed, standing up because now I was ready to fight. I think I was readier to fight because she said something about someone being okay with being with me. Koda acted like he was okay with it, all while he was embarrassed of me. Yeah, what she said was out of line, but I wanted to fight her because my feelings were hurt. Not because of what she said.

"Whoa, chill out," Mia said, now standing between us.

"Man, hell nah. Who the fuck she think she is coming in my house and talking shit to me? Bitch, I'll fuck your nigga, record it, and put that shit all over Facebook. I'll even tag you in it so everyone knows! Don't try me!"

Mia glared at me. "I *said* chill out." I didn't know what the fuck it was, but the way she said it made me feel some type of way. It hit me right between the legs, and I had to take a step away from her because I shouldn't be feeling like that anymore. Not about Mia.

I sat back down and started drinking some more. Mia and Leah started talking amongst themselves, and I just sat there staring at Mia like she was my next meal. I tried to shake the thoughts about Mia, but for some reason I couldn't. I just started having flashbacks about how good her sex was. How she looked like a dangerous ass bitch, but when it came to sex, she knew exactly what she was doing.

I clenched my legs together as I watched her run her fingers through her hair. I tried to force my mind to think about other things, but it kept coming back to Mia. In my room or her room, with our clothes off.

"I'm sorry," Leah said, looking at me, pulling me from my thoughts of Mia. "My emotions are all over the place. I didn't mean to come at you like that. There's nothing wrong with how you make your money."

"I know it isn't," I scoffed.

"I just... I just wanna beat him up. I wanna destroy all his shit that I know he likes. I wanna—"

"No," Mia interjected. "What you can do is go get some of your things so this time, he knows it real, and you can stay here a few days while you figure out where you're going to go."

I looked at Mia like she was crazy because why the hell was she just inviting people we barely knew to stay here?

"Really?" Leah asked with her eyes lighting up. "Y'all would do that for me?"

"No, Mia would do that for you. Clearly, I don't have a say so in this," I spat as Mia picked up her car keys.

They both ignored me. I knew they heard what I said, but they didn't give a fuck. I sighed to myself as I got up from the couch and followed behind them out the house, still making sure I had the liquor in my hand.

Leah got in the back of Mia's car, and I got in the front. I'm glad she knew to get her ass in the back because I really didn't feel like arguing about some shit like that. I would've just drug her out the seat and got in like I didn't do anything wrong.

I didn't care to participate in the conversation they were having on the way to Leah's boyfriend's place. My thoughts were still about Mia, and at this point, I didn't try to fight it anymore.

The more I thought about Mia's mouth on me, the tighter I clenched my legs together. Mia knew exactly what I liked. Sex with her was out of this world, and when she got locked up, it was one of the things I missed the most about her. Honestly, I was actually shocked that we hadn't messed around since she'd been out of jail.

I glanced over at her, and she was already looking at me.

"You okay?" she asked as I looked at her through low, lustful eyes. At this point, I didn't even care anymore. I wanted her, and I didn't care if she knew or not.

"Yep," I said, watching her focus her attention back to the road.

"Just making sure," she said. "You looking like you're about to pass out over there."

I didn't bother responding to her. I wasn't about to pass out. Not before I got what I wanted from her.

The rest of the ride, I didn't say anything. I just kept replaying flashbacks of me and Mia in my head.

"I'll be right back," Leah said when we pulled up to her boyfriend's house. "I shouldn't be long at all." She quickly got out the car before we could say anything back to her, and that's when Mia turned her attention to me.

"What's up?" she asked. "You sure you're good?"

I nodded. "I'm gooood, Mia. Just over here thinking."

She lifted a brow. "What you thinking about?"

"The first time we had sex." I knew I had caught her off guard with what I said, but she gave me a small smile.

"Why you thinking about that? Out of all the things you could be thinking about, you're thinking about us—"

"So, you don't be thinking about it?" I asked in a low voice, moving in so that I was closer to her. I started rubbing my hand up her exposed thigh, and Mia tried to laugh it off.

"Yeah, I think about it. Some of the best sex I've ever had, but—"

I licked her ear, causing her to stop in mid-sentence and tense up. I knew where all her spots were just like she knew where all mine were. She pulled her bottom lip between her teeth, and I knew she wanted it just as bad as I did.

I stopped licking on her ear, then pulled her face closer to mine, and put my lips against hers. The kiss alone made me want to let out a moan. The feeling of her tongue exploring, then her biting down on my bottom lip opened the floodgates in my underwear.

Mia's kisses were way different from Koda's. Hers didn't feel rushed, and it didn't feel like she was trying to overpower me, either.

Mia slipped a hand down my sweats, and in my panties and gently rubbed against my vulva. I spread my legs wider and let out a small moan against her mouth as I shuddered against her hand. Mia smiled because she knew she had me right where she wanted me.

She knew exactly what she was doing. She wasn't being overly rough because she knew I didn't like that. Well, I didn't have a problem with it rough, but with Mia, she didn't even have to do all that to make me cum.

"Cum for me, baby," she said in a low voice, lips still against mine.

I wanted to be closer to her. I wanted to feel her body against mine, but the arm rest, cup holders, and gear shift were all in the way. That didn't matter, though. I was still trying to pull her body closer to mine.

"Make me," I breathed as Mia pressed down on my clitoris with her thumb. I let out a loud moan that Mia caught with her own. Mia was the type to get pleasure from giving it to other people, so she was probably about to cum just from what she was doing to me.

Mia went from toying with my labia, to sticking a finger inside me. My head went back with a moan loud enough for the entire neighborhood to hear. She stopped kissing me, and started sucking on my neck, knowing that shit drove me crazy. I could feel my peak coming as I fed Mia my moans.

She inserted another finger, causing my moans to get louder. She took her free hand and pulled my shirt up, causing my breasts to pop out. She wasted no time assaulting my already hard nipple with her tongue. I tangled my hand in her hair, and let her name escape my lips over and over.

I felt myself about to climax, so I pulled her up from my breast and invaded her mouth with my tongue. Mia picked up the pace with her fingers and I erupted all over them.

"Oh my Goddd," I let out as Mia snatched her fingers from inside me, then put them in her mouth.

"Yeah, I missed this shit," she said with small smirk as I came down from the high of my orgasm. "Don't think I'm finished with you either."

Mia's sex drive was crazy. She would want it all the time, and it didn't matter where we were. She had no problems sticking her fingers in my honey pot.

I was all smiles thinking about how Mia was going to make me feel when we got back home. That smile quickly faded when I saw Leah rushing back to the car empty handed.

She was crying as she slid in the car, and when I looked at her, I saw that her lip was busted.

"We can leave," she said quietly. I was already shaking my head and coming out of my seatbelt.

"Where's your stuff?" I asked.

"He won't let me get anything. He had the same girl in there that I caught him out with earlier," she let me know with more tears streaming down her face.

"So, you tried to fight her?"

She shook her head. "No. He slapped me because I was talking shit. Then—"

I had heard enough. I popped my door open while retrieving the taser from the glove compartment that I knew Mia kept in there.

Mia got out too. The only thing she had was the pepper spray that was on her keychain, but we didn't care. One thing me and Mia didn't play about was a dumb ass nigga putting his hands on a woman.

The front door wasn't locked, so we barged right in there and walked around until we heard voices.

"Okay, but you didn't have to hit her like that!" the girl yelled. "She just came in here to get her things, but you wanted to throw a fuckin' fit—"

"Ayo, shut the fuck up!" he hollered. "She pepper sprayed my dick! I should've beat her ass!"

"I wish you would, nigga," I said, causing them both to turn and look at us. "You're one of those bitch ass niggas who thinks it's okay to put your hands on a woman? After your dirty dick ass cheated on her?"

His brows came together in confusion. "Who the fuck are you, and why are you in my house?"

I smiled at him right before I ran up and started beating his ass. Mia was right behind me, punching him with one of her car keys between her fingers. He was trying to fight back, but once I stunned him with the taser, he fell to the floor like he was getting electrocuted.

The girl started screaming, and I shot her a look that instantly shut her ass up.

"Go get Leah," I demanded, taking the keys from her. There was blood on them from her digging in that nigga's skin, but it didn't even bother me. I only needed the keys for one thing.

I didn't know what it was about spraying people with pepper spray, but it was one of my favorite things to do. I loved it. It made me feel powerful.

I looked at the girl who was scared out of her mind. She looked like she was about to shit bricks, and I had to contain my laughter because I was trying to be serious right now.

"You knew he had a girlfriend?" I asked, watching her nod her head.

"He would always wait for her to go to work to invite me over," she said with her voice barely above a whisper.

"And you would come? Knowing his girlfriend at work? Knowing you were in the house they shared together? Knowing you were fuckin' him in the bed he fucks his girlfriend in?"

"He told me he was about to break up with her. He told me—"

I pepper sprayed her mid-sentence. She deserved it, just like her dumb ass nigga did. He was still laying on the floor with his body convulsing, and now, his little bitch was on the floor too, screaming and rubbing her eyes like a dumb ass.

I pepper sprayed him, too. I mean, it wouldn't be fair to just pepper spray one of them, right?

Leah came into the room and looked at the damage I had done.

"What happened?" she asked.

"I gave them both what they deserved. Get your shit so we can get the hell out of here."

She nodded, grabbed a few suitcases from the closet, then began putting whatever she could in them.

Mia stood by the door looking even better than she did in the car. Just thinking about how she just made my body feel moments ago had me weak in the knees. She knew it too, because she started smirking at me.

I walked past her without saying anything, only because I knew she wanted me too. It didn't surprise me when she followed right behind me.

"You running from me?" she questioned once we were outside.

I lifted a brow. "Why would I be doing that? We rode together, and we live together. That wouldn't make any damn sense, would it?"

She pushed me against the car and gently put her lips on mine.

"Why would you do this, Dime?" she asked against my lips. She let a hand gently come to my neck, knowing what that did to me.

"What are you talking about?"

She pulled away and looked at me.

"Re-open this door. You know how crazy I get over this," she said, letting her hand travel in my sweats until she found what she was looking for.

"Don't get crazy," I said as I kissed her again. "Just think of it as having fun."

She moaned into my mouth as she let her fingers play some more. I closed my eyes and she deepened the kiss. This car ride home was about to be a long one.

"Uhh... I don't even know what to say," Leah said, causing us to pull apart. Mia snatched her hand from inside my sweats, and we both looked at Leah.

I smiled to myself as I went to get back in the car. The only thing that was on my mind was getting home and letting Mia finish what we started.

Leah put all her things in Mia's trunk, then they both got in the car. I didn't say anything to either of them. I could tell Leah felt awkward, though.

"So..." Leah started. "Are y'all like a thing or something?"

Mia let out a small chuckle. "We used to be. We found it was best if we just went our separate ways."

"Then, what was that? Y'all were just kissing like y'all were about to fuck right then and there."

"Mmmm," I gushed, closing my eyes while I thought about how good Mia could make me feel. "I can't wait to, though."

"So, y'all broke up, but y'all still fuck around from time to time? How are you two even still friends? Y'all didn't get mad at each other after the break up?"

I shook my head. "No. We're both grown. What's the point of being mad when we can still be cool?" I turned to look at Leah, and she had a look of confusion written all over her face.

"That's just so crazy to me. You just broke up with your boyfriend, so now y'all are gonna get back together?" Leah asked, causing me to catch an instant attitude because thinking about Koda just put me in a sour ass mood.

I turned around and didn't say anything else the entire car ride back to my place. I think Mia sensed that I was feeling some type of way because she kept shooting glances in my directions.

Remembering I had the bottle of Patrón with me, I picked it up, and took a few more shots. I was drunk as hell by the time we pulled back up to my house. I could barely walk, but I managed to stagger into the house and into Mia's room and laid out on her bed.

The room was spinning, and I felt like I was about to be sick, but I tried to ignore the feeling. I didn't wanna get sick before Mia came in here. That would just ruin the mood.

A few moments passed, and Mia finally entered the room. No

words needed to be exchanged as she slowly walked over to me. Maybe me and Koda breaking up wasn't such a bad thing.

TWO WEEKS LATER

Having sex with Mia was fun, but after a week of having sex with her, I realized I was only doing it to help me forget about Koda, which wasn't working. I woke up thinking about him and went to sleep thinking about him. Of course, I didn't let it show that my feelings were hurt over him, but it was eating me up on the inside.

I blocked his number, so I had no idea if he was trying to get in contact with me or not. To keep myself from thinking about him, I was using the drugs. I was doing drugs more than I did before, and I knew it was bad, but that still didn't stop me from doing it.

As I sat on the couch staring aimlessly at the TV, my phone began to ring. The number wasn't saved, but I already knew who it was. I blew out an annoyed breath as I answered the phone.

"What?" I spat.

"Well, that's not any way to answer the phone or your mother. You know, I'm the only reason you're alive, right?" Tanya said as I rolled my eyes.

"Actually, if it wasn't for my daddy nutting inside you, you would've never gotten pregnant. Give him some credit, too."

She smacked her lips. "I didn't call you for that."

"Don't really care what you called me for. Especially after you called the police on your own child. That ass whoopin' wasn't enough for you? You still trying to talk to me?"

"What did you expect me to do, Diamond? You went crazy, attacking the whole family! I couldn't just sit there and do nothing!"

I let out a cold laugh. "Girl, fuck you. You got five seconds to tell me what the hell you called me for before I hang the fuck up."

"Your sister is still in a coma, and not once have you been down here to check on her or see how the rest of the family is doing."

I twisted my face up so bad. Who the hell did she think I was? She thought I was supposed to just be okay with the entire family blaming me for getting raped? She thought I wanted to be around them after that? She thought if and when I saw them all again that I wouldn't beat some ass?

"Fuck her." I laughed. "She deserved it. That's what she told me, right? That I deserved getting raped?"

"Diamond—"

"Girl, shut the hell up. I'm not coming down there to see her. I don't wanna see Michael, and I damn sure don't wanna see you. Next time I see you, it's going to be at your funeral, so I can twerk right in front of your casket and let everyone know what a terrible mother you were. Don't call me no more, Tanya. I'm no longer your child." I ended the call before she could say anything and let out a small sigh.

I felt like my life was falling apart. I felt sad more than I felt happy. I cried myself to sleep last night, and I didn't even know why. Well, I knew exactly why, but I don't even wanna give Koda that satisfaction.

"I think you should go see your sister," Mia said, coming to sit down next to me on the couch. Leah was still staying here with us, but she was almost always at work. She wasn't annoying like I thought she would be. Now that she was finally realizing her worth, she was actually pretty cool to hang with.

"You think I should do what?" I asked, looking at her to make sure I heard her right.

"You heard what I said. You should go see her. I know you don't like them, but just because they're terrible people, that doesn't mean you have to be one. Plus, what if she wakes up after you go see her? You can't sit here and say—"

"I'm not going to see her, Mia. That's the end of that."

She stared at me for a moment without saying anything. It's like she was reading me, because she always knew how.

"I heard you crying last night," she finally said after a while of just staring at each other. I slumped down into the couch. I thought I was crying quietly last night, but I guess not.

"It happens sometimes," I let her know.

She gave me a knowing look. "Call him."

IN THE ARMS OF A THUG   171

"What? Call who?"

"Call your albino boy. You miss him, and he misses you—"

"He's a liar," I snapped. "How the hell you know he misses me? He's probably somewhere lying to some other bitch."

Mia let out a small sigh like she didn't wanna tell me what was about to come out her mouth.

"I've been messing around with this dude... Sani. Him and Koda are friends. Close friends. Like, they live together and everything. Koda hasn't stopped talking about you since you left him. It's getting annoying."

I didn't know what to say back to that. The fact that Mia was fucking Koda's roommate was one thing. I would've never guessed that was the nigga she was messing with. I'm not gonna sit here and lie and act like I wasn't happy that Koda missed me, but that didn't change the fact that he was still a liar.

"So..." I said. "You got a boyfriend?"

"No." She laughed. "We're not serious. Just having sex with him from time to time. Nothing major because you know I don't do relationships."

"Mhmmm."

"Don't try to change the subject. We're talking about you and *your* boyfriend."

"He's not my boyfriend." I flipped.

"He gave you your space. Either you call him, or he's gonna pop up on you. That's how it always happens."

I waved her off. He could pop up all he wanted. That still wouldn't make me forgive him.

"And he can keep giving me my space," I let her know as my phone lit up on my lap. I looked down at it and saw a random number calling. I rolled my eyes and ignored it. If it was important, they would leave a voicemail.

Right after the phone stopped ringing, a text message from the same number came through.

Unknown: Come outside

"What the fuck?" I muttered, slowly getting up from the couch. Reluctantly, I looked out the window and saw an all-black Ferrari parked right behind my car. I turned to look at Mia, but she was already gone.

My blood started boiling. I thought about just ignoring the message all together and sitting my ass back down on the couch, but now, I had some shit to say. I swung the door open, and stormed out, heading straight for his car. Once he saw me, but opened his door and stepped out, looking like a totally different person.

He was wearing an all-black Armani suit. He had a Rolex on his left wrist. I didn't know what type of sunglasses he was wearing, but I knew they were expensive, Gucci loafers on his feet, and his dreads were in four braids going straight back. It was amazing how much better he was looking right now, but I wasn't going to let him know that.

"What's up?" he asked, taking a step closer to me. "Unblock my number so I can—"

"No," I spat. "Fuck you."

"Man, it's been two weeks. You're still mad at that shit? You're still—"

"Yes, I'm still mad! You lied to me for three months, and you told me the reason was because you're embarrassed of me. You think I'm just gonna forget about that shit? You think I'm gonna get my little space, then be ready to take you back after you hurt my feelings like that?"

He let out a loud sigh. "I didn't even mean it like that. I'm not embarrassed... I mean, yeah, at first the shit bothered me a little bit, but I don't give a fuck about none of that shit."

"You just care about what other people will think?"

"Nah, man... I just..." He let out a long sigh like he couldn't get out what he wanted to say. He took his glasses off and pulled a hand down his face. "Can we start over?"

I twisted my mouth up. "Oh, so now you wanna start over? You think—"

"What's up?" he asked, giving me a small smirk. "I'm Koda Mitchell. What's your name?"

"Koda, I'm not doing this with—"

"What's your name, ma?" he pressed, taking a step closer to me. "Ain't no way you came out this pretty and don't have a pretty name to match."

I bit my lip to suppress a smile. "Diamond," I said, rolling my eyes because I didn't wanna play the game he was trying to play.

"You got a man?"

"Nope. He was a liar, so I'm good on men. I don't even want them to look in my direction. Go ruin the next bitch's life." I folded my arms as I looked at him.

He gave me a small smile. "True shit. You should let me take you out though. Come back to my place and chill."

I shook my head. "You think I'm gonna go with you just because you have that nice ass car and a little bit of money? What kind of girl do you think I am, *Koda?*"

He grabbed me by my hand and led me to the passenger side. From there, he opened the door for me and motioned for me to get in. I looked at him like he was crazy.

"Koda, I'm not about to go with you to—"

"Get in the damn car, Diamond. Why you always gotta make shit harder than what it has to be? I gotta show you some shit."

I let out a breath but got in the car. He smiled at me again, then shut the door. I had a right mind to get out of the car and run back in my house, but I decided against it. I was gonna see what it was he had to show me before I decided anything else.

SEVENTEEN

KODA

Diamond sat in the passenger seat with an ugly ass expression on her face, and her arms folded. Honestly, I was just happy she agreed to get in the damn car with me.

"Can't even believe this," she muttered.

I glanced over at her. "What?"

"That I'm sitting here with your lying ass." She scratched her nose a little and remained looking out the window.

"Stop playing." I laughed. "Don't sit here and act like you didn't miss me—"

"I didn't—"

"Like that pussy didn't get wet as soon as you saw my ass."

"It didn't—"

"You can deny it all you want, but I saw it all over your face."

She cut her eyes at me but didn't say anything. She knew I was right, but she didn't wanna say it.

"Where the hell are you taking me anyway?"

"I told you I had something to show you, right?"

She smacked her lips. "Well, what is it?"

"You'll see when we get there."

"Swear to God, if it's something stupid, I'm gonna put my hands on you."

I let out a small laugh. "You ain't putting your hands on shit. Why you always gotta be so violent?"

"Why did you have to be a liar?"

I could tell that Diamond just wanted to argue, so instead of replying to her, I just turned the radio up. I didn't come get her just so we could argue. I understood that she was mad at me, and she had every right to be, but arguing about it wasn't going to make anything better.

For the past two weeks, Diamond had been the only thing on my mind. I could barely focus because I was too worried about who she was with and what she was doing. Sani was laughing at me because he thought me actually loving and missing my girl was so damn funny. It was only funny to him because the shit had never happened to him before. When the tables turned, he was gonna see that ain't shit funny about missing your shawty when she's not fucking with you. Swear to God, this had been the longest two weeks of my life.

About twenty minutes later, we were pulling up to my crib. Not the one that I stayed at with Sani, but my real one. The one I go to when I needed to get away from everyone and everything.

Diamond let out a sigh as she turned the music down.

"I'm not in the mood to meet anyone right now, Koda," she let me know.

"Chill. Who said I was about to take you to meet someone?"

Her brows came together in confusion. "Then, why the hell you got me in this white ass neighborhood? You better not be planning anything stupid."

I didn't respond. I just pulled into my driveway and opened the garage.

"Come on," I said, stepping out the car. She hesitated for a moment, but she slowly got out the car and followed me through the garage and into the house.

"So, this must be your real house or something," she said, looking around the large kitchen.

"I mean... it's one of my houses."

"Of course it is," she scoffed, walking away from me. "You probably got like ten houses."

"Nah." I laughed. "Fuck I need all those for?"

She shrugged. "Don't know. I don't know what goes through a liar's head."

"Shut that shit up," I said, making my way to the stairs.

"Why? That's what happened, right? You lied to me, and I still don't understand it. You really should've just left me alone. Who said I even wanted a rich ass nigga? Maybe my type is broke niggas. You didn't think about that, did you?"

"Go get you a broke nigga, then." I started up the stairs, and she followed behind me.

"I will," she mumbled. "Or get me a broke bitch."

"Like Mia?" I asked, looking at her as her eyes widened. She quickly tried to hide the look on her face, but it was too late. I had already saw it.

"Mind your business," she snapped as we stepped into the master bedroom.

"You are my business, though."

"I'm not."

"You are." I laughed, coming out of my suit jacket.

She crossed her arms and sat down on the edge of the bed.

"If you have all this money, then why don't you act like it? Why do you still act like a hood nigga that doesn't have any damn sense? You carry yourself like you're broke and don't have shit to lose. You were doing that before you met me too, so don't try to sit here and say it's because of me."

I loosened my tie as I looked at her.

"Honestly, this shit is overwhelming at times. Sometimes, I just wanna have a normal life again, so that's just how I act."

"A normal life? All that money you have, and you just wanna have a normal life? That's crazyyy."

"You're only saying that because you don't know what it's like. You never went through no shit like this, so I wouldn't expect you to understand it."

She rubbed her nose and she rolled her eyes.

"So, why did you bring me to your house? I really would've been fine without seeing it. I promise I would've."

"You're gonna be in here as much as me, so I felt like it was a good idea—"

"Who said that? So since you brought me to your house, you think I'm gonna take you back? No apologies or nothing?" she shrieked.

"I apologize," I said, walking over to her and grabbing her hand so she was standing up right in front of me.

"That's it? That's your weak ass apology?"

I pulled her closer to me.

"I apologize for lying to you, Diamond. I should've just kept it a hundred from the jump, but a nigga wasn't thinking like that."

She still had her arms folded.

"And what else? You're missing something."

I sighed to myself.

"Sorry for saying I was embarrassed of you, mama. You the shit, aight?"

"Oh, nigga, I know that. I'll always be the shit." She took a step away from me and lifted a brow. "You been fucking other bitches?"

I chuckled lightly. "Have *you* been fucking other bitches?"

"I mean..."

"Damn. You come in here questioning me, when you're the one that was out here doing it? Shit crazy, bruh."

I wasn't trippin' off that shit, though. We weren't together, she was able to do whatever the hell she wanted.

"You didn't answer my question, though. You just flipped it around on me," she said, rubbing her nose some more.

"I might've gotten my dick sucked—"

"By who?"

"Chill, shawty. I was single, right? Single for two whole weeks, so—"

"I'll beat you and her the fuck up," she spat as I laughed.

"Nah. Shit would be uncalled for." I glanced up at her and saw that her nose was starting to bleed. "Aye, your nose is bleeding."

Her hand quickly came to her nose, then she looked around the room and headed straight toward the bathroom.

"What the fuck?" she muttered once she was in the bathroom. I was gonna let her do her thing in there, but after five minutes had passed, I made my way into the bathroom with her.

"You good?" I asked as she looked at me.

"Yeah. I must've gotten too hot or something."

"Too hot? But when I was just touching you, you were cold as fuck."

She shrugged as she looked at me through the mirror.

"Well, I don't know. I guess my nose just decided to bleed."

I didn't say anything. I already knew why her nose was bleeding. Yesterday, while Mia was over, she damn near begged me to get back with Diamond because Diamond was going crazy with the drugs. I didn't wanna believe it, but I knew Mia wouldn't lie about no shit like that. She wasn't the type of person to ask for help either, so I knew it was serious.

When I saw Diamond walking up to me earlier, I could tell she was losing weight. She'd been rubbing her nose since I picked her up, and now her shit was bleeding?

"Why you looking at me like that?" she asked.

"Like what?"

"Like you have something you wanna get off your chest."

"Nah," I said, shaking my head. "Do you have something you need to get off your chest?"

"Something like what?" she asked. "You know something that I don't?"

"What's the real reason your nose is bleeding?"

She rolled her eyes and turned to look at me.

"Well, since you're asking, I'm sure you know already. Instead of beating around the bush, why don't you just come out and ask me?"

I couldn't understand what the hell she had an attitude for. I just asked a simple question.

"So you're still on drugs? You quit the pills to start coke? Where the fuck does that make sense?"

"You knew this shit before you came and picked me up, didn't you?" she asked, looking at me through squinted eyes.

"I mean... I might've."

"You ever tried to quit something you were addicted to?"

I let out a small laugh. "I tried to quit you."

"Boyyy, fuckin' bye. I quit you. You didn't quit me." She turned back to the mirror to make sure her nose was finished bleeding.

"The fuck you doing drugs for, Diamond? You think that's a good way to—"

"Wow. I swear, we've had this conversation before."

"Stop that shit."

She ignored me as she walked past me and went to sit on the bed again.

"You could've at least told me to bring my phone so I wouldn't be bored over here and shit. Damn."

"Don't act like you don't hear me talking to you," I said, following her.

"Well, what the fuck do you want me to do, Koda? I tried to quit the pills, but that shit was hard. I couldn't get in contact with Lawrence, so I decided to do something else."

I gritted my teeth at the mention of that bitch ass nigga's name. She shouldn't have been trying to get in contact with that nigga to begin with.

"Sounds like you didn't even try to me. And that nigga wasn't answering his phone because he's no longer with us."

She lifted a brow. "What? You killed him, didn't you?"

"That's not what's important right now. The only thing I'm worried about is you and those got damn drugs you need to give up."

"I can quit at any time," she said, but even I didn't believe that shit.

"Aight, then quit."

She looked at me for a moment, and I could see the uncertainty in her eyes.

"Alright," she said confidentially, but I knew deep down, she knew this shit was about to be way harder than she expected.

"I'm serious, Diamond."

She rolled her eyes to the ceiling. "I know you are. Otherwise, you wouldn't still be talking about it. Damn, nigga."

"Nah, come on," I said, making my way out the room.

"Whyyy? Where are you trying to take me now?" She came out the room and stood at the top of the stairs.

"I said come on, Diamond. I really don't wanna throw you over my shoulder."

She muttered something under her breath as she angrily made her way down the stairs.

"You could at least let me know where you're taking me this time," she spat once we were both in my car.

"I'm taking you back to your crib because you think I'm playing with yo' ass."

"So, now you're dropping me off because you're mad that—"

"Shut the fuck up, bruh. Who said anything about dropping you off?"

She snapped her head in my direction as I backed out of the driveway.

"Then what are we doing? You know, it would be nice for you to tell me what we were doing before you start forcing me in the car."

"It would be nice for you to stop snorting that shit up your nose, but here we are."

She folded her arms and didn't say anything else. I might've hurt her feelings, but shit, she shouldn't have been on drugs to begin with. Why couldn't she be like most people and smoke weed to solve her problems? No man wants to find out that their girl is doing no shit like that.

"Put yo' ass in therapy," I mumbled to myself.

"Excuse me?" she almost yelled. "You have something to say?"

"Hell yeah. I'm 'bout to put your crazy ass in therapy. You need to find a healthy way to cope with—"

"I'm fine, Koda."

"Nah, shawty. If you were good, you wouldn't be doing that shit to begin with."

"So, you mean to tell me, it's sooo crazy that a rape victim is doing—"

"Hell yeah, it's crazy! I know I said this before, but there's hella people in the world who have gone through shit worse than you. They're not out here doing drugs. I really don't wanna hear that shit."

"You can't tell me how to cope with it, Koda. You just can't."

"Aight, ma." I said, not wanting to talk about it anymore because it was starting to piss me off.

"Exactly nigga, so shut the fuck up," she muttered. I didn't bother responding. That was another argument I was trying to avoid.

We finally pulled back up to her house, and she quickly hopped out the car. I followed right behind her mad ass.

"Where's the shit at?" I asked, walking into her room.

"What are you talking even talking about?"

"Don't try to act stupid. Where's the drugs, Diamond? I know you got some in here."

She hesitated for a moment, but then she slowly started walking toward the dresser beside her bed, and pulled out a small, wooden box.

"Here." She exhaled. "It's all in there."

She handed me the box, and I opened it. After that, I made my way to her bathroom and flushed all that shit down the toilet.

"You happy now?" she asked, as I left the bathroom.

"Nah. I shouldn't have had to do that. You should've never had that shit to begin with. Now since you can't be trusted, I'm gonna have to keep an eye on you."

"Well, how are you going to do that when we live in two different houses? You can't be with me all the damn time, Koda." She had a small smirk on her face like she was satisfied with what she'd just said.

"You funny," I let her know. "Get your purse and shit, though. You won't be coming back here for a little minute."

"Boy, bye. You're not about to keep me stranded in that big ass house."

"Let's go, shawty." I walked out her room, then out the house all together.

I already had this shit planned out. I knew after Mia had told me everything that Diamond was doing, I knew I was gonna have to keep an eye on her. I didn't care if she wanted to or not, she was moving in with me.

A few minutes later, Diamond came walking out her crib, and I could see the look of displeasure written all over her face.

"So, you're not gonna let me pack any clothes? I'm just going to be at your house with nothing to wear?" she asked when she was finally in the car.

"Yep." I laughed driving off.

"Are you fuckin' serious? Hell no. I'm not about to be over there with nothing to wear, so you might as well just take me back home now."

"You really think I'm about to let you stay in my crib with nothing to wear? That shit make sense to you?"

"Just stop talking to me, Koda. You're really getting on my nerves."

I chuckled lightly and didn't say anything else to her for the rest of the way back to my crib. She had an attitude, but I knew that shit would go away when she wanted some dick.

We got back to my place, and she didn't say a word to me as she got out the car. Her attitude wasn't bothering me. She could be mad all she wanted.

"Can I have my own room?" she asked, sitting on the couch across from me. I looked at her, then turned the TV on like she didn't just say that stupid shit to me. "You hear me, Koda. Don't try to act like—"

"The fuck you need your own room for? You don't wanna sleep with your man?"

"My man?" she popped. "I don't have a man. I broke up with him about two weeks ago." She shrugged and started picking at her nails.

"Nah, you can't have your own room. You gotta sleep with me."

"Why? Why would I want to sleep with a man that's not mine?" She waved me off, then slumped down into the couch.

"Ain't nowhere else to sleep, Diamond. I don't know what to tell you."

"You got like seventeen rooms in here, nigga! I don't have to sleep with you." She crossed her arms and twisted her mouth.

"I don't have seventeen damn rooms in here, but all my other rooms are taken. You can't just come up in my shit demanding rooms and shit. What the hell you think this is?"

She covered her face with both hands.

"So, this is how you're gonna act the whole time? You're not gonna let me do shit?"

I shook my head. "Don't know what you're talking about, ma." I shot her a smile, but she wasn't feeling it.

"Whatever, Koda. I'll sleep in the same bed as you, but don't think we're having sex."

"Okay." I laughed. "You'll crack before I do."

"You'll crack before I do," she mocked. "Boy, fuck you." I ignored her. She knew like I knew that it wasn't gonna be me that cracked first. "So what do you do during the day since yo' lying ass doesn't really work at Walmart."

"You really wanna know?"

"Duh, nigga. I wouldn't have asked if I didn't wanna know."

I nodded. "Cool. Say less."

THE NEXT DAY

I thought Diamond would've gave in last night and asked to have sex, but she didn't. Instead, she took a long ass shower, and got in the bed next to me, naked. I should've known she wasn't gonna play fair because that's just how she is.

"Wake up, ma." I said, throwing the covers off her.

She let out a small groan. "Nooo."

"Come on. We got shit to do."

She opened one eye and looked at me. She eyed my outfit and sat up in bed.

"You're about to work out?"

"Nah, *we're* about to work out."

"Whyyy? I barely got any sleep last night. I just wanna go back to sleep."

"Nah. Get that ass up. You'll feel better once you start moving."

"Oh my God," she huffed. "You're like hella annoying in the morning. You could've went by yourself and let me sleep."

"You're the one who asked me what I did during the day, so I'm about to show you."

"I asked because I thought you were gonna tell me. I didn't know you were about to do stupid shit like this." She got off the bed, then realized she was still naked. "What the hell am I gonna wear? I'm just gonna be working out naked?"

I gave her a small smirk. "I mean, if we were working out in here, then hell yeah, but we're going outside. Go look in the closet. You'll know which side is yours."

She looked at me like I'd grown two heads, but then she slowly made her way to the closet and pulled the door open.

"What the fuck?" she muttered, stepping in it. "Why... Nigga, how? When did you do this? You bought all these clothes for me, or was it for one of your other bitches?"

"The only bitch I have is you, Diamond. Put some shit on so we can go. This shit shouldn't be taking this long."

She smiled to herself and found some spandex tights and a sports bra to wear.

"This shit is crazy. How do you even know what size I wear? You got shoes too?" She opened the Nike box and pulled out the tennis shoes that were in there.

"That ain't none of your business. Come on."

She quickly got dressed and put her shoes on, then we both made our way downstairs. I walked into the kitchen to grab bottles of water for us, then we made our way out the door.

"So, what gym are we going to?" she asked, trying to walk to the car, but I stopped her.

"We're not about to go to no damn gym, shawty. Fuck I look like going to one, when I got one in the crib? Nah, we're about to run a mile."

Her eyes almost popped out of her head.

"A mile! You want me, a bitch that hasn't worked out...ever, to run a mile? You don't think we should start off small? Like, why can't we walk a mile? That sounds so much better."

"Gotta push yourself, Diamond. Come on. We can jog at first," I let her know, stepping off the porch, hoping she would bring her ass.

"Wow," she huffed. "I can't even believe you're about to try to kill me like this."

EIGHTEEN

DIAMOND
This nigga is trying to kill me.

Was it so hard to tell me that he ran a mile every morning when he woke up? He had to wake me up to run it with him? Then he had the nerve to say we can start off by just jogging, but that didn't make anything better! I was still over here about to pass out.

I was slowly jogging behind him, not even trying to keep up with him at this point. He was jogging so effortlessly. He would glance back at me to make sure I was still good, then laugh. So not only was he trying to kill me, he thought this shit was funny.

"I'm gonna fuckin' puke," I said, slowing down to a walk. He stopped too, but from the look he wore on his face, I could tell he didn't want to.

"Come on, Dime. You're good. It's all in your head."

I held my finger up. "Hold on." I was so out of breath, it didn't make any damn sense. I really did feel like I was gonna vomit. I didn't want him to watch me throw up, so I turned around.

"Damn, we haven't even been running that long," he let me know, walking closer to me.

"Koda, leave me alone unless you want me to throw up on you." I put my hands on my knees and tried taking a couple deep breaths. That didn't stop the nausea, though.

"You good," he said grabbing me by my hand. "We can walk the rest of the way. By the end of the week we're gonna be back to running, so prepare yourself."

I didn't even wanna walk. I just wanted to go back to his place so I could hop in the shower again and get back in the bed.

He handed me a bottle of water, and I quickly opened it. At first, I thought I was feeling like this because I was out of shape, but after thinking about it for a second, I knew exactly what it was.

The drugs.

Quitting was always hard for me, and I knew this time it was gonna be even harder, but I wanted to prove to Koda that I could actually quit... even though the only thing on my mind was cocaine right now.

"I'm starving," I let him know as we walked. "McDonalds sounds so good right now."

"Hell nah." He laughed. "You gotta stop eating that shit. It's not good for you."

I rolled my eyes. "So, are you a health freak too? Is that something else you lied to me about?"

"No, I'm just letting you know that shit ain't good for you. There ain't no point of working out if you're just gonna go and eat junk. They cancel each other out."

"But that's what I want to eat, so..."

He shook his head. "While you're with me, you won't be eating that shit. Go ahead and get that thought out of your mind, aight?"

"What the hell, Koda? I shouldn't feel like I'm in prison living with you. You won't let me do anything fun."

He let out a small laugh. "You'll be alright. I'm worried about your overall health right now. I know for a fact it's not where it's supposed to be."

I didn't say anything back because honestly, I had no idea what I should say back to that. I never had anyone to care about my health like he did. Yeah, they would make little comments about my drug use here and there, but that was about it. They wouldn't actually help me try to quit like Koda was doing.

"Well thank you," I said in a small voice after a while of just walking in silence. "But I'm still hungry. I'm starting to get stomach cramps."

"Because you need to eat some fruit. You'll be good when we get back to the crib."

I let out a small groan. Eating healthy wasn't what I wanted to do right now. I mean, I knew I should be doing it, but it was a little hard when the only thing I wanted to do was stuff my face with greasy foods that I knew weren't healthy for me.

"I don't want fruit," I muttered.

"And I don't want an unhealthy girlfriend," he shot back.

"Nigga, when did I become your girlfriend? You never asked me. All you did was apologize, then force me to move in with you."

He chuckled. "So, I gotta ask you to be my girlfriend again? Even though you already know you're gonna say yes?"

"You don't know what the hell I'm gonna say, nigga. I could say no. Then what?"

"You know like I know you wouldn't say no."

I laughed to myself. "Just for that, I don't wanna be your girlfriend again. Don't got time for liars, or that devil dick you got. Go fuck up another bitch's life with that shit."

"Devil dick?" he asked, with his blond ass eyebrows coming together. "That's what you call it? Damn. That's some new shit I ain't never heard before."

"Yeah. That's what it is. Keep that shit away from me."

He scoffed. "Yeah, okay."

By the time we finished walking, I really felt like I was dying. We got back to his place, and I rushed to the bathroom to throw up. I felt like these stomach cramps were about to take my ass out. I knew I wouldn't be no good for the rest of the day.

When I was done puking my guts out in the bathroom, I went to collapse on Koda's bed. He was downstairs, probably trying to get me something to eat, but with the way I was feeling, I didn't want to eat anything.

"You good?" he asked, once he returned to the room.

"No," I groaned, pulling the covers over my head. I was cold, but I was sweating. Honestly, I just wanted to go back to sleep.

"Here. Eat something. You'll probably feel better."

"I'm not even hungry anymore. Just let me lay here and die."

He let out a laugh as he pulled the covers off me. "Come on, ma. You need to eat." He handed me a bowl of strawberries, and I just looked at it. He then sat a glass of water next to me with lemons in it. I twisted my face up.

"You couldn't have just given me regular water? You had to be extra and put lemons in it?" I asked, finding the strength to sit up in bed. "I don't even like lemon water." My attitude was on another level right now.

"Have you ever had it?" he asked as I picked up a strawberry and bit into it.

"Nope, and I damn sure didn't plan on it."

"Try it. See if you like it."

I let out a small sigh. "Why are you doing this to me? Why are you trying to force me to eat this shit when you know I don't want it?"

"It's not about what you want. It's about what you need. You like lemons, right?"

I nodded. "I mean, there's nothing wrong with them. I just don't prefer them in my water."

"When's the last time you even had water? Every time I'm with you, you're drinking nasty ass Sprite."

"Because Sprite is the shit, Koda! At least it tastes good."

"You don't think water tastes good? That just means you don't drink it enough, shawty."

I rolled my eyes and didn't reply to him. The strawberries were delicious. Some of the best strawberries I'd ever tasted. I didn't want to let him know that, though.

Reluctantly, I picked up the glass of lemon water and looked at it. It didn't look good at all. I hated when shit floated around in my drinks.

"Drink it, Diamond," he demanded.

I sighed to myself and brought the cup to my lips. It was so bitter, but it wasn't nasty. Honestly, I didn't know how to explain the taste, so I just took another sip. Then another sip, and another sip, and before I knew it, I had drunk the entire glass.

"Whoa," I said to myself as I put the glass back on the dresser. "I didn't expect that."

"Exactly. You're so quick to talk shit about something that you've never even tried before."

"Who drinks lemon water because they want to, though? That's some weird ass shit."

He shook his head as he sat down on the bed. "You ain't never heard of detox water?"

"Hell no. Sounds like some vegan shit."

He laughed and stood up. "Damn. You got so much shit to learn about. I'm about to hop in the shower, though. You coming?"

I gave him a small smirk. This nigga thought he was slick, trying to take a shower together so I could see how beautiful his pale ass looked when he was naked, and I could crack first. Nah. Not today.

"No thanks," I said, watching him come out his clothes. "I'm perfectly capable of taking a shower by myself."

"I never said you weren't capable. I just asked if you wanted to take a shower with me."

"I said no, Koda. Get your white ass in the shower."

He flashed me a small smile, then proceeded to make his way into the bathroom.

It was getting harder and harder for me to contain myself around him. I thought he'd be the one to break first. Shit, I thought getting in the bed last night naked would've got his ass, but he went right to sleep like I wasn't lying right next to him with my goodies out.

I felt like I was going through withdrawals with everything; dick, drugs, and good food.

"What the fuckk," I muttered to myself. I quickly pulled out my phone and called Mia. I needed to talk to her ass since she decided she wanted to have loose lips all of a sudden.

"Hello?" she sang into the phone.

"Bitch, I should beat yo' ass!"

"What? Why? What did I do?"

"You know exactly what you did. You really told all my business to Koda? For what? I was fine!"

She smacked her lips. "You were fine? So, crying, doing coke, and barely eating is fine to you? Diamond, you were spiraling out of control. I've never saw you like that, and I damn sure didn't like it. I knew if I would've tried to get you to stop, we would've ended up fighting, so I just got your boyfriend to do it since that's the only person you listen to."

I was quiet for a moment because she was right. I wouldn't have listened to anything she had to say.

"He's not my boyfriend," I let her know.

"Girl, bye. You love that man, and that man loves you back. Get your life together so y'all can live happily ever after and you can pop out his damn babies because I know you want to."

"What?" I shrieked. "I do not wanna have any babies right now. Me and him aren't even having sex. I swear it feels like I'm in prison."

"Don't think of it as prison," she said with a light laugh. "Think of it as rehab that your boyfriend is willing to help you through. He could've been like one of these bitch ass niggas and left because you're on drugs, but he's not. Be grateful, Dime. What he's doing is good for you. He really cares about your health."

I wanted to roll my eyes, but I couldn't. Just like I wanted to be mad at Mia for telling on me to Koda.

"He keeps telling me I need to find a different way to cope—"

"You do. Drugs is fun and all, but not the way you're using them."

"Well, how? What am I supposed to do? I still think about it. I still think about getting blamed for it. I still think about how many family is okay with him coming around them."

"Fuck them! Fuck that nasty ass nigga for raping you, fuck your family for blaming you, but mostly, fuck your mom because she ain't shit for that. She should've been ready to go to war with that nigga's entire family. If some shit like that would've happened to my daughter, someone would've popped up dead. That ain't no shit to play with. Maybe, you should try talking to other rape victims. You know, there's support groups for—"

"Hell no," I immediately interjected. "I'm not about to talk to strangers about some shit like that."

"Why not? It could be good for you. You need to have an open mind about this."

I was shaking my head like she could see me. "That shit isn't for me, Mia. You're one of my closest friends, and you see how long it took me to tell you. It's not something I want to go around shouting and shit."

"Okay, but you're talking to other people who's been through the same thing. They're not gonna judge you. I promise."

"No thanks," I said, rolling my eyes. I already didn't like people in my personal life, then telling them on purpose? Nope. I didn't like the way that sounded.

"Whatever, Diamond. I think it's a good idea. Being able to relate to people that's—"

"I said no, Mia. Stop talking about it," I snapped. I didn't mean to catch an attitude like I did, but I just needed her to stop talking about it.

"Okay, nigga. You don't need to catch an attitude with me. I'm just trying to help. I want you to know that I'm going to support anything you do. If you tell me you want to go to his house in the middle of the night and beat him the fuck up, then I'm all for it. I don't have any problems doing that."

I laughed lightly. "No, girl. It's been years since it happened. It would be stupid to run up in his house just to beat him up."

"Excuse me?" She flipped. "Who am I talking to? I know this isn't Diamond Carter. The one who beat up her entire family and walked out without a scratch on her. Can't be."

I wasn't gonna sit there and lie. I thought about killing that nigga almost every night. Just knowing that he still walked this earth, and probably raped other women, made my skin crawl.

"You know what? We should do that. We should run up in his mama's house and beat her ass too. She's the one who raised that nasty mothafucka," I said, listening out for Koda. I wanted to be off the phone before he was finished.

"His mom, though? I mean... You have every right to be mad, but I don't think—"

"Girl, fuck what you think! She's the root of the problem! She should've turned his ass in once she found out he raped me! That shit didn't happen, though. So, she needs to catch an ass whoopin', too."

She sighed loudly. "See, I should've never got you started. Now, you're talking about beating up his mom? How would we even find her?"

"She lives right in front of me. I see her almost every Sunday rushing off to church. We could wear something over our faces so she wouldn't know it was us."

"You're talking crazy, Dime."

I wanted to smack my lips because now. This was sounding like a great idea. I didn't know why I didn't think of this shit earlier.

"No I'm not," I responded, hearing Koda turning off the water. "I gotta go, though. I'll probably call you tonight."

"Alright. If I don't answer, it's probably because I'm somewhere getting dicked down. Unless you want me to answer while—"

"Actually, I'm good. If I don't talk to you tonight, then I'll just call you tomorrow."

"Alright." She laughed. I ended the call and waited for Koda to come out the bathroom. I just knew he was about to come out here trying to provoke me to have sex with him.

He did.

Koda came out the bathroom with nothing but a towel wrapped around his waist. His torso was still wet, but for the first time since we'd been together, I noticed how perfect his body was. I mean, yeah, I had noticed it before, but right now, it looked different. He didn't mess up his perfectly sculpted body with tattoos, either. Like the first time we had sex, it looked like he was glowing.

"Damn, you staring at me like you're ready to risk it all." He chuckled.

"Boy, bye," I said, trying to downplay it. "I'm not risking shit for a liar."

He smiled at me, then quickly moved to the closet to find himself something to wear.

"You know, you're not really good at lying. Your facial expressions always give you away."

I waved him off because I didn't care what he was talking about.

"Where are you about to go?" I saw that he pulled a suit from the closet, so I knew he wasn't going to put it on for no reason.

"Work." He laughed. "You think I just sit at home on my ass all day?"

I shrugged. "Well, actually, I thought you worked at Walmart, so..."

"Get dressed," he said, ignoring my last statement. "You're coming with me."

"What? Is that even allowed?"

"Is it allowed? I'm the boss. I can do whatever the hell I want to. I could walk up in that bitch naked, and they couldn't do shit about it." He dropped his towel and I tried my hardest to keep my eyes above his waist. I wasn't about to give him the satisfaction of looking at his penis.

"So, I'm just gonna go with you and be bored?"

He smiled at me. "Just get dressed, shawty."

I hated when he did shit like that. Why couldn't he just answer the question? He always ignored it like I didn't even say anything to him.

I let out a breath as I got off the bed and stormed into the bathroom. I was starting to realize that I got annoyed very easy when I wasn't getting any dick. For a moment, I wanted to go back out there and tell him I wanted it, but I couldn't. I didn't wanna give him the satisfaction.

"You got this," I muttered to myself. "You got all of this."

I quickly hopped in the shower, making sure not to take too long, and when I was finished, I decided that I was going to air dry.

I brushed my teeth and ran my fingers through my hair. Then, I stepped out the bathroom.

"Should I dress up, too?" I questioned, looking at Koda who was sitting on the edge of the bed, half dressed.

He looked up at me and eyed my body for a moment. He wanted me just as bad as I wanted him. I didn't know why the hell he was playing with me.

"I mean... you don't have to. You can wear whatever the hell you want."

"You sure? I don't wanna go to your job looking busted or anything."

His brows came together. "Did you even dry off?"

"No. I thought I'd air dry today. I do it at home all the time. It's not a problem for you, is it?"

He smirked at me. "Get dressed, ma. I don't have all day to wait on you."

"Wait on me? You're not even dressed." I walked to the closet and tried to decide on what to wear. Koda was wearing an expensive ass suit, so I didn't wanna be walking next to him looking basic.

The clothes that he had bought for me were nothing like the ones I would've picked out for myself. I wasn't complaining because I was grateful that he would go out his way and do something like this for me, but I missed all my clothes I had at home. I missed my car, too. I was definitely going to go home and get my things.

There were mostly dresses hanging up. Everything still had the tags on them.

"What the hell?" I whispered. Who knew finding something to wear would be so hard?

I scanned the closet one last time before my eyes finally landed on a navy-blue tube dress. Grabbing it, I saw the price tag that was attached to it, and my eyes almost popped out of my head.

"This dress was eight hundred dollars?" I asked, looking at Koda.

He shrugged. "Honestly, I just told my assistant to buy a woman's wardrobe, and this is what she came back with."

"Your assistant? You have an assistant?"

"Hell yeah. I wouldn't get shit done if I didn't have an assistant. That's what you're wearing, though? I got a tie that matches that shit." He was smiling, but I rolled my eyes.

"Don't call it shit, Koda. That makes it sound bad."

He ignored me because he was too busy looking through his drawers to find that damn tie. While he was doing that, I slipped the dress on and immediately fell in love with it.

"Sheesh," I gushed, looking at myself in the full-sized mirror. "This makes my body look immaculate."

"Because it is," he said, holding up his tie next to my dress. The colors matched perfectly. I smiled at him because I thought it was cute that he wanted his tie to match with me like we were going to prom or something.

While I was still admiring myself, he slapped me on the ass as hard as he could.

"Ow!" I shrieked as he pulled me closer to him. He pressed his erection into me, then gave me a soft kiss on my neck.

"You see what you're doing?" he asked in a low voice. Instantly, the flood gates opened. "You want some dick?"

I let out a small laugh. "Nope. I'm good, actually. I don't think you deserve my vagina yet."

"What? Why?"

I turned to look at him. "Did you forget you lied to me, nigga?"

"How we gonna get past that if you keep bringing it up? How is that helping us in any way?"

"I might give you some pussy when I feel like you deserve it. Right now, you don't deserve it."

"Damn." He sighed. "That's fucked up. I wouldn't do no foul shit like that to you."

I shrugged. "We're two different people, aren't we?"

He grabbed a handful of my ass and pulled me closer to him After that, he put his lips on mine and made my knees weak. We were so close. The only thing separating us was the thin fabric of this dress.

He slipped his tongue in my mouth, and I wanted to take my clothes off. Before I did anything I regretted, I took a step away from him, then made my way back to the closet. I needed to find some bomb ass shoes that went with this dress. I knew there were some in there.

Koda didn't say anything as I found a pair of simple black heels to wear. At first, I thought about just wearing sandals, but that would've just taken from the dress. I needed some cute ass shoes to go with this cute ass dress.

"Okay," I said, after I had the shoes on. "I'm ready."

"About damn time."

He led the way out his place, and I didn't bother saying anything back. I didn't even take that long to get ready, so I didn't know what he was complaining about.

Once we were in the car, my stomach started yelling at me. I needed to eat a meal. Not fruit that wouldn't do anything but make me hungrier.

"Are we gonna eat?" I asked, watching him as he drove.

"Eat? You ate, didn't you?"

"What? I ate like two strawberries! Why can't you just take me to McDonalds. I swear, we're about to pass one."

"Aye, around me, you're not about to be eating no damn McDonalds. Fuck that."

"Why? What did McDonalds even do to you? You're really—"

"I'll get you something to eat. It just isn't gonna be nasty ass McDonalds."

I gave him an ugly expression. "It's soo crazy how you get a little bit of money and started acting like you're too good for McDonalds. You forgetting where you came from, nigga."

"A little bit of money." He chuckled. "If I know the shit is bad for me, and have the money to eat healthy, don't you think it's smart to do that? Why you wanna put poison in your body? You wanna die early or some shit?"

"I'm here for a good time, not a long time, Koda."

He shook his head and didn't say anything else until we pulled up to Subway. I rolled my eyes so hard, but I didn't say anything as I got out the car. I was just happy that I was about to eat.

"I don't even remember the last time I'd been to Subway," I said as we approached the counter.

"Why? You don't fuck with Subway?"

"Not really. But I'll eat it because you won't take me to McDonalds. We wouldn't even have to get out the car if we were at—"

"What you still talkin' about it for? I already told you that shit dead."

I blew out a breath through my nose, then turned my attention to the worker who was ready for us to tell him what we wanted.

It felt like we were in Subway way longer than we should've been. I didn't know if homeboy had just started or something, but he was so damn slow. My patience was thin, but I held it together.

I didn't wanna say something to him because he could've been new, for one, and also, he *was* doing his job... just a little slower than I preferred.

"Are we eating here, or in your car?" I asked Koda after he paid for everything.

"Your messy ass ain't about to eat in my car." He laughed as we walked to a table.

"Messy? I'm grown as hell. I know how to eat."

"You don't. Especially when you're really hungry. You be going in and making a mess in the process."

"Shut up. You can't even name a time when I made a mess while I was eat—"

"That time we were at Waffle House. You dropped a waffle on you. Got syrup everywhere."

I thought about it for a moment. I did drop a whole waffle on my shirt, but that was because it had fell off the fork I was using.

"That didn't happen because I was eating too fast. It fell off the fork, and—"

"Because you were eating like a savage."

"Fuck you," I spat, opening my sub. I made sure to be extra careful while eating it. I didn't wanna prove Koda right, and this dress was too damn cute to mess it up.

"Let me ask you something," he said after a while of silence. "How your money looking?"

The question caught me off guard. He had never asked me about my money before, so I was wondering why he was asking now.

"It's good," I lied. I had enough money to pay my bills because I was good at saving my shit, but since I wasn't having sex with niggas for money anymore, I was going to go broke unless I found another way to make money.

"You sure?" he countered, lifting a brow to look at me.

I nodded. I didn't know why I didn't want to let him know that I was running out of money.

"I have some saved," I let him know. "It's enough to keep paying my bills." It would've been way more if I hadn't been spending my money on drugs.

"So, it's not good?"

I let out a sigh. "I mean... no. Not really. I stopped making money because of your pale ass, and your pale ass dick."

He smiled at me. "But you haven't been complaining about me or my pale ass dick."

He was right about that. When it came to his penis, there was nothing to complain about there.

"As long as you don't do no stupid shit like try to cheat on me, then there won't be any complaints. Oh, and you already know I'm not with that lying shit. Next time you lie to me, and I find out, I'm beating your ass." I smiled innocently at him while he looked at me like I was crazy.

"There you go, threatening me again." He laughed. "You wouldn't do shit."

I raised both eyebrows in amusement. "Why do you think that, Koda? I'll beat your whole family up and not give a single fuck."

I wouldn't fight his family. I *would* fight him, though. I would beat that nigga like he stole something from me, and I wouldn't have any regrets afterward.

"Damn. My family, though? They don't have anything to do with me sticking my dick in another bitch. I think you should leave them out of it."

I looked at him through squinted eyes. "Nigga, you cheating on me?"

"We ain't together, right? That's what you told me, right?"

"Fuck that. If you're cheating, tell me now so I can beat your ass then be on my way."

He shook his head. "Nah, I'm not cheating. Chill."

"You better not be. Swear to God, you'll be in a river floating somewhere."

He waved me off like what I was talking about wasn't important. It was all good, though. I could show him better than I could tell him.

When we were finished eating, we threw our trash away, then was on our way to where he *really* worked.

"I still don't understand," I said, as he drove. "If I was established like this, you think I'd be walking around here acting like a damn hood rat?"

"I don't act like a fuckin' hood rat," he spat. "I act how I acted before I started getting money. I didn't want niggas to think the money shit changed me."

"That's some of the dumbest shit," I scoffed. "Who gives a fuck what they think? You're the one making money, not them."

"You're saying that shit because you're a female. That shit is different for y'all. I act the same so I never forget where I came from. All my niggas in the hood still fuck with me because I didn't switch up on them. It's a respect thing."

I rolled my eyes because he was talking stupid. I just know that wouldn't be me. Of course, I wouldn't forget about my friends that had been with me since day one, but other than that, I would be acting like I had some damn sense. I wouldn't act like I was straight out of the hood.

About ten minutes later, we were pulling up to a huge building.

"This is yours?" I asked while he parked his car right out front.

"Yeah." he laughed. "One of them."

How much money did this nigga really have?

I was so in awe of the building, I didn't see him get out the car and come to the passenger side to open the door for me.

"Close your mouth, Diamond. Bugs might fly in it." I didn't even realize my mouth was hanging open, but I snapped it shut as I stepped out the car.

Already, my feet were killing me. I wasn't used to wearing heels. Honestly, I hardly ever wore them, so I knew by the time we left, my feet were gonna be in excruciating pain.

We walked through the doors and headed straight for the elevator. He got greeted by everyone. I could tell by how friendly they were being that they enjoyed working here.

"Fuckin' hate elevators," I muttered when we stepped on it. I didn't know why, but ever since I was younger, I never liked riding them.

"Whattt?" he asked once the doors shut. "Don't tell me big, bad, Diamond is afraid of elevators."

"Shut the fuck up, Koda." I gritted, gripping the bar attached to the wall as hard as I could.

This will be over before you know it.

I closed my eyes and imagined I was somewhere else.

"It's not even that serious." He laughed. My eyes shot open and I glared at him.

"It is."

"No it's not. You're being dramatic as hell."

"Koda, just stop talking. You're not making me feel any better about anything."

He let out another laugh and pulled me closer to him. His scent invaded my nostrils, and for a quick moment, I forgot that I was even on the damn elevator. That was until it chimed, and the doors slowly opened.

I damn near ran off the elevator, and he was laughing behind me like something was funny.

"Damn. I never thought I'd see the day you get scared over something like this." He chuckled, pushing the door open to his office.

"What the fuck is funny?" I asked, folding my arms.

"You are. Why you afraid of elevators? What—"

"Hey, Kodaaa," some light skinned bitch said walking into his office, but she immediately stopped once she saw me. "Oh, I didn't know you had a...guest."

"Yeah, this is my girlfriend, Diamond," he let her know. "Diamond, this is my assistant, Sundai."

I had to bite my lip to suppress a laugh. Her mom really named her that? What the hell?

"Hi," she said in a dry tone. I swear, when Koda said I was his girlfriend, she twisted her face up a little.

I turned to Koda. "You let your assistant call you by your first name? That's a little unprofessional, don't you think?"

He lifted my chin with his finger and smiled at me. That nigga knew he could get me wet just from smiling at me and showing me those perfect ass teeth.

"It is." He turned his attention to her. "You know better than that, Sundai."

She nodded. "My apologies, Mr. Mitchell. I moved your meeting to tomorrow like you asked me to, and I have a few brand ambassadors trying to get in contact with you."

"Aight," he said, basically dismissing her, but she still stood there, glaring at me.

Sundai wasn't ugly. She was skinny, but she had a nice body. She was wearing a black pencil skirt with a white blouse and a burgundy blazer. I could see how shapely she was. She had little to no makeup on, but she didn't need it. I wasn't sure if her hair was real or not, but it stopped right past her shoulders, and it was jet black. Off gate, I felt like something had went on between them two.

Koda walked around his desk, and Sundai finally left since he wasn't going to say anything else to her.

"What?" he asked. "Why you looking at me like that?"

"You fuck her?" I crossed my arms and waited for him to answer.

"My assistant?"

"It's a yes or no question, Koda."

"No, man. I'm not fucking my assistant."

"Were you?"

He chuckled. "No, Dime. I haven't fucked her, and I damn sure don't plan on it. The only girl I'm fucking is you."

I nodded, but something didn't feel right. I caught the look she gave me, then she just barged into his office, calling him by his first name? Nah.

"If I find out you're lying, I swear to God—"

"I'm not lying, Diamond. Just chill." He shot me a smile, but I still wasn't feeling it. I was going to let it go for now, but if something else happened, I was definitely gonna start an investigation.

NINETEEN

KODA

"A girlfriend?" Sundai snapped as I blew out a breath. "You really have a girlfriend, Koda? Then you had the nerve to be parading her around work like that! What the fuck is wrong with you?"

I pulled a hand down my face. I already knew Sundai was gonna be on some bullshit the moment she saw Diamond.

"I know you didn't call my work phone on no bullshit like this, Sundai."

"No, I know *you* didn't have that bitch—"

"Watch your fuckin' mouth, yo."

"Don't tell me to watch shit! See, this is why I don't like fucking with you! You're a liar!"

"What did I lie about?" I asked, picking up the remote, and flipping through the channels.

"Everything! I should've known there was a reason you've been hitting me up for the past two weeks. Calling me and telling me you wanna chill and shit. You just want some company, but you know every time you come over here, your dick is gonna be in my mouth!"

she hollered. I was just glad Diamond wasn't around because that would've started a whole new problem.

"Well, whose fault is that? I don't force that shit in your mouth. You willingly do it. You pull it out and everything, so—"

"That's not the point, Koda! You had a girlfriend the entire time! That's why you cut me off three damn months ago! Telling me it's best if we have a platonic relationship. Well, it's a little too late for that. You've already fucked me and fucked my whole head up!"

"Get to the point, Sundai." I rushed because Diamond would be back at any moment.

"You ain't shit. That's my point. The only reason you've been hitting me up for pussy is because y'all were probably having problems! You used me."

I let out a breath. "Look, bruh. I don't see a problem with the shit you're talking about right now. I hit you up for some pussy, and you gave that shit to me. I never said anything about wanting to be with you, so you really don't have anything to be mad about."

"Are you being serious? You already know how I feel about you! I've told you plenty of times, and what do you do? Show up to work with a fuckin' girlfriend."

"Aight," I said, tired of being on the phone with her. "I don't wanna be with you, I wanna be with her. Instead of being mad about finally getting some dick from me again, you should be happy that I even hit your ass up. Get your feelings in check, Sundai. This shit ain't cute."

"Cute?" She flipped. "Who the fuck said anything about being cute? My feelings are hurt! You don't give a fuck about anyone but yourself!"

"Nah. I give a fuck about my girl." I let out a small chuckle because I knew that shit got under her skin. "But anyway, I was doing some shit before you called, so I'ma get back to that. If you wanna keep your job, I suggest you get yourself together." I ended the call before she could respond.

I met Sundai three years ago. She was looking for a job, and she fit all the requirements, so I hired her. For a whole year, she was one of the best assistants I'd ever had. She did her job, and she did it well.

After that first year, shit started changing with her. At first, Sundai would dress normal. Her skirts, and dresses always came past her knees. She would never wear makeup, and honestly, fucking her had never crossed my mind.

One day, she showed up to work wearing a tight ass dress that stopped mid-thigh, she had on makeup, and her hair was done, opposed to being in that bun she always wore.

She looked good. I'll admit that, but having sex with her was still out of the question because I wasn't the type of nigga to mix business with pleasure.

Obviously, that shit didn't last long. We ended up fucking a few times, and I swear, she caught feelings hella fast. I told her what it was from jump, though. I wasn't looking for a relationship, because at that time, I was still fucking around with Melanie, but Sundai didn't care. She kept fucking with me and always felt the need to let me know how she felt about me. She gave me a list of reasons to why I should give her a chance.

I didn't, though.

Sundai came off as desperate to me. That shit was a turn off. I needed a girl with confidence, like Diamond.

I stopped fucking with Sundai once I knew I wanted to get serious with Diamond. I might've slipped up and had sex with Sundai once or twice since I'd been with Dime, but that was on some drunk shit.

The past two weeks, Sundai was just something to do. She should've known that. I didn't feel like going to find a new bitch, so I just called her.

My phone rang beside me with her number popping up. She was really in her feelings behind this one. She was trying to start some bullshit that I didn't have the patience or energy to deal with, so I ignored her call then went back to finding something to watch on TV.

Diamond had went back to her crib to get some clothes and her car. I was glad Sundai called while Diamond wasn't here, but I had a feeling in the back of my mind that Sundai was about to be a problem for me. I paid her ass good money to be my assistant, so if she knew what was good for her, she would stop acting crazy.

About twenty minutes later, Diamond was pulling up into the driveway, and I made my way outside to help her because I knew she'd probably brought a lot of shit that she didn't even need.

She stepped out the car then smiled at me when she saw me.

"I'm so tired," she let me know, falling into my arms. "I'm tired, I have a headache, my feet still hurt from wearing those damn heels all day, and I'm horny as fuck."

My dick instantly got hard at her revelation.

"Sounds like you need some dick to put you to sleep."

She rolled her eyes then pushed the button on her keychain to pop the trunk. "No thanks. I brought my vibrator with me."

I smacked my lips. "You're not about to be using that shit when I have all this dick—"

"I don't want your dick, Koda. You don't deserve—"

"Shut the hell up," I cut her off then moved toward her trunk to get her bags out.

"Don't be mad, I told you we weren't having sex."

"And I told you, you're not about to be using no damn vibrator in my shit. You got me fucked up, Diamond."

She gave me a light shrug as she followed behind me into the house.

"I mean, you won't even know I'm using it because once you go to bed, that's it. You be knocked the fuck out," she let me know.

"What? Nah. I'm a light sleeper."

She let out a small laugh. "You're really not. I be fucking with you so much in your sleep. You never wake up either."

"No the fuck you don't. Stop playing." I set the bags down by the door then returned outside to get some more.

"You think I'm lying?" she asked, pulling out her phone. "Look." She shoved the phone in my face, and I took it from her.

It was a picture of us. I was sleep of course, and she was smiling.

"What the fuck?" I questioned, after looking at myself and seeing there was makeup all over my face. "The fuck is this shit on my eyelids?"

"Eyeshadow." She laughed. "Look at your eyebrows, though! Them shits look nice."

"No the fuck— why you be putting makeup on me and shit? I ain't with that—"

"Boy, shut the fuck up. It's proof that you're not a light sleeper. So like I was saying, I can use my vibrator when you go to—"

"Aight," I said, jostling the phone back to her then grabbing the rest of her things out the trunk. "You think I'm playing with you."

"It's just a vibrator. I don't understand why you don't want me to use it."

I set her bags down, closed the front door, then started unzipping every bag she had.

"Koda? Koda, what are you— Stop!" she yelled, once I started pulling everything out of her bags, piece by piece.

"Where's the shit at, Diamond?"

"What are you talking about? You're throwing all my clothes on the floor!"

"Where's the fuckin' vibrator, bruh? Which bag is it in?"

"Stop!" she yelled, trying to pull me away from the bags, but I was too strong. "I'll find it! Just stop throwing my shit on this nasty ass floor!" She took the bag from me and started searching through it.

It wasn't in that bag, so she moved on to the next one.

"Stupid ass nigga," she muttered. She finally found it, then pushed it into my chest. "Here, bruh."

I gave her a small smirk and headed straight for the back door. "Shouldn't have brought this shit over here in the first place," I said as she followed me.

"I didn't know you were gonna act like a little bitch over— Koda!" she shrieked after I opened the back door and flung that shit as far as I could. "Are you serious?"

I turned to look at her. "As a heart attack. You don't need that shit. You wanna play with your pussy then you come get me. Fuck you need a piece of plastic for to pleasure you anyway?" I lifted a brow as she gave me the ugliest expression.

"I don't want you anywhere near my vagina, nigga." She crossed her arms.

"Why?" I asked, walking up on her. "You don't miss this?" I pressed my erection into her, and she gave me a small smirk.

"Nope. Plus, you gotta pay for this pussy."

I stuck my tongue in her mouth before she could say anything else.

"I'm cool with that." I scooped her up in my arms and headed straight for the stairs. It was still a mess from where I was throwing all her clothes out her bags, but I would clean that shit up later. It had been way too long since I felt the inside of her, and she was trying to hold out on me? Nah, this shit wasn't about to work for me.

When I got her upstairs, I gently laid her on the bed and she looked at me with nothing but lust in her eyes.

"You love me?" I asked with our faces just inches apart. I let my hands roam up and down her exposed thighs and she smiled at me.

"Yes."

"Then why you tryna hold out on a nigga?" I put my lips on hers just as I pulled her dress up a little. She still had on the same dress from earlier, and I was ready to rip that shit off of her.

While she was busy sticking her tongue down my throat, I slid my fingers up and down her slit, and she moaned into my mouth.

"Baby." She sighed, once I slid a finger inside her. She threw her head back, and I started kissing and biting on her neck, causing her to shudder against me.

"You missed this shit?"

"Mhmmm."

"What? I can't hear you." I grabbed her face with my free hand, forcing her to look at me.

"Yes." She breathed, and I stuck another finger inside her. "Fuck-kk." She tried to close her eyes, but I wasn't having that shit.

"Nah, baby, keep them eyes on me." She slowly opened her eyes and I shot her a smile. "You wet as hell, mama. This my pussy?"

She shook her head. "Hell no."

I raised a brow. "Word?" I snatched my fingers from inside her and watched her twist her face up.

"You play too much, Koda," she spat, pushing me away from her. "And before you ask, no. I don't want you to finish."

"You sure?" I asked, showing her my fingers that were coated in her juices. Before she could respond, I put those fingers in my mouth, and she grinned at me.

"I'm good. I don't even wanna have sex," she lied. I could see it all over her face that she wanted it. My dick was pressing up against my zipper, so there was no way I wasn't about to get inside of her.

"Well, I'm not," I said, standing up to remove my clothes. She just sat there watching me then stared at my dick like it was the best thing in the world. "Take that shit off," I demanded.

She wasted no time coming out of her dress and tossing it to the floor. After that, she slowly crawled to the edge of the bed and grabbed my dick in both of her hands.

She started off by just sucking the tip. I wasn't complaining or anything because she was making that shit sloppy.

"Fuck," I grunted, pushing myself further into her mouth. "Suck that shit, Dime. Why you playing with it?"

As soon as the words left my mouth, I felt my dick touching the back of her throat. I bit down on my lip to keep from screaming out like a bitch. She had me in here thinking about what type of rings would look good on her finger because I was definitely marrying her ass.

"Damn, baby," I damn near yelled when she started sucking and licking on my balls. "Do that shit. Show me how nasty you are."

I could feel my nut rising, and I wasn't ready to cum yet. Not off head, and not this damn quick.

I pushed her away from me then watched as she laid back on the bed and spread her legs for me.

I grabbed her ankles and positioned myself at her entrance. The anticipation was all over her face, and it caused me to smirk at her.

"Koda, please don't," she pleaded.

"What? I'm not even doing anything."

"Exactly. Are you gonna give me the dick or— Koda!"

I slid all the way in while she was trying to talk shit.

"What was that?" I asked, slowly starting to move my hips. "You were saying what? That you love this dick?"

She nodded and grabbed both her breasts to keep them from bouncing too much.

"What? You know I can't hear you."

"I love ittt!" She moaned, closing her eyes again. I wasn't going fast. Nah, I wasn't trying to beat her shit up right now. I needed her to feel every inch of me.

"Eyes on me, ma," I demanded in a low voice. She opened her eyes, and I could feel her clenching around my dick. "Tell me you love me, Dime. Let me hear you say it." I let her ankles go so I could get closer to her.

Once I was on top of her, she took my face in both hands and said, "I love you, Koda." She gave me a quick peck then gently bit down on my bottom lip. "Fuck, baby, I'm gonna cum!"

"Yeahh, cum all over this dick." Feeling her pussy clenching around me had me ready to cum all up in her.

"Shit." She threw her arms around me and gripped on to me like she never wanted to let go.

"You better not let anyone in this pussy, Diamond. You hear me?" She nodded. "I can't fuckin' hear you! Say that shit."

"I won't!" she screamed, squeezing her eyes shut.

"You won't what?"

"I won't let anyone in this pussy, baby! Fuckk!"

"I'll body you and that nigga," I let her know, putting one of her legs on my shoulder.

I started pounding her ass because I was about to cum. Two weeks was too damn long for me. She better not ever try to pull some shit like this again.

"Ohhhh shittttt," I said, hitting her with one last deep stroke and releasing all my cum inside her. "Damn."

I collapsed next to her on the bed, and we both laid there for a moment trying to catch our breaths.

"It was still rude what you did to my vibrator," she said, looking at me.

"Fuck that vibrator, shawty. I got all this dick. I shouldn't hear you talking about vibrators ever again."

She rolled her eyes. "Whatever you say, Koda. Whatever you say."

TWENTY

DIAMOND

4 MONTHS LATER

Checking my appearance in the mirror, I applied a fresh coat of lip gloss, then grabbed the Japanese food that was sitting in the seat next to me. I was wearing a Gucci dress that showed all my curves, and a pair of Jimmy Choo heels that Koda had just brought for me last week.

I was feeling real good. I hadn't been doing drugs anymore, and I was starting to gain weight, but it was all going to the right places.

I smiled to myself as I walked through the doors of Koda's building. At first, it took me a little minute to get used to Koda having all this damn money, but I got used to it. He went to work almost every day, but usually, he wouldn't work long hours because he didn't have to. He honestly didn't have to show up at all, but he just did it. He never gave me a real explanation as to why, so I just dropped it.

When I made it past the door, everyone stopped what they were doing to watch me. That's how it always was when I came in here.

You'd think they would be used to me by now, but nope. It was the same reaction every time.

I gave everyone smiling a small wave since they acted like they couldn't speak. I was beyond happy when I got halfway up the stairs because I couldn't see them anymore. I took the stairs every time I came her alone because I wasn't getting on that damn elevator by myself. Plus, the stairs were a workout for me.

Koda still had me running with him every morning. He had me eating right, too. At first, I complained and bitched about it because I didn't want to do it, but after about two weeks of doing it, things got better. Now, I was so used to starting my day running, if I didn't, everything would be thrown off.

I finally made it to the floor Koda's office was on, and I flipped my hair.

Sundai was sitting at her desk, and she turned her nose up when she saw me. That's how it'd been for the past four months. Either she would give me a stank ass look, or she would act like I wasn't even there. The shit didn't bother me, and Koda had already let me know she tried to get with him a while ago, and he rejected her ass. As long as she never came out her mouth crazy, then I was good. What the hell I looked like wasting time over someone irrelevant like her?

"Koda is in a meeting," she said smugly.

I chuckled. "Girl, shut up. I didn't ask you all that." I continued walking.

"That means you can't go in there." I could hear the attitude dripping from her voice.

"Stop talking to me before you lose your job, Saturday. Also, stop calling my man by his first name. That shit isn't professional." I didn't wait for her to respond. I just walked through the doors of his office, stepped in, and closed the door behind me.

Koda was standing in the middle of the floor watching the TV that was mounted to the wall. Sani was sitting on the couch scrolling through his phone.

Koda turned to look at me then a big smile formed on his face.

Every time he would see me, his eyes would light up like a kid on Christmas morning. That would only make me return the smile like a Cheshire cat.

"Hey, chocolate," he said, making his way over to me. "I didn't think you'd come by today." He pulled me in for a kiss.

We had only been away from each other for about five hours, but it felt like forever.

"I brought you some food," I said, holding the bag up. "Hey, Sani. I would've brought you something if I knew you were going to be here."

"You good," he let me know. "I was gonna pick up something on the way home anyway."

I nodded and turned my attention back to Koda. He looked so good today. He was dressed simple in a plain black shirt and a pair of jeans, and he let his dreads hang free today. That's something he didn't do too often because he said they got on his nerves.

"Your stupid ass assistant told me you were in a meeting. She told me not to come in here, too. I'm tired of her."

"Word? I haven't even had any meetings today. I don't know why she would tell you that shit."

I smacked my lips. "Because she doesn't like me, Koda. For no damn reason. And why the fuck does she keep calling you by your damn first name? You let her walk around calling you that?"

He shrugged. "I don't know what you want me to do, Dime. She's good at her job."

"Good at her job? She lied to me just now." I folded my arms and looked at him.

"Aight." He nodded. "I'll talk to her."

"Good. Because I'm not gonna let her keep getting away with those dirty ass looks she keeps giving me." My phone vibrated in my purse, and I quickly pulled it out.

It was Mia like I expected because we were supposed to be spending the day together.

MIA: DAMN BITCH. WHERE U AT?

MIA: YO BLACK ASS PROBABLY SOMEWHERE SUCKING DICK

MIA: BITCH GET OVER HERE NOW! IT'S URGENT

I let out a small chuckle as I looked up at Koda.

"Who the fuck you texting that got you smiling at your phone like that?" he asked.

"Mia. She's rushing me to come over there. I guess I'll see you tonight," I let him know then gave him a quick kiss on the lips. "You can have my food, Sani. I'll probably go get something to eat with Mia."

"We're about to get up out of here, too. I'll probably chill at Sani's crib for a little bit," Koda said, pulling me close to him again.

"Okay, daddy." I laughed. I gave him another kiss then said bye to Sani. As soon as I walked out of the office, Mia was calling me. Whatever she needed to tell me must've been important.

"I'm on the way, Mia." I said, answering the phone.

"How far are you?"

"I'm leaving Koda's job now. I'll be there in about twenty minutes."

"Alright... just hurry up." She ended the call, and I damn near ran to my car. I didn't know why, but I was nervous. I felt like Mia was about to hit me with some bad news.

I tried to shake the feeling as I drove, but it wouldn't go away. I took a couple deep breaths to calm myself down. I was probably just overthinking. Mia was probably only doing this so I would rush over there. That sounded like some shit she would do.

The twenty minutes it took for me to get to my place felt like twenty hours. I took another deep breath as I stepped out the car and made my way to the door.

Before I could lift my hands to turn the knob, the door flew open.

"About damn time," she said, watching me step into the house.

"I didn't even take that long. Did you want me to speed over here?"

"Yep. I told you it was urgent."

I rolled my eyes. "Well, what is it?"

She sighed like she didn't wanna tell me. "Sit down, Dime. I don't think you want to be standing up for this."

The nerves hit me like a ton of bricks. What was she talking about? Was what she had to tell me that bad?

I quickly went to sit down on the couch, then Mia handed me her phone.

I looked at it for about five minutes straight without saying anything. I couldn't form the words because of the lump that had formed in my throat.

"I met her yesterday at the hair salon," Mia said after I didn't say anything. "She told me to follow her on Instagram, so I did. I just went through her pictures today, and that's when I saw it."

It was a picture of Sundai and Koda. She was kissing him on the cheek, and she was also the one who took the picture. I quickly looked to see when the picture had been uploaded.

Yesterday.

Koda had on that outfit yesterday.

I shook my head as I clicked on her profile and started going through her pictures. There were so many of her and Koda. The one that really caught my attention was her laying on his pale ass chest. The caption said, "The love of my life" and that was all I needed to see.

I handed Mia her phone back and just sat on the couch staring at the wall.

"Say something, Diamond," she said in a low voice, but I couldn't. There was nothing to be said.

Here I was, thinking this nigga was all for me, but he was fucking his assistant. The assistant that he told me I didn't have to worry about. He lied straight to my face.

I could feel the tears stinging my eyes, but I didn't wanna let them fall.

"Nah," I said with a light chuckle. "Hell no."

This nigga was cheating on *me*? On Diamond Nicole Carter?

"Kill his ass," Mia said. "I'll help you hide the body." I ignored her. I knew she was being serious, but no. I didn't want to kill Koda. I didn't know what I wanted to do right now.

I didn't say anything as I got up from the couch and headed straight for Mia's room. Koda had me all types of fucked up. My entire body was shaking with rage.

I couldn't believe he'd lied to me like that. Not only was he lying, but he was cheating, too. This right here was the main reason I never did relationships. Niggas thought everything was a game. Niggas thought a woman's feelings were something to play with, but nah. Koda played with the wrong bitch.

I walked into Mia's closet and grabbed the first sweat suit I saw. All my clothes were at Koda's place, so I didn't have anything to wear. I still wasn't sure what I wanted to do, but I knew it would result in fighting. I wasn't about to do anything in this expensive ass dress and heels.

I was out of my clothes and in the sweat suit quick as hell. After I was dressed, I found a pair of Mia's sneakers and slid them on. Her feet were one size smaller than mine, so the shoes were tight as hell. It didn't bother me too much, though. It was better than trying to fight in some heels.

"Oh shit," Mia said when I made it back in the living room. "Look who's ready to beat some ass."

"I'll be back," I let her know, grabbing my keys and walking out the door.

"Hold on," she huffed, doing a light jog to catch up with me. "You really think I'm gonna sit here while you go fight a nigga by yourself? Nah."

I rolled my eyes and got in the car. I didn't want Mia to come with me because I knew she would talk too much. Right now, I just wanted to be alone with my thoughts so I could think about what my next move should be.

Mia smiled as I pulled off. "I hope that nigga hits you back so I can shoot his ass. You know I always keep the strap on me."

"Bitch, no. I'm not gonna let you shoot him."

"What?" she snapped. "Why not? He deserves it! You don't know who this girl is, do you?"

I nodded. "Yeah. She's his assistant. She had an attitude with me the first day we met, and it's been that way ever since. Koda told me it was because she tried to get with him and he wasn't having it."

"What?" she flipped. "You believed him? What grown ass woman is gonna be mad at *you* for some dumb shit like that? Why didn't you put two and two together, Diamond? Her not liking you should've been a damn red flag!"

She was right. That should've been something that I looked into even more, but I trusted Koda. I didn't think he would've violated me this bad.

"I trusted him," I said quietly. "I love him, so I didn't think—"

"Fuck that, Diamond! Why would you trust him? He cheated on Melanie to be with you right? I mean, there's nothing wrong with trusting your man, but you should've had your damn guard up. Him and that bitch needs to die!"

I didn't say anything as I gripped the steering wheel harder. I needed her to shut the hell up. Just shut up for five minutes.

Let me think bitch, damn!

"Couldn't be me," she continued. "I'd kill that nigga's entire family. Fuck you mean?"

"Shut up, Mia." I gritted, breaking all types of traffic laws trying to get to his house. I was glad he told me they were about to be at Sani's place. I didn't know if they were there or not, but I was gonna sit my ass out there until they showed up.

"She's probably not the only bitch, either. There's probably hella bitches that he's telling the same shit to. All y'all out here sharing a nigga."

Oh my God, if this bitch doesn't shut the fuck up.

"Hush!" I yelled.

"No! You need to hear this! That nigga made you soft, bruh! You being loyal to him, not even looking in another nigga's direction, and he's out here sticking his dick in the bitches that work for him? He got you looking like a dumb bitch, bruh. Can't believe you were letting that nigga fuck for free. You sucking a dick that's been up in other bitches. That's—"

Her sentence was cut short because my fist connected with her mouth.

"Bitch, I swear to God, if you say some more shit, I'm gonna stab yo' ass!" I hollered, watching her bring her hand to her lip.

She gave me a small smile. "You mad?"

Bitch what? What kinda question was that?

"Hell yeah, I'm mad!"

"You mad at me for saying some real shit, or you mad at that pale ass nigga?"

"I'm... shit, I'm mad at both of y'all! I need you to shut the fuck up, Mia, damn!"

"And I need you to beat this nigga like he fuckin' stole something. Beat that nigga like you would beat yo' daddy if you ever met him. I need the old Diamond to come out right now, aight? Don't get soft when the nigga tried to plead his case. You know what? Don't even let that nigga talk! Do you hear me?"

I glanced at her lip busted from where I'd just punched her. I started to feel bad because she was only telling me what I needed to hear.

"I hear you," I said, voice barely above a whisper.

"And when we leave from beating this hoe ass nigga, I better not see you shed one tear over his ass. Go make you some money, then take yourself shopping."

I nodded. Even though I wanted to cry right now, I didn't. I was doing a great job of holding everything in. I wanted to scream and fight. So, that's what I was going to do.

When we pulled up, I saw Koda's car parked in the driveway. I was glad because I honestly didn't feel like waiting for his ass to get here.

I didn't say anything to Mia as I grabbed my pepper spray and pocket knife from the glove compartment.

Sani was sitting on the porch, smoking a blunt like always, and his eyes lit up when he saw Mia.

"Don't say shit to me, nigga. You a liar just like your bitch ass friend in here," she snapped at him. He gave her a look of confusion, but we didn't stay out there to hear what he had to say.

"Pull up her Instagram on your phone right quick," I said to Mia as I stepped through the door. Koda wasn't in the living room. I could hear moving coming from in the kitchen, so that's where we headed.

Mia handed me her phone, and I clicked on the first picture of them, and walked into the kitchen where Koda was standing in front of the microwave. He turned to look at me then gave me a small smile.

"What's up, bae? What you—" I hit him straight in the mouth. "What the FUCK? Fuck you coming in here hitting me and shit for?"

I showed him the picture of him and Sundai and watched as the guilt play out on his face.

"But you never fucked her, right?" I laughed, bitterly. "You never plan on fuckin' her, right?"

"Dime—" I threw Mia's phone at him, clocking him right in the face.

"Beat his ass, Diamond." Mia chuckled.

That's exactly what I did. Every time I closed my eyes, I pictured him laid up with Sundai. That shit was only fueling my anger.

"You a bitch ass nigga!" I yelled, throwing punch after punch. "You had me look stupid as fuck, bruh!"

"Yo chill! Mia, get ya girl!"

I heard Mia laugh. "Hell no. You deserve this ass whoopin'."

At this point, he was trying to run from me.

Don't run now, bitch! Take this ass whoopin'!

"Diamond, you're doing too much!" he hollered.

I picked up the frying pan that was sitting on the stove and swung it at him. I swear, the whole neighborhood heard the noise it made when it connected with the side of his face. He fell to the floor but was still trying to get away.

"Stop running, Koda!" I screamed at him, shaking up the pepper spray that was connected to my car keys.

"Diamond—" I refused to let him finish his sentence. I didn't care about shit he had to say.

His screams were like music to my ears when I sprayed him in his face. Sani ran through the door, with his late ass. I'm sure he heard all the noise we were making before now.

"Aye!" Sani yelled, hurrying toward me.

Dumb ass nigga.

I pepper sprayed him, too. I had two bitch niggas on the floor screaming. I wasn't satisfied, though.

"You done?" Mia asked.

"Nah," I said, out of breath. Koda decided he wanted to get up as soon as I flipped open my pocket knife.

"You wanna fight me like you're a man, so I'm about to beat your ass like one," he said, pulling his pants up, and walking closer to me.

Nah. Not today, Koda.

I started swinging the knife like I was crazy.

"Get his ass, bitch! Stab that white ass nigga in his heart!" Mia encouraged.

I knew I wouldn't be able to stab him in his heart, even though that's what it felt like he did to mine. I stabbed him in his arm instead. This nigga needed to know that I wasn't the one to be fucked with.

"Fuck!" he yelled.

I quickly pulled the knife out of his arm and stabbed him in the other one.

"Go, bitch!" I yelled at Mia, as she picked up her phone off the floor. "Go!"

She didn't protest. She ran out the house and I glanced at Koda.

His face was swollen and bloody, blood dripping down both

arms, and tears streaming down both cheeks from where I'd pepper sprayed him.

"Fuckin' crazy," he said, rubbing his eyes. Just looking at him pissed me off. So I kicked him in his dick and ran out the house. Mia was already in the car waiting for me.

I smiled to myself as I got in the car and pulled off.

"Welcome back, bitch," Mia said.

My phone vibrated in the cup holder. I thought it would've been Koda, but I was shocked to see Lawrence's name popping up. It kinda threw me off because I thought Koda had killed him.

I thought about not answering it, then I said, fuck it. Why not?

"Hello?" I answered.

"What's good? Haven't heard that sexy ass voice in a little minute," he said. Yeah, it was definitely Lawrence.

"Yeah. I thought you were dead or something."

"Nah. I've just been laying low. How you been, though? You good?"

"You know what? I am good. You got some pills, though? I need the strongest ones you got."

He let out a small chuckle. "You know I got you. Come see me right quick."

I smiled and hung up the phone. Fuck Koda's white, cheating ass.

TWENTY-ONE

K ODA
THE NEXT DAY

"Told yo' ass she was gonna find out," Sani said, as I looked down at my phone. "Because of you, Mia won't fuckin' talk to me. She knows that I knew." He'd been bitching about Mia all damn day, and I was ready for him to shut his ass up.

Diamond had me on the block list. Shawty wasn't even trying to hear what I had to say. She beat my ass and dipped. I gave her an entire day to calm down, but she didn't. I was calling her private, and she still wasn't answering.

"She got me fucked up," I muttered.

My lip was busted, face was sore from where she hit me with that fuckin' frying pan, and my right eye was swollen. The swelling in my face had went down, but that was because I held ice over that shit all throughout the night. I could still see out of my eye, but the shit still hurt.

"Nah, nigga. You had her fucked up. She straight beat yo' ass like she was a nigga. Never in my life have I saw some crazy shit like that."

"Nigga, shut up."

"She stabbed you, bruh. Twice. In both fuckin' arms. She pepper sprayed us both, and you're over there trying to call her? Nah, son. Leave that crazy ass bitch where she's at."

I mugged him. "Don't call my girl a bitch, yo."

"She ain't ya girl no more. You just need to accept it. Ain't no coming back from an ass whoopin' like that. You just need to be happy that she didn't kill yo' ass because she damn sure tried."

Right now, Sani talking wasn't doing anything but making me feel worse. Yeah, I knew what I did was fucked up, but she thought I was gonna let her leave my ass that easy? Hell nah. It didn't work like that.

"Lemme use your phone," I said with my hand out. He looked at me like I was crazy.

"Nah, nigga. You're going out sad. There's too much pussy in the world for you to be acting like this," he said, while shaking his head.

"Man, shut the fuck up. You were just over there crying about Mia. Let me see the fuckin' phone,"

"Fuck Mia. I bet she'll be calling me before I call her ass again. Fuck these bitches." He handed me his phone, and I laughed at his dumb ass. He knew like I knew, Mia wasn't gonna be calling his ass.

I quickly dialed Diamond's number and waited for her to pick up.

"Nigga," I heard Mia answer. "I know you're not calling my best friend's phone from your home boy's phone."

"Stop playing, and put Diamond on the phone," I said. I wasn't in the mood for this shit.

"No! If she wanted to talk to you, she would've answered when you were calling private like a little hoe!"

"Mia, ain't nobody playing with you, yo!"

Sani looked up at me. "You're talking to Mia?"

I nodded while I listened to Mia go off.

"Wasn't that ass whoopin' you got yesterday enough? She doesn't have shit to say to you. My nigga, stop fuckin'—"

Sani snatched the phone from me before I even realized what was going on.

"Mia? Baby, I need you to talk to me." He walked away, and I smacked my lips.

"Nigga, I thought you said it was fuck that bitch!" I called after him.

"Nigga, fuck you!"

I sat there on the couch for a second, not knowing what I should do. I didn't wanna act like no crazy ass nigga, but I felt like that was the only way I would get Diamond to talk to me.

"Fuck it," I muttered as I got up from the couch. I quickly went to my room, grabbed my car keys, and left. Sani was on the porch begging for Mia back, but from the sounds of it, she wasn't trying to hear it.

I couldn't even talk shit about him right now. I was prepared to beg for Diamond, too. I just hoped when she saw me, she wasn't trying to fight again. I didn't have time for that shit. She'd already fucked up both my arms.

I sped the entire way to her crib. I didn't give not one fuck about traffic laws. As soon as I pulled up to her house, my phone started to ring, I didn't even have to look at it to know who was calling.

"Wassup?" I answered.

"What the fuck, Koda? Why you acting like you can't answer your phone?" Sundai yelled.

"Look." I sighed. "Don't call me no more."

"Don't call you no more? You want me to tell your little girlfriend about us? You want me to tell her that the only way I would keep quiet about us fucking was if you kept fucking me? Nigga—"

"She already knows because yo' dumb ass wanna be posting pictures of us on your fuckin' Instagram! I don't want you, Sundai! I never wanted to be with you! I was just fuckin' you so you would keep your mouth shut, and she still found out! You know what? I'm firing you. You're done. I'll find me another assistant."

"What?" she asked with her voice trembling. "You're really gonna do this? I've been working for you for three damn years, and you're just gonna drop me over some bitch?"

I gritted my teeth. Why the fuck was everyone calling me girl a bitch today?

"Tomorrow when you come in, I need you to get all your shit. If you're not gone by the time I come in, I'll call security on your ass. Don't call me no more, bruh. Lose this fuckin' number."

"So you're serious?! Koda, I—" I hung up because I saw Diamond leaving her house. I quickly got out my car and did a light jog over to her.

"Diamond—"

"Nigga, you got two seconds to get the fuck off my property," she spat quietly.

"Nah. I just need you to talk to me."

"Talk? You cheated, my nigga. There is no talking. Go talk to Sundai. I'm sure she'll listen to whatever the fuck you have to say." She looked up at me with two red, puffy eyes.

"I know, ma, but—"

She held her finger up, then she turned around and started puking. I had to look away because that shit had me ready to throw up, too.

"Koda, just leave," she said, wiping her mouth with the back of her hand. "You can tell all your hoes you're single now. It doesn't really matter since you were already acting like it."

"No man!" I took a step closer to her, and she took a step back. "I'm not single, you're not single. Stop fuckin' playing with me, Diamond!"

"Nigga, get the fuck on! You've been fucking other bitches the entire time we've been together! You made me look fuckin' stupid! But you wanna know the worst part? You broke my fuckin' heart, Koda. You ripped that shit out and stepped on it."

Her eyes started watering, and I swear to God I felt my heart sink to my stomach. She quickly turned around and started throwing up some more.

"You good? You sick?" I asked.

"Diamond!" Mia snapped, coming out the house and over to her. "Nigga, why are you even here? Sani, don't call this phone no more!" She hung up the phone and started pulling Diamond toward the door.

"Let me—"

"Nigga, leave! Diamond is done with you, alright? She's gonna find her a real nigga! A dark skinned one with melanin! Take yo' white ass on!" She went in the house then slammed the door.

"Fuck, bruh." I sighed, pulling a hand down my face. I thought about staying out there, but I decided to just leave. There was no point.

The entire ride home, Sundai blew my phone up. I was about to block her ass. I should've never even agreed to that bullshit. I should've just fired her when she started threatening to tell Diamond about us.

When I pulled into my driveway, Sani was sitting on the porch looking like he'd just lost his best friend. Nigga was hurt that Mia wasn't fucking with him.

I didn't say shit to him as I went in the house. He was gonna start blaming me for everything like he'd been doing, and I wasn't trying to hear that shit. The only person I was trying to hear right now was Diamond, but she wasn't trying to hear me.

I took my mad ass into the kitchen since I hadn't eaten anything yet. I noticed how hungry I was on the ride home.

"Man, hell nah," I heard Sani say, coming through the front door. "I don't have time for this shit."

My brows came together. "Fuck you talkin—"

"Sani! Where that bitch at?" I heard from outside. I knew that voice all too well.

Jewel Spencer.

Jewel was Sani's younger sister. She was the youngest out of all four of them. They were all crazy. Sani was probably the craziest, but so was Jewel when someone fucked with her brothers.

"I didn't even tell her ass what happened with Diamond. I told Chosen."

I chuckled. "I don't know what the fuck you did that shit for. You knew he was gonna tell everybody."

"Sani!" Jewel hollered once she came through the door. "Nigga, you got me so fucked up!"

She came into the kitchen looking like the fine ass chocolate goddess she was. She had a nice ass shape with some long legs. Her hair was always done, and it didn't matter if she wore makeup or not. She was still fine as fuck.

"I got you fucked up? I didn't even do shit!" Sani had his hands up in surrender already.

"You weren't gonna tell me some dusty ass bitch put her hands on you yesterday? Why did I have to hear it from Chosen and Zeke? Huh?" She stood directly in front of him with her arms folded.

"She didn't put her hands on me. She put her hands on Koda. She just pepper sprayed me." He shrugged like it was nothing, but his ass was crying like a bitch when his eyes were burning and shit.

"That's the same thing, nigga!" She glanced at me then her mouth fell open. "Nah, who the fuck is this bitch?"

"Koda's ex. He cheated and that was the result. She hit that nigga in the face with a fuckin' frying pan and stabbed his ass twice." Damn. Why was this nigga over here snitching?

"She stabbed you?" she asked. I nodded as Sani walked off because his phone started ringing.

Jewel made her way over to me then gently grabbed my face to examine it.

"These are the type of bitches you like fucking with, Koda? This is what you left me for?" She made sure to keep her voice low because Sani would've had a fit if he knew what went on between me and his sister.

"How can I leave you if we were never together? That doesn't make sense—"

"You know what I mean. You cut me off for what? For some hood ass prostitute?" The attitude was dripping from her voice, but I wasn't quite sure why she was mad.

"Jewel, you're in a relationship. Been with yo' nigga for years. You were using me when you were mad at that nigga. Don't come in here acting like your feelings hurt and shit because I have a girlfriend."

I knew she had a nigga when we started fucking around. That shit didn't bother me, though. I didn't wanna be in a relationship with her anyway.

"Nigga." She laughed. "You *had* a girlfriend. The way she beat yo' ass, ain't no coming back from that. You broke that girl's heart."

I smacked my lips. "Fuck you. I'ma get her back. I just gotta give her time.

"Yeah, you're gonna give her time, and she's gonna already be on to some new dick. Good luck with that, though."

See, Jewel used to be cool as hell until we started fucking. How was she jealous of who I was dealing with, but she had a whole nigga? They had been together for at least two years.

Diamond had me fucked up, though. I'd kill her and whatever nigga she thought she was gonna fuck.

ONE WEEK LATER

I thought those two weeks when Diamond had broken up with me was hard, but nah. This had been the hardest week of my life. I couldn't focus on anything because the only thing that was on my mind was Diamond. I had shown up to work, and Sundai wasn't there. I called her ass and made her delete all the pictures of us that she had on her Instagram. I didn't know why she was uploading pictures of us in the first place.

"Nigga, you look like you haven't had sleep in days," Sani said when he walked into the living room.

"I'm good," I lied. I hadn't been getting any sleep. My days were spent sitting outside Diamond's house in a car she'd never seen before, and my nights are spent calling her from different phones, then staying up all night wondering what the hell she was doing.

"Nah," he said. "You're not good. I know you miss your shawty, but you're gonna drive yourself crazy—"

"I'll be back later," I said, getting off the couch and heading outside. I usually only followed Diamond around in the day time, but since the sun was going down, and I knew I wasn't gonna be sleeping tonight, I might as well see what she had planned for tonight.

Sani didn't follow me outside like I thought he would. I was glad because I didn't feel like hearing his mouth about what I needed to do. I was fine with what I was doing. Diamond just needed some more time to cool off. I mean, she could answer the phone for a nigga, but it was all good. She'd be talking to me sooner or later.

Once I was in my car, I picked up the half drunken Hennessy bottle I had lying on the floor. I wasn't a drinker, but for the past week, I'd turned into a straight alcoholic. Honestly, I didn't even know how I was functioning right now.

I sped all the way to Diamond's house like I always did. I took a few shots as I was driving. This shit wasn't making me feel better, though. It was actually making me feel worse. I just needed her to talk to me. I needed to let her know that I wasn't gonna do no more stupid shit like this. I needed a fresh start.

I let out a loud sigh as I sat across the street from her crib. I turned the bottle up a few more times then I started to feel a little tipsy. All the lights were off in her house, but I knew she was home because her car was parked in the driveway. It was all good, though. I was about to make myself comfortable right here. I didn't care if I had to sit out here all night either.

I had probably been sitting in my car for a good hour before I saw Diamond's front door open, and she walked out. She was wearing a short ass dress that barely covered her ass, and some high ass heels. I instantly got heated because where the fuck was she going in that dress?

She had her phone glued to her ear, and it looked like she was smiling from ear to ear. Who the fuck was she on the phone with? But she wouldn't answer the phone for me, though?

Diamond got in her car and pulled off, so I started my car and discreetly followed behind her. I had no idea where she was going, but something told me she was about to go see another nigga. I felt like Diamond would go fuck another nigga just to try to get over me. The thought of it was making my blood boil. It wasn't helping that I was also drinking.

I followed behind Diamond for about ten minutes before she pulled into a neighborhood that was too familiar. She parked in front of a house, and I parked a couple houses down, making sure I was still able to see everything.

She sat in her car for about five minutes, but then she finally got out, smoothed her short ass dress down, and ran her fingers through her hair. She sashayed to the door and lifted her hand to knock.

I thought my eyes were playing tricks on me when I saw that nigga Onyx open the door. They engaged in a long ass hug, and he even had the nerve to have a handful of her ass.

"Nah." I laughed once Diamond had stepped in the house, and the door was closed. "Nah, she thought I was playing with her ass, bruh."

There was no way Diamond didn't come over here to fuck. I quickly grabbed the strap from the glove compartment. I sat there for a few more minutes trying to get my thoughts together. I didn't wanna walk in there and catch them fucking. I didn't wanna kill Diamond, but I was a different person when I lost my temper.

I let ten more minutes go by before I finally said fuck it and hopped out my car. I didn't bother putting my gun up because I knew I was about to put it to use as soon as I walked up in this bitch. I just wanted to know why this nigga was trying me like this. Also, why the fuck was this the first nigga she ran to after some shit went down with us?

I swear, somebody could see them steam coming out of my ears as I approached the front door. I quietly turned the knob, and to my surprise, that shit was still unlocked. That's where he fucked up at.

He saw how good Diamond looked in that dress, and his mind was on one thing.

Fucking my bitch.

I clenched my jaw together and quietly shut the door behind me. They weren't in the living room, but I could hear voices coming from upstairs. Quietly, I started walking up the stairs and headed straight for the room the voices were coming from.

"Nah, nah," he said. "You got gold between your legs. I've been thinking about that pussy for a long ass time now."

Diamond let out a small laugh. "Boy, shut up. You had my number. You just didn't wanna call me."

I poked my head in the room. Diamond was sitting on the bed, naked, and that nigga was standing at the end of the bed in nothing but basketball shorts.

"It's all good, though. I'm about to fuck the shit out of you right now, though."

Diamond bit down on her lip, and I'd had enough. I was the only nigga she was supposed to be looking at like that.

I aimed the gun at the back on his head then pulled the trigger. His head exploded, and Diamond let out the loudest scream. When his body hit the floor, I slowly made my way over to her. I could see the fear all in her eyes, but I didn't even care about that shit right now.

I pressed the gun into her temple.

"Give me one reason I shouldn't blow your brains out all over this bitch!" I barked.

She looked up at me with the tears forming in her eyes.

"I'm pregnant."

TO BE CONTINUED...

AFTERWORD

I want to start off by saying, if you bought/downloaded this book, thank you!!! I hope you all enjoyed it as much as I enjoyed writing about Diamond and Koda. Let me know how much you enjoyed the book by leaving a review. It means a lot!

Also, add me on Facebook: Raya Reign
Join my Facebook reading group for sneak peeks and more: Raya's Reading Palace

Thank you for the support!

Coming Up Next!

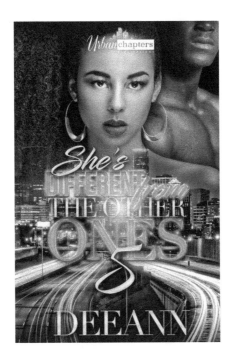

CPSIA information can be obtained
at www.ICGtesting.com
Printed in the USA
LVHW041950110119
603610LV00016B/323/P